"A wonderful story of romance and love; betrayal and heartbreak; friend and foe. If you have not had a chance to read the Bad Boys of the Highlands I would suggest you move the series to the top of your TBR pile."

—*The Reading Café*

Praise for *X Marks the Scot*

Winner, *RT* Reviewers' Choice Award, Best Medieval Historical Romance

"For a complex story brimming over with pride and passion, betrayal, trust, and most of all the power to make a bad boy a hero, pick up this read."

—*RT Book Reviews*

"This is one author who just keeps on getting better... One of the most exciting Highland romances I have read. Definitely worthy of five stars!"

—*Night Owl Reviews*, 5 Stars, Reviewer Top Pick

"As a fan of historical Highlander novels, this one was perfect."

—*Mrs. Condit & Friends Read Books*

"Roberts blends in just enough seventeenth-century English history to set the reader firmly in the time and place. *X Marks the Scot* is a keeper."

—*Long and Short Reviews*

"*X Marks the Scot* is a wickedly good romance."

—*Joyfully Reviewed*

Praise for *Temptation in a Kilt*

"An exciting Highland adventure with sensual and compelling romance."

—Amanda Forester, acclaimed author of *True Highland Spirit* and *A Midsummer Bride*

"Well written, full of intrigue, and a sensual, believable romance, this book captivates the reader immediately."

—*RT Book Reviews*

"Roberts's debut features appealing characters and an interesting background of ancient clan feuds and spurned lovers."

—*Publishers Weekly*

"Everything a Scottish romance should be. Beautifully written, this story will captivate you from the very first page, bringing the Highlands to life right before your eyes."

—*Romance Junkies*

"Given a lass in distress with the hounds of hell on her heels and a muscle-bound length of maleness dressed in a kilt and you got youself some challenging, steamy scenes."

—*Yankee Romance*

"Filled with everything I love most about Highland romance."

—Melissa Mayhue, award-winning author of *Warrior Untamed*

My
Highland
Spy

Victoria Roberts

sourcebooks
casablanca

Copyright © 2014 by Victoria Roberts
Cover and internal design © 2014 by Sourcebooks, Inc.
Cover art by Jon Paul Ferrara

Sourcebooks and the colophon are registered trademarks of Sourcebooks, Inc.

Published by Sourcebooks Casablanca, an imprint of Sourcebooks, Inc.
P.O. Box 4410, Naperville, Illinois 60567-4410
(630) 961-3900
Fax: (630) 961-2168
www.sourcebooks.com

Printed and bound in Canada
WC 10 9 8 7 6 5 4 3 2 1

To Maisy Jane, my beautiful niece, who is always one publication ahead of her favorite aunt. Enjoy what you do, and one day you will inspire the world.

Suspicion is a heavy armor and with its weight it impedes more than it protects.

—Robert Burns

One

London, England, 1609

SHE HAD MADE A DEAL WITH THE DEVIL, KING JAMES to be precise.

Lady Ravenna Walsingham silently cursed her liege as she stood huddled against the darkened wall of an alley near the London docks. She closed her eyes as a light rain misted her face. Although she felt miserable, she knew the information she sought would assist the Crown in discovering the latest conspiracy against it.

She pulled her heavy cloak tighter around herself, shivering from a sudden chill. The cold could have been due to the scantily clad clothing she wore underneath, but she quickly pushed back the thought. All she needed was to catch a glimpse of who dastardly Lord Cobham was conversing with in the latest string of unsavory establishments.

She wiped the drops from her face and had just taken a step forward when a couple of drunken men walked out of the Devil's Tavern. As the sound of laughter approached her, she backed hastily into the shadows. The men passed her and she studied them closely. To her regret, neither man was Lord Cobham. Although the light barely illuminated their features, she knew the man she sought was shorter—at least a head shorter than she was.

The rain hardened as Ravenna quivered against the wall like a drowned rat. Lord Cobham was more than likely not coming out any time soon. That's when she decided to hurry things along and make her move. Besides, if she didn't meet her driver, George, within the hour, he would undoubtedly come looking for her. The faster she could determine the person or persons with whom Lord Cobham was conspiring, the better. She was tired, cold, and wet, and wanted to be home where a warm bed awaited her.

She made her way toward the back of the brick building. The stairs leading to the door were dark. Of course they were. Was it too much to ask for at least one assignment that worked in her favor? She climbed the steps carefully and tried not to stumble over her own two feet. Fumbling for the door, she found the latch and discreetly entered.

The small room looked like a crowded hovel, and she suddenly had a strong desire to bathe. More than a handful of women readied their hair in the looking glass as the sound of boisterous laughter came from the adjoining room. The women wore little clothing, which reminded Ravenna to remove her cloak. She tossed her protective garment into the corner and placed her arm over her chest. She suddenly felt very open to the view of others—not to mention that her laced bodice left very little to the imagination.

A large-bellied man came into the room and waved the women out. "Make haste, ladies. My customers need to be served. You can't do that if you spend all your time in here pampering yourselves." As one of the women walked by, the burly man slapped her on the bottom. He looked up, and his cold, dark eyes met Ravenna's. "You're the new girl, but you will quickly learn your place. Don't just stand here staring at me. Get out there."

Ravenna nodded and rushed past the man, feeling his gaze upon her. She followed the lead of the other women and picked up a tray from the table. As she looked around the smoke-filled room packed with men, she noted the large barrels and ship masts built right into the structure. Being so close to the River Thames, she could see why. The tavern was often frequented by men of the sea, but she knew not to be fooled.

The Devil's Tavern held many secrets.

The establishment was notorious for housing smugglers, cutthroats, thieves, and pirates. If Lord Cobham was meeting anyone here to further promote his illicit behavior, she was going to find out.

Without warning, Ravenna was roughly pulled down onto a lap. The man's breath reeked of ale and he smiled, fingering her locks.

"This place keeps getting better and better. I haven't seen you here before." He lowered his head and sniffed down her body. "Mmm...you smell of lavender."

She didn't think it wise to tell the man what he smelled like so she politely nodded. When she tried to stand, he pulled her back down and held her with a firm grip.

"Let me tell you a little secret." He lowered his voice and leaned forward. "I think you are by far my favorite." His hand encircled her breast, and it took all of Ravenna's might not to slap him. And that's when she looked up and noticed the men.

Dear God.

Lord Cobham was walking straight toward her. She hastily glanced to Cobham's right and saw Charles Paget. What was he doing here? She couldn't risk being spotted, so she did the first thing that came to mind. She turned in the lap of the man who held her and brought his lips to hers.

The man's comrades cheered him on, and his hands roamed all over Ravenna in places they shouldn't. She had to endure quite a repulsive kiss and felt as though she needed a cloth to wipe away the slobber that had escaped the man's lips. How she despised this part of the masquerade! Only when she was confident that the two men had departed did she dare pull back, attempting not to think about the bile that rose in the back of her throat.

She placed her finger to the man's lips. "I have something for you. I'll be right back." When the man nodded, as she knew he would, she made her escape to the back room. She didn't want to spend another moment in that place. Grabbing her cloak from the corner, she bolted out the door.

She did not look back.

What was Lord Cobham doing with Charles Paget? She thought Paget was still in Paris. No matter, she would simply give the information to her uncle. She wrapped her cloak tighter around herself as the cool breeze whipped her cheeks. She walked with long, purposeful strides, clutching the dagger in her pocket. She didn't like walking the streets of London by herself, let alone by the docks in the darkened hours of the night. One of these days her luck was going to run out. She prayed it was not at this moment.

Her uncle's carriage waiting at the end of the dimly lit street was a welcome sight. George climbed down upon her approach and extended his hand. He was a large man with graying hair at the temples and stood well over six feet tall. He always aided her when she needed protection from places like the Devil's Tavern.

"Lady Walsingham, did you find what you were looking for?"

"Thankfully, yes."

"Home, my lady?"

"Yes, please."

Ravenna climbed into the coach and breathed a sigh of relief. She sat back, closed her tired eyes, and fell asleep to the gentle, rhythmic movement of the carriage and the sound of clomping hoofbeats. When the carriage suddenly stopped, she was jolted awake.

"My lady, we have arrived."

She took George's hand and climbed down. "Thank you. Could you please ask my uncle to pay me a visit on the morrow?"

He nodded. "Of course. Have a pleasant evening, Lady Walsingham."

Ravenna walked to the front of the manor house and quietly opened the heavy door. It was nearly midnight and the house was silent. Her sisters were already in bed. She hated when she had to be away from them, but at least she would be there in the morning as the girls broke their fast.

She lifted her cloak and climbed the steps on the tips of her toes. As she made her way down the hall to her bedchamber, she passed the family portraits that hung on the wall. She could feel her father's gaze upon her and couldn't help but wonder what he would think of her now. She closed the door to her chamber, and when she heard the soft click of the latch, she sighed. Removing her cloak, she tossed it onto a chair as a faint smell of smoke invaded her senses.

A voice spoke from her bed and Ravenna jumped.

"Where the hell have you been? And *what* in the name of God are you wearing?"

Ravenna placed her hand over her heart to make sure it didn't leap from her chest. "Grace…"

Her sister sat up on the bed. "What's his name? I want to know."

Ravenna wasn't in the mood for this. All she wanted was to be in her warm bed—alone. Ignoring her sister's prodding, she donned her nightrail and nudged her sister over. "Grace, it's late. Why don't you seek your own bed? Please?"

"You may fool Elizabeth and Kat, but you don't fool me. You sneak out of the house at all hours of the night, and now I find you dressed as what? Some type of harlot? Who is he, Ravenna? Why do you have to hide him from us? Is he wed? You must tell me."

Ravenna shook her head and prayed for her sister's silence. "There is no man, Grace. I'm telling you the truth."

The light of the candle reflected on her sister's

worried brow. "Did Uncle Walter spend our coin? Is that it? Are you selling yourself?"

Ravenna crawled under the blankets and stifled a groan. "I beg you to please lie down and close your eyes. The time is after midnight. I'm weary."

Her sister huffed and punched the lumps out of the pillow. "Why won't you talk to me? I'm seventeen. I'm old enough to understand what's going on with you. You take care of everyone around you but yourself. You won't even let me help you. I'm not a child anymore, and you don't need to face this burden alone. Talk to me."

Ravenna didn't see Grace roll her eyes or hear her sister curse under her breath when a little snort escaped Ravenna. It wasn't as if she deliberately fell asleep in the middle of Grace's rant.

❧

The next Ravenna knew, the door flew open and she was crushed on the bed by Elizabeth and Katherine. She must have slept sometime during the night, since the sun peeked through the windows and Grace no longer slumbered by her side.

Ravenna let out a grunt. "Why is it you two can never let me be?"

Elizabeth, the elder of the two, sat down on the chair. She was fourteen years old, and she had the quietest disposition of all the sisters. Her reddish-brown locks were pulled back with a ribbon. She still wore her nightrail, while Katherine and her golden curls bounced annoyingly on Ravenna's back.

"It's time to get up, Ravenna. We want to go

below stairs to break our fast, but Elizabeth said we had to wait for you."

"Kat, go get dressed and I'll meet you soon."

"We know you are just going to go back to sleep as soon as we leave." At eight years old, Kat was wise beyond her years. She sat on Ravenna's back and sighed. "We're not leaving until you get out of bed."

"All right." Ravenna rolled over and quickly grabbed Kat, tickling the little girl relentlessly. "I'm up! I'm up!"

"Let me go, Ravenna!"

Elizabeth stood. "Come, Kat. Let's get dressed."

"Off with you both, and I'll meet you after I dress."

Ravenna walked to the washbowl and splashed cool water on her face. These long evenings had started to take their toll. Her reddened eyes made it look as though she'd been in a brawl. She dressed quickly and descended the stairs. When she made her way into the dining room, her sisters were already seated at the table along with an early-morning visitor.

"Uncle Walter, what a pleasant surprise. I'm so glad you're here with us on such a lovely morn," said Ravenna, pulling out her chair.

He swallowed his oatmeal and smiled. "I have to meet with His Majesty later this morn and I thought to pay you girls a visit."

Lord Walter Mildmay, her mother's brother, had been appointed the Walsingham family's guardian, but their situation was more pretense than anything. Uncle Walter had his own estate and family, while he permitted Ravenna and her sisters to stay under their own roof. At twenty-five years old, Ravenna handled all the accounts, managed the servants, and had served as a mother figure to the girls since the deaths of their parents.

Uncle Walter, with his dark hair and tanned skin, was the complete opposite of Ravenna's fair-skinned mother. No one would ever think they were of the same relation, especially because his hair was as black as night. Ravenna always thought the man looked like a bloody pirate.

Ravenna's father, Lord Francis Walsingham, had been Queen Elizabeth's principal secretary until his death. Little did anyone know that her sire had also been the queen's spy. Given that Ravenna's father had handled all of the royal correspondence and had determined the agenda of the council meetings, he had been a very influential man in his time, which fortunately now worked in Ravenna's favor.

In short, she was a spy for King James and the Crown, the same as her father had been under Queen Elizabeth's reign. When Ravenna was old enough to show an interest in political matters, her father had educated and conditioned her to one day take his place. She lived in a man's world, but that's why she was so proficient at doing what she did—a mere woman was the last thing anyone would expect. Her family meant everything to her, and she was determined to keep her siblings sheltered and protected for as long as possible.

Especially from unsavory establishments like the one last eve.

After everyone finished their meal and polite conversation, Ravenna and Uncle Walter excused themselves and met behind the closed doors of her father's study. With the dark wooden furnishings, the large desk, and her father's books lining the wall, the room always reminded Ravenna of her father. At times, she could swear she even smelled his scent, almost as if he wanted her to know that he still watched over her.

"What did you find out?" asked Uncle Walter, tapping his fingers on the desk.

Ravenna sat in her father's chair. "I followed Lord Cobham into the Devil's Tavern. The man he met with was Charles Paget. I thought he was still in Paris."

Her uncle sat forward, his eyes narrowing. "I suppose it should come as no surprise. His Majesty gave Paget back his manor of Weston-on-Trent and his other homes in Derbyshire, but we'll be sure to keep an eye on him. As usual, I'll pass along the information to the king's advisors. You did well, Ravenna."

"Grace is questioning my sudden disappearances, and I don't know how much longer I'll be able to keep the truth from her."

"You know as well as I do that it's better she doesn't know what you do. Perhaps we should start thinking about arranging a marriage for her."

Ravenna rubbed her fingers over the bridge of her nose. "I really want to give her some time. She doesn't show an interest in anyone at the moment, and I'm not quite ready to force her into a marriage." She paused. "Let me think about it."

He bobbed his head. "There is another assignment from His Majesty."

"So soon? I just completed this one." She sat forward, frowning. "What is it this time?"

"The Highland lairds are completely out of control and the men refuse to listen. Between their squabbles among themselves and increased rebellions against the Crown, the king has required that all Highland lairds send their heirs to Lowland Scotland to be educated. Futhermore, the men are to regularly report to Edinburgh to stand for their actions. King James demands conformity and hopes that by abolishing the Gaelic language and destroying Scotland's culture, he will get it. The lairds won't conform on their own so the king is left with no choice but to force their hand."

"And what does that have to do with me, precisely?"

"There is a man in the Highlands whom the king's men have been watching—Laird Ruairi Sutherland. He has not sent his heir to be educated, and he has not made an appearance in Edinburgh for quite some time. Although he claims his wife is gravely ill, the king's advisors think this is nothing more than another clever plot to refuse King James's authority. They also believe Sutherland's absence in Edinburgh is because he's conspiring with other lairds in the Highlands to raise arms against the realm." He sat back casually in the chair.

"Whether these rumors are true or not, an example is to be made of Sutherland. The king grows tired of these...*Highlanders*"—he sniffed—"and their constant disobedience. These barbarians need to understand they cannot do whatever they please and pay no heed to the authority of the king. Sutherland has a formidable stronghold in northern Scotland. He could be a powerful enemy. He's been told a governess will be sent to his home to educate his son, since his wife is ill. You will travel to the Highlands. Find out if what he says is true, or if he and others conspire against the Crown."

Ravenna's eyes widened and her voice went up a notch. "A governess?" She cleared her throat. "Uncle Walter, surely my...*talents* would be much more valuable closer to home. I have spied on men who've conspired against the realm, uncovered a wealthy lord's machinations in selling secrets to the French, discovered a traitor before he made his escape to the colonies, and now you ask me to masquerade as a governess for some Highland laird's child?"

He chuckled. "Not me. His Majesty."

"Surely there is a more *appropriate* assignment for me. A governess—I have no idea what or even how you expect me to teach a boy anything, especially one who doesn't speak English. And travel to the Highlands? The place is completely uncivilized. More to the point, you know I can't be gone for that long. What about the girls?"

"I understand this assignment will take a few months. I will, of course, see to their welfare while you're away. As a woman, you have the perfect disguise. You'll be safe, Ravenna, and you've certainly been placed in more dangerous circumstances than in the Scottish Highlands as a governess. I'll have George and Mary escort you."

She groaned. "I don't like this."

He gave her a sympathetic smile. "I know. At times, your father didn't, either."

"I've been managing to live in two worlds quite well. You know how strongly I desire to follow in Father's footsteps, but I can't be traveling to Scotland or God knows where. There are more than enough troubles in England. As always, I will fulfill my duty to the Crown, but please recognize how imperative it is for me to be here for my sisters, my family. I want the girls to have an ordinary life. How can they do that if I keep disappearing for long periods of time?"

"I tried to speak on your behalf. You don't have a choice."

She let out a heavy sigh.

Her uncle rose and walked around the desk to embrace her. "Passage is being made two days from now."

She stepped away from him, her mouth pulled into a sour grin. "The girls are not going to be happy."

He patted her on the shoulder and then walked to the door. "They never are. Safe travels, Ravenna." The door closed and reality struck.

Damn. Damn. Damn.

The fact that she clearly had no voice in the matter grated on her very last nerve. Why would anyone want to travel to Scotland? That wild country had nothing to offer but a bunch of unkempt men in kilts waving broadswords and screaming battle cries. She didn't mind when her assignments were closer to home, but the Highlands? With no mother or father to guide her sisters, Ravenna had become their anchor—and now that rock was uplifted once again.

She gave herself a moment alone in her father's study to decide exactly what to say to her sisters. How could she make them understand? What could she possibly tell them that would be believable? There was no sense delaying the conversation. She knew she'd think of something. She always did.

Ravenna walked out into the fresh air to find the girls in the garden. The sun was shining, roses were in full bloom, and a rabbit scrambled out of her way on the garden path. She tried to show an ease that she didn't necessarily feel. She was bothered by the fact that instead of enjoying a lovely day with her sisters, she found herself once again spinning tales to them. Sitting on a bench, she gathered her sisters around. Grace looked suspicious, Elizabeth bit her lip, and Kat couldn't stand still.

"I want to tell you how proud I am of all of you. We have really pulled together as a family since Father passed and I know he would be pleased."

Elizabeth smiled sadly. "I know Mother would be happy, too. Family was important to her."

"Of course she would be. I wanted to tell you that I will be traveling soon."

Grace had a disgusted look on her face. "When?"

"Two days."

"When will you be back?" Grace folded her arms over her chest.

"I will be gone for a few months."

Grace's jaw dropped. "*Months?* You're leaving us for…months?"

"Uncle Walter will see to your welfare."

Kat sat down beside Ravenna. "Where will you go?"

"Uncle Walter asked me to do him a favor. The wife of his friend is gravely ill, and they need a governess to care for their son for a few months. I'm doing this as a kindness for all the wonderful things that Uncle Walter has done for us."

Elizabeth smiled easier. "Where will you go?"

"The Highlands."

Grace gasped and her face was bleak. "Scotland? The country is full of nothing but barbarians. I didn't think any of them were educated, let alone that someone would actually need a governess for their son."

Kat embraced Ravenna, followed shortly by Elizabeth. "We will miss you, Ravenna."

Ravenna looked up and tapped the girls with her hand as Grace glared at her. "Why don't you play in the garden so I can talk with Grace?"

She'd had enough experience with her sister to know the conversation that followed was not going to be an easy one. Perhaps Uncle Walter was right and they should arrange a marriage for Grace. On second thought, her sister's loose tongue would more than likely drive her poor husband mad.

The girls ran off and Grace's expression did not lighten.

"I know what you're doing," said Grace. She sat down beside Ravenna and actually growled. "You do not fool me for a moment—coming in at all hours of the night, having your secret meetings with Uncle Walter. There is only one reason why you would travel that far away from us for *months*."

Ravenna closed her eyes and prayed for patience. "Grace…"

"You're with child."

Two

"She's here."

"Damn."

"Aye, well 'tis too late to turn her away now, Ruairi. What did ye expect? How long did ye think ye'd be able to hold King James at bay? Ye havenae shown your face in Edinburgh and didnae send Torquil—"

Laird Ruairi Sutherland thundered his way to the great hall and didn't even wait for the captain of his guard to finish his comment. Why would he? Fagan knew how Ruairi felt about the Crown. As if he would send his only son to the Lowlands to learn the King's English. King James had no respect for Scotland or its people. And Ruairi would be damned if he'd give in without a fight.

He entered the great hall and walked toward the English lass. Her brown hair was pulled back into a tight, unflattering bun. Her face was austere, her manner haughty. The woman acted as if she graced him with her presence. He didn't like her at all.

"A bheil Gàidhlig agad?" Do you speak Gaelic?

The woman merely stood there mute.

He looked at Fagan and smirked. Turning back toward the woman, Ruairi's eyes darkened. *"Thalla dachaigh."* Go home.

"Just place the trunk right there. Thank you."

Ruairi's eyes widened in surprise as another woman entered the great hall. Her smooth ivory skin glowed. She had a wealth of red hair in loose tendrils that softened her face, and her lips were full and rounded over even teeth. She was elegant and graceful. He wasn't sure what an English governess was supposed to look like, but she wasn't what he'd expected.

She wore a blue traveling dress with tight sleeves and a low-pointed waist that clung to her slender body. And for the first time since he could remember, he had no words to express the sight before him. The woman was simply beautiful. She lifted her skirts and walked over to him, greeting him with a warm smile.

"I see you've met my driver's wife, Mary. You must be Laird Sutherland. It is a pleasure to make your acquaintance. I am Mistress Denny."

Carried away by his own response, Ruairi failed to notice that the woman waited for him to answer. He also had one hell of a time trying to suppress his admiration. When her cheeks reddened under the heat of his gaze, he cleared his throat and nodded at Fagan.

"'Tis a pleasure to meet ye. I am Fagan, the captain of Laird Sutherland's guard." The lass looked puzzled, and then Fagan added, "My laird doesnae speak English."

Her eyes widened and her jaw dropped. "I see. And what of Lady Sutherland?"

Fagan paused. "Lady Sutherland has passed away."

Ruairi eventually came to his senses when the pounding of his heart finally quieted. Although the woman was pleasing to the eye, she could keep her English ways to herself, as far as he was concerned. He was determined not to make this easy for her—as if he would roll over like a good dog because his liege demanded obedience. As soon as King James gave the Highland lairds the respect they deserved, perhaps he would feel differently. But for now, Ruairi certainly wasn't going to tell the lass that he understood every word she spoke.

∽

With all her might, Ravenna held back a groan. The laird didn't speak a word of English. How would she be able to figure out if the man conspired against the Crown if she didn't understand a word of Gaelic? Praise the saints. This was nothing short of a disaster. She was stuck in the Highlands with a widowed laird and his son. She didn't like this at all.

As she stood in the great hall trying to suppress the urge to flee, Ravenna noticed tapestries hung on the walls that depicted swords, shields, and men in the throes of battle. Laird Sutherland certainly had an odd way of making his guests feel at home. Perhaps that was his intention. A stone fireplace dominated the far wall, and there were long tables and benches on the floor in front of a raised dais.

Trying to compose herself, Ravenna gave Laird Sutherland a sympathetic smile for the loss of his wife. She stretched her neck to look up at him because the top of her head only reached the middle of the massive man's chest. These Highland men were definitely different from their English counterparts. The English lords didn't look that formidable in their waistcoats, whereas the Scottish men looked big, brawny, and battle-ready.

Laird Sutherland and Fagan sported the traditional kilt of green, black, blue, white, and orange, which Ravenna presumed was the Sutherland tartan. They also had large swords sheathed at their waists. She'd never met a Highlander before and realized she'd made a grave error in judgment by believing the words of her countrymen. She had foolishly assumed these Highland men were nothing but a bunch of chest-pounding barbarians.

She was never so happy to be wrong.

The laird's green eyes continued to study her intently. His straight, long chestnut hair hung just past his shoulders and had traces of red. He had an air of authority and the appearance of one who demanded instant obedience. The set of his chin suggested a stubborn streak, but his boldly handsome face held a certain degree of sensuality. Somehow she knew she would never forget a single detail.

When their eyes locked, her heart turned over in response. Her gaze roamed to his powerful set of his shoulders, and he stood there like he didn't give a damn about her or what she thought of him.

Ravenna cleared her throat. "You have my sincere condolences on the loss of your wife."

When he raised his brow, Fagan spoke, and she presumed the man translated her words. The laird must have understood because he nodded in response and then left without as much as a backward glance.

"Your trunk will be carried up to your chambers," said Fagan. "Ye must be weary from your journey. I will escort ye to your room and leave ye to rest." He was about to walk away when Ravenna spoke.

"Might I at least meet Torquil?"

His eyebrows shot up in surprise. "Ye arenae weary?"

"Captain, I've come all of this way. Perhaps you could introduce me to the boy?"

The man was just as big and imposing as Laird Sutherland. He had a strong, chiseled jaw and his dark hair hung well below his shoulders. He had a kind, almost tender smile that was difficult not to notice.

"Fagan, if ye will."

Ravenna nodded in response.

"I donna know where the lad is at the moment, but I will be sure to introduce ye when he returns."

"Very well. I suppose I will unpack my trunk."

Ravenna was placed in a modest chamber of her own, while Mary and George were given rooms with the other servants. The two of them would depart in the morning and tell Uncle Walter that she was safely delivered into the lion's den. For a brief moment, Ravenna silently wished this would all be over and she could return to her family, but she quickly reminded herself of the greater good. After all, that's why she did what she did.

She gazed around the room, which had a bed, a table, and two chairs that weren't nearly as lavish as in her bedchamber at home. No matter, she was determined to get this assignment over with as quickly as possible, even if the dastardly man didn't speak a word of English. She needed to find a way to communicate with him and obtain the information she was sent to retrieve. And she couldn't very well go home until she got what she came for.

Ravenna lifted the lid on her trunk. She pushed the clothes aside and her fingers tapped around the bottom until she uncovered what she searched for. She pulled out her five daggers and placed them on the bed. She would keep one strapped to her thigh at all times. Who knew what dangers lurked in the Highlands?

She placed the second dagger under her pillow and the third one under the mattress. Her eyes searched around the room. A small stone fireplace took up the center wall, and other than the table, the chairs, and the bed, there wasn't another useful place to conceal a weapon. She wrapped up the remaining daggers and secured them back in her trunk.

With the most important task complete, she shut the lid and took a deep breath. If she was to be successful, she needed to first familiarize herself with her surroundings. Ravenna opened the door to find a young boy standing in the hall with his back pressed against the wall. With his reddish-brown hair, green eyes, and pale skin, the boy was no doubt Torquil. He was the picture of his father, especially since he wore a much smaller version of the Sutherland kilt.

"Hello there," she said with a warm smile.

The boy stood to his full height, the top of his head reaching about Ravenna's midriff. He returned a smile and said, "*Ciamar a tha sibh? Is mise Torquil. Dè an t-ainm a tha ort?*"

Her eyes widened at the many foreign words that escaped his mouth. The only thing she could discern was the boy's name. "Torquil?"

"Aye. *Dè an t-ainm a tha ort?*"

Ravenna wrinkled her nose and shook her head.

"A bheil Gàidhlig agad?" When she shook her head again, the boy smiled and pointed to himself. He spoke slowly, speaking each word articulately. *"Is mise Torquil."* He placed his small hand on Ravenna's arm and said, *"Is mise…"*

She tried to repeat his words the best she could, something her tongue clearly wasn't meant to do. She pointed to herself and said, "My name is Mistress Denny."

When Torquil tried to say her name, he couldn't get through "Mistress." He continued to struggle and she said, "Ravenna." She smiled when he repeated her name fluently.

She ruffled the boy's hair and he grabbed her hand, pulling her down the hall. Many portraits of men hung on both sides of the stone walls, and she presumed they were of past Sutherland lairds. She realized that her manor house was akin to Laird Sutherland's home in that way. Perhaps family was important to him, too. She walked down the stairs with Torquil, and when they entered the great hall, Fagan approached them.

"I see ye've met Torquil."

"Yes. He's a delightful boy."

"Mmm… Mayhap some days. Please join us." Fagan gestured to the raised dais. When she reached for a chair, he pulled it out for her.

"Thank you." She sat down and smiled at him.

"'Tis my pleasure, lass. My laird will be along shortly. I know 'tisnae proper for a governess to sit with the clan at the meal, but my laird requests that ye eat your meals with us here at the table so that Torquil continues to learn from your guidance. And I will be joining ye on most eves to sup. Ye may find the conversation a wee bit easier to understand that way."

"I appreciate your kindness. Thank you."

While they waited for Laird Sutherland, Ravenna glanced around the great hall. Trying to not pay any heed to the tapestries of blood and battle, she counted roughly two score of men and women who sat at the tables below. When she looked at the fireplace, something caught her attention. Imbedded in the mantel was a clan crest that looked like a giant cat sitting upright. There was something inscribed below the animal which she had difficulty making out.

She noticed Fagan watching her and asked him, "What do the words mean?"

"Sans Peur," he said proudly. "The meaning translates as 'fearless.'"

∽

Ruairi took his seat at the table and felt the lass's eyes upon him, judging him. The woman undoubtedly thought he was some kind of barbarian, as all those pampered English bastards did about his kind. He wasn't thrilled to have her here, but the sooner Torquil took to his lessons, the faster the lass would be back in her own country and not underfoot. Maybe he wasn't thinking about this the right way. Perhaps instead of working against her, he should assist her with Torquil so that she could be on her way. In spite of everything, she was only a woman and doing as she was told. Ruairi liked the lasses—not necessarily English lasses—but lasses nonetheless. And this particular woman was not so sore on the eyes.

He gave her a brief nod. *"Ciamar a tha sibh?"*

"He asks how ye are," Fagan translated.

She sat forward and took a sip from her tankard. "Tell me. How do I answer him that I am well?"

While Fagan instructed Mistress Denny, Ruairi sat and listened, surprised the lass wanted to answer him in his native tongue. After several botched attempts, she turned and gazed at Ruairi with an intense look on her face.

"Tha gu math." I am well.

Torquil clapped, and his eyes lit up at his governess's efforts to speak Gaelic. Ruairi hadn't seen that look on his son's face in quite some time.

"She would like a tour of your home. Will she teach Torquil in the library?" asked Fagan in Gaelic.

"Aye. I will take her after we sup."

Fagan's eyes grew openly amused. "Must I come along to translate?"

"I think I can manage," Ruairi said, annoyed.

Fagan smiled at the lass. "My laird will escort ye and show ye his home after we sup."

Ruairi didn't like the way her face lit up when Fagan—his captain under his command—spoke to her.

"That would be delightf—"

"Ravenna, I want to come, too," said Torquil in Gaelic.

Ruairi's brow rose when he heard Mistress Denny's Christian name spoken from his son's lips. "Torquil..."

Her gaze became puzzled at the sight of Ruairi's displeasure, and the lass placed her hand over her heart. She leaned forward in the chair. "Fagan, is the laird upset because Torquil called me Ravenna?"

"Aye."

"Please tell Laird Sutherland that I asked the boy to call me by my given name because it was much easier on his tongue. And if it suits the two of you, you may both call me Ravenna as well."

Fagan turned up his smile a notch. "Ravenna...a verra bonny name for a verra bonny lass. The name suits ye."

Ruairi scowled. What the hell did Fagan think he was doing? Was he actually trying to woo the lass? God's teeth! The chit was English, a sworn enemy. Ruairi was perfectly aware that he shouldn't have been so aloof toward her. After all, she would report back to the king. But hell, he wasn't about to woo the lass in the middle of the great hall. When he gave his captain another dark look, Fagan only lifted a brow and then had the audacity to smirk. The man would pay for that one later.

For the remainder of the meal, Ruairi sat and listened while the woman laughed at Fagan's jesting, cast smiles at Fagan, and asked him questions about Ruairi's home. Clearly, Ruairi couldn't answer, so his only option was to sit mute. Perhaps this wasn't one of his most brilliant ideas. Mistress Denny must think him daft. He took another drink from his tankard and tried to think of all the ways to kill the captain of his guard.

Her gentle laugh tinkled through the air. Her nearness was overpowering, but it had been quite a long time since he had shared his bed with a woman. When visions suddenly appeared of the sultry temptress lying beneath him, a cynical inner voice cut through his thoughts. He hated when his cock ruled his mind.

Ruairi brought his tankard to his lips and took another big gulp, quickly realizing he needed something much stronger than what was in his cup.

∽

Ravenna was by no means blind to Laird Sutherland's attraction. Her instinctive response to him was powerful, but she mentally took a step back. What was she thinking? What had she become? And what kind of man made her mind race with purely wicked thoughts? He had recently lost his wife. Furthermore, since he didn't speak English, she was forced to obtain information elsewhere.

She deliberately switched her attention to Fagan. If anyone would know what was afoot, it should be him. He was, after all, the captain of Sutherland's guard. She didn't like the thought of using her feminine wiles against him, especially since she unexpectedly favored the rugged, dangerous looks of the handsome laird who sat beside her. But she needed to be home where she belonged. Who knew what mischief her sisters were up to? Grace in particular.

When Laird Sutherland abruptly stood, Ravenna presumed the meal was over. She thanked Fagan for his hospitality and followed the laird. His kilt rode low on his lean hips, and the movement of the muscles under his tunic quickened her pulse. He appeared to fill out the material quite nicely.

She continued to follow him, not minding the view at all, as he led her from the library to the kitchens and then to the ladies' solar without speaking a word. He gestured with his hand, and when they reached the end of the hall, he opened a door and they walked out into the fresh air of the gardens.

The last of the summer blooms lined the path. Yellow and red flowers led to a waist-high stone wall where the laird had stopped and was waiting for her. She walked up beside him and looked over the wall. The white waves of the ocean crashed below on jagged rocks. She inhaled the fresh saltwater air and closed her eyes, letting the breeze comb through her loose tendrils.

When she opened her eyes, he was watching her. He shifted his weight and stood so close that a piece of his long hair whipped her cheek. She could easily drown in the depths of his emerald eyes. She suddenly found it difficult to breathe and caught the smell of his spicy scent as it wafted through the air.

For a brief moment, Ravenna forgot who she was and what she was sent there to do. It was as if something intense passed between them, making her tingle in the pit of her stomach. No man had ever looked at her that way.

What was the matter with her?

The man had enough burdens. He was mourning the loss of his wife and now had to raise his son alone. And here she was acting like some silly chit floundering over the man's good looks.

She cleared her throat. "It's quite unfortunate that you do not speak English." When she saw a slight hesitation in his hawk-like eyes, she added, "Praise the saints. I don't know what's wrong with me. You stand there, so handsome, sporting your kilt. Frankly, I don't remember any of my other assignments being quite so…desirable."

The smoldering flame she saw in his eyes startled her.

"Ye are my son's governess, but I would take ye verra willingly to my bed."

Ravenna paled.

Three

Ruairi couldn't say what surprised him more—the fact that Mistress Denny so blatantly approved of his handsome visage or the look on her face when she realized he understood every word she said. He had a feeling he'd remember that particular moment for a very long time. It wasn't often he found a lass who spoke her mind. As her jaw continued to tremble and she quickly averted her eyes, he found that her discomfiture amused him.

He lifted her chin with his fingers. "Ye already said the words, lass. Why is it that ye can nay longer look me in the eye?"

"Because I presumed you didn't understand English. This whole time you did. Why would you do that?" He was about to speak when she silenced him with a glare. "Let me make something perfectly clear. I am here for the sole purpose of educating your son. I assure you that I have absolutely *no* intention of sharing your bed." The woman turned on her heel and walked along the stone wall without him.

He couldn't help it when his lips lifted into a

roguish grin. "We'll have to see about that," he said under his breath.

When she reached the outer wall, she stopped and stretched her neck to see over the cliffs. Her skirts billowed behind her and her hair whipped in the wind. If she had taken flight, he wouldn't have been surprised. She looked like an angel sent from the heavens.

"Have a care and donna wander beyond this wall. The cliffs are dangerous. Torquil knows it's forbidden."

"I can see why." She turned to him and asked dryly, "So tell me. Does Torquil speak English as well, or does the boy truly need my assistance?"

"My son doesnae speak English."

"Did his mother?" As soon as she said the words, she reached out and touched his arm. "My apologies. I didn't mean to—"

"Nay, my wife didnae speak English."

She nodded. "I will begin Torquil's studies on the morrow in the library, if that suits you. During this time, may I suggest that English is spoken in front of your son so that the words we speak are not so foreign to his ears? I believe that the more he hears it, the easier the language will be for him to grasp."

"Whatever ye think is best. The faster my son learns the ways of the English, the faster ye can depart." When her eyes widened, Ruairi realized his words came out harsher than he had meant them to. But to his surprise, her expression only lightened.

"I understand this is a difficult time for you. I will try my very best to see that Torquil takes to his studies.

I'm sure that with the sudden passing of your dear wife, you have enough worries."

The woman had no idea.

❧

Ravenna closed the door to her bedchamber and started to pace. She slapped her hand to her head and growled. "What are you doing, Ravenna? You are never this careless." She threw herself onto the bed and buried her face in the pillow. "You actually told the man you didn't remember any of your other assignments being quite so desirable. Are you completely mad?"

When she paused to hear herself answer, she thought she might be. She couldn't afford to be so reckless. Perhaps she was weary from the long journey and needed to rest. Things had to look brighter in the morning. They always did.

She donned her nightrail and climbed into bed. With one last look around her modest chamber, she blew out the candle and brushed the loose tendrils away from her face. She pulled the blanket up to her chin, closed her eyes, and let out a loud sigh.

A brutal ending to a less-than-perfect day.

When Ravenna rose in the morning, she felt a bit more refreshed than she had the evening before. Praise the saints for small favors. She needed to have her wits about her and knew she shouldn't dwell on her own stupidity. She dressed quickly and went straight to the courtyard, where George and Mary were ready to depart.

"Is everything all right, m'lady?" asked George. "You're certain you don't want us to remain?"

"No, George. It would look far too suspicious. I am supposed to be a governess, of all things. Please tell my uncle everything is fine. I shall contact him at once, should I discover anything."

He nodded and gave her a slight bow. "As you wish, Lady Walsingham."

She placed her hand on his arm and he stilled. "And George. Please make certain Uncle Walter…"

"Of course, m'lady. Rest assured the ladies are in good hands."

Ravenna nodded her thanks and turned to find Laird Sutherland approaching her. His eyes twinkled with amusement.

"Having second thoughts?" he asked. "'Tisnae too late to turn back."

"I'm only thanking my driver for his and his lady wife's hospitality."

"Torquil has already broken his fast. Ye will find him in the stable when ye're ready to begin his lessons."

"Already? I'm surprised he's awake. It's still rather early."

"Aye, well, we Highlanders donna lie in bed all day when there is work to be done."

She detected his barb against her English upbringing and tried to hold her tongue, but her words came out faster than she could stay them. "Tell me, Laird Sutherland. Should I expect the noon meal to still be at noon, then?"

Ravenna pretended not to understand his scolding look and brushed passed him to the great hall. She quickly went to the kitchens and broke her fast before the man accused her of eating too slowly simply because she was English. At least the kitchen maids were kind enough to let her sit at the kitchen table, even though she was the enemy.

When she finished her meal, she found Torquil in the stable. He was standing in one of the stalls brushing a light-colored mare and didn't appreciate it when she led him away to begin his first lesson. The look on his face was not one of excitement, not that she blamed him.

As they entered the library, she paused. For being this far north in the Highlands, the laird certainly had a vast array of books in his collection. And that was another misconception. She didn't think these barbarians even knew how to pick up a book, let alone read one. Then again, what else would Laird Sutherland do in the dead of winter to occupy his thoughts?

A large wooden table surrounded by six chairs sat in the center of the library. Two chairs were placed in front of a stone fireplace that looked like a lovely place to sit and curl up and read. One wall of the library was lined with several wooden shelves that held many books that she couldn't wait to explore. When she spotted a tapestry of another bloody battle hung on the wall surrounded by shields and swords, she shuddered. Why the man wanted nothing but brutal scenes of war displayed on the walls of his home was beyond her comprehension.

She pulled out a chair and sat next to Torquil at the table. She took out a piece of paper and drew a picture of the sun while he watched.

"Sun," she said. "Good morning."

His green eyes studied her intently.

Ravenna pointed to the picture. "Good morning, Torquil." She yawned and stretched her back.

He slowly repeated her words and she smiled. She took the paper and drew a picture of the moon beside the sun.

"Moon," she said. "Good night, Torquil." She closed her eyes and pretended to sleep.

When the boy realized what she meant to convey, he nodded his head in understanding. Seeing the smile on his face made Ravenna feel saddened for him. Kat was only two years younger than Torquil, and Ravenna knew how much her sister needed and missed her mother. The loss must be devastating to him.

Ravenna spent the next few hours drawing pictures and having Torquil repeat her words. When it was time for the noon meal, they made their way to the great hall. She had just taken her seat when Fagan and Laird Sutherland entered with a score of men. Seeing kilted warriors flow into the hall and hearing their deep masculine laughs made Ravenna feel like her breath was cut off. These men were a massive, self-confident bunch.

Fagan sat down beside her and gave her a polite smile. "Ravenna."

"Fagan."

"Ravenna," said another voice in a captivating Scottish accent that she tried not to think about.

"Laird Sutherland."

"Och, lass. I think we are more than beyond formalities. Donna ye think? Ye will call me Ruairi."

When he gave her a knowing look, she felt her face turn to crimson. She lifted her tankard to her lips before another witty—or daft—remark escaped from her mental arsenal. The room was suddenly silenced as a man was escorted to the dais. He gave a slight bow as a troubled expression crossed his brow.

"My laird. Two more have been found."

❧

Ruairi stood and gave a brief nod to Fagan.

"Pray excuse us," said Fagan to Ravenna. They promptly escorted Calum to Ruairi's study and closed the door.

"Please sit." Ruairi gestured to a chair. "Where were they found?"

"North of the cliffs. Both of the cattle found much the same as the last, my laird. Slaughtered and left for dead. It was nay animal that killed them," said Calum.

Ruairi ran his hand through his hair. "Have them removed."

"I already gathered the remains, my laird. I came as soon as I found them."

"Verra good."

Calum looked uneasy and shifted in the chair. "And should the men still watch the border, my laird?"

"Aye. I donna want anything in or out without me knowing it. See to it."

Calum rose. "Aye, my laird."

The door closed and Ruairi sat down in the chair with a heavy sigh. "I donna like it. That makes five of our cattle slaughtered."

Fagan sat on the edge of the desk. "And ye still believe 'tis your wife's clan?"

"Who else could it be? Even though the Gordon doesnae say as much, I know he blames me for Anna's death. Howbeit we have nay proof and I cannae verra well accuse the man with naught before my eyes. He is clever. I give him that. Make certain the men watch the border. If 'tis Anna's clan, I will deal with them."

"Ye neglected to mention," said Fagan. "I assume since ye sit here hale that the lass didnae kill ye when ye told her ye speak the king's tongue."

"She wasnae exactly thrilled," he said dryly.

"Ye must admit she is a fine-looking lass, Ruairi."

He shrugged with indifference. "There are many fine-looking lasses who arenae English."

Fagan waved him off. "I wouldnae hold that against her. She's only doing as she's told."

"The woman isnae my concern. Speak English in front of Torquil. The faster he takes to his lessons, the faster she departs."

"Och, aye. And if I didnae know ye any better, I would say that almost sounded convincing."

"If ye didnae take notice, we have more pressing matters upon us."

Ruairi didn't need to remind Fagan of the Highland clans who attempted to rally against the king. Nor did he have to remind his captain that the lairds barely tolerated one another, so the idea of working together to form an alliance against the realm was completely absurd. But until either came to fruition, Ruairi was determined to keep his clan as far out of harm's way as possible. He knew his wife's father had other ideas, but Ruairi was not a daft fool. The Gordon should not be starting trouble, especially in political matters. Men had been hung for less.

"Let's ride to where Calum found the cattle. If we're lucky, mayhap there is still a trail," said Ruairi.

He walked out into the courtyard, and no sooner did he approach the stable with Fagan than a shrill scream rang through the air.

⁓

Ravenna had a difficult time trying to convince Torquil to return to the library while the sun was shining. He kept shaking his head "no" and pulling her by the hand out into the garden.

A warm breeze tickled her nose, and she stopped to brush back the hair that had fallen into her face. "All right. You win," she said with a smile.

Torquil didn't need to understand her words to comprehend their meaning. His face lit up from ear to ear. Elizabeth and Kat were much the same. At times it was difficult to gather them inside on a nice day. What Ravenna wouldn't give to be that young and innocent again.

She sat down on a garden bench, and when she heard the sound of crashing waves, she walked to the edge of the wall. She had to admit that she was pleasantly surprised. Laird Sutherland had such a beautiful home. The gardens and paths were quite exquisite, and so was the view from this very spot. She stood silently and watched the water that rolled in and out on the sandy shore. The feeling was so serene that she didn't want to move—until Torquil called her name.

Ravenna turned as he gestured for her to follow. They walked through the bustling courtyard, and as they strolled beyond the gate, she noticed that the curtain wall had to be at least twenty feet thick at the widest point. While Torquil ran ahead of her in the mossy field, jumping over rocks and simply enjoying being a boy, she turned and gazed at the fortified castle, with its round turrets and square watchtower.

To her left were the dangerous cliffs and to her right was a lush forest. Uncle Walter was right. With the large number of guards she'd seen standing on the castle walls, Sutherland could be a powerful enemy. When she and Torquil started to stray farther away from the castle, she stopped.

"Why don't we turn around now? We've walked quite a way from home." Ravenna waved her hand for him to return, but the boy shook his head and turned abruptly away from her. "Torquil," she said sternly. "We've gone far enough."

He raised his hand in the air to silence her. Bringing his fingers to his lips, he let out a piercing whistle. His eyes searched the trees as he patiently waited for something.

"Your father will be wondering where we are. Torquil…"

When he still didn't move, she walked toward him with long, purposeful strides. She grabbed his shoulder and gently spun him around. "You've had your fun. Now it's time we return." She gave the boy the same look that frightened her sisters when they misbehaved, and thankfully, no further words were needed since he nodded in agreement.

They were starting to walk back when the tiny hairs rose on the back of Ravenna's neck. She had a feeling she was being watched. She turned her head and thought she caught something move out of the corner of her eye. If danger was near, she would by no means chance Torquil being hurt. Feeling her dagger strapped securely on her thigh, she increased her pace until they reached the courtyard.

But to her dismay, Torquil didn't follow her and walked into the stables. She let out a long, audible breath. If she didn't set rules now, he would never respect her authority. She grudgingly went after him.

And then she froze.

A giant wolf had Torquil splayed on the ground. The beast's massive paws were on the boy's chest and a head was lowered in Torquil's face. The animal was a mass of black fur and stood as tall as Ravenna's waist.

"Do. Not. Move," she said in a calming voice.

Ravenna lifted her skirts and fumbled for her dagger as the wolf turned and glared at her with soulless eyes. Once she felt the hilt of the blade securely in her hand, she slowly unsheathed her weapon. As long as the boy remained still, she'd be able to throw her dagger into the side of the beast. She never missed—ever. And she would not start now.

Torquil sat up abruptly and hugged the animal close to hold the massive jaws at bay. Ravenna couldn't help but scream when she realized she didn't have a clear shot. The boy's life hung in the balance. Sheer black fright swept through her and she gasped, panting in terror. Her heart pounded furiously.

Without warning, Ruairi and Fagan clamored into the stable with swords drawn. The men looked around, back and forth, a shadow of alarm touching Ruairi's face. His eyes finally met Ravenna's.

"What is amiss?" he asked, resuming his search in the stable.

She looked back at the wolf with confusion. And that's when she noticed Torquil's smile. She slowly felt the color returning to her face as Ruairi and Fagan sheathed their weapons at the same time.

"Why did ye scream? Tell me ye arenae afraid of Angus."

She lifted her fallen jaw. "Angus? You call that wicked beast 'Angus'? But that's a *wolf*." She didn't miss the chuckle that escaped Fagan when he promptly took his leave, and there was a trace of laughter in Ruairi's voice when he spoke.

"Lass, Angus has been with us for many years. He will nae trouble ye." He patted the creature on the head. "Right, Angus?"

Torquil rose to his feet and walked over to Ravenna. He gestured for the animal to come toward him. The wolf crept slowly forward, eyeing her as if for his next meal. She found herself renewing the grip on her dagger.

"Ravenna, put down the knife and hold out your hand. Let Angus approach ye."

She couldn't stay the tremor in her voice. "I think not. Tell him to stop right where he is."

"Hold out your hand and let him get to know ye. Let him smell your scent."

"I have enough friends and I don't need any more companions, especially the four-legged kind. Please tell him to go away," she blurted out.

"Angus is Torquil's protector. He wouldnac harm the lad."

"Be that as it may, I will not be giving *Angus* a chance to harm me. Please keep that beast as far away from me as possible."

Ruairi rolled his eyes and spoke in Gaelic to Torquil. She breathed a sigh of relief when the boy left with the wolf in tow. She knew the Scottish Highlands were a dangerous place, but she was discovering that the men were not the only wild things in Scotland.

Four

RUAIRI WAITED UNTIL THE WEE HOURS OF THE NIGHT.
For the past two weeks, he had made certain he knew
when Ravenna was sound asleep. She was a stranger in
his home, and he couldn't chance her stumbling across
him as he stalked through the darkened halls. He also
couldn't risk anyone discovering his secret, especially
an English lass.

The main torches were extinguished, but he could
find his way easily in the dark. He knew every inch of
his home. The castle was silent except for his footsteps
as he treaded lightly across the stone floor. When he
reached the kitchens, he stopped. He thought he heard
a noise, but perhaps he was mistaken.

He pushed back the cloth and entered the pantry.
Once the material had fallen, closing the opening behind
him, he approached the shelved wall. Lifting the false
shelf, he pulled the lever, and when the wall creaked
open, he paused a moment to make certain he was alone.
When he didn't hear anything, he pushed open the partition and walked through. He fumbled to light a candle
and kicked the wall closed behind him with his foot.

The air had changed to cold and damp. Holding up
the light in front of him, Ruairi proceeded through
the stone enclosure and descended through the tunnels. He wiped away the cobwebs that clung to his
face. There were many passageways underneath his
home, but only a handful of trusted men knew of
their existence.

Ruairi walked several hundred feet and then turned
east toward the sea. He could hear the sound of the
ocean waves crashing in the distance. The tunnel narrowed and then the natural room widened, straight
out into the bottom of the cliffs. Through the years,
he had learned to study the tides, so he knew when it
was safe to enter the cave. The only time he had that
chance was at low tide. When the waters rose, the
room flooded and was impassable.

Now was the perfect time.

Inside the cave, he bent over, his arms encircling a
giant rock. He was able to nudge the rock a little farther each time he pushed, and after four attempts, he
had uncovered the hole in the floor. Ruairi removed
the pouch from his sporran and lowered himself to the
wet ground. His fingers reached around in the hole,
and when he grasped a handful of coins, he pulled
them out and tossed them into the bag. After a couple
more handfuls, he shook his hand, feeling the weight
of the bag.

There. That ought to do it.

He shoved the pouch back into his sporran and stood,
then inched the rock back in place until the opening was
covered. While other greedy clans raided and pillaged,
Ruairi made sure his clan's wealth was protected. The

bastards may slaughter his cattle, but they would never steal Sutherland coin. His enemies would never be that successful. And besides, Ruairi knew money bought anything and anyone. Coin had certainly secured the future of many Sutherland lairds that came before him.

He made his way back through the tunnels. When he reached the stone enclosure, he snuffed out the candle, lifted the latch, and pushed open the wall. He paused a moment to make certain he was alone. Once he was sure, he turned and pushed the shelf down into its rightful place, then lifted the cloth to the pantry. When he heard the material fall behind him, he caught a familiar scent in the air.

Lavender.

❧

Ravenna pressed her back so tightly against the darkened wall that she dared not breathe. *Good God*. The man stood a hairbreadth away from her. If she was discovered now, her assignment would be over before it had begun. She closed her eyes and silently prayed for a miracle.

That's when she heard a slight banging sound, followed by a chuckle.

"Angus, what are ye doing here? Are ye hungry?"

Ravenna felt both relieved and panicked. She felt momentary relief because the sound was only that of a wagging tail. At least the dreaded beast had distracted Ruairi from her. But she was panicked because she knew that tail belonged to a large wolf with extremely sharp teeth. What she wouldn't give to make the two of them go away!

"Here's a piece of bread. Now off with ye."

She heard Angus's massive jaws devour the bread. She didn't dare move until she was certain Ruairi and his odd choice of a companion had left. Ravenna wasn't sure which beast would be more dangerous if she was found wandering alone in the dark—the handsome Highland laird or his wild protector. Only when all threat of discovery was removed did she dare move from her wall.

Knowing the wolf was under the same roof, Ravenna walked with hastened purpose through the halls. She needed to reach the safe confines of her bedchamber, suddenly longing for the security of its four walls. Over the last two weeks, she hadn't been privy to any conversations among Ruairi and his men. And to her dismay, she was unable to determine the reason for the guard's disruption in the great hall. When she'd asked a few of the servants if they knew anything about it, no one was forthcoming. She couldn't say she was surprised.

Ravenna had just rounded the bend to her chamber when she saw a darkened figure rise from the stone floor at the end of the hall.

She froze and tried not to scream.

A big, black shadow crept slowly forward. She. Was. Going. To. Die. She caught herself glancing uneasily over her shoulder, praying for some sign of rescue by a certain Highland laird. She became more uncomfortable by the moment as the animal approached her, seemingly studying her every move. She began to shake with fear.

One bite.

That's all it would take to tear into her soft flesh. Ravenna's breath was choked and she could barely get enough air into her lungs. When the wolf stopped in front of her with his deadly stare, a cold knot formed in her stomach. She dared not move while memories of the past suffocated her.

The animal held his ground with purpose, and she didn't want to wait to find out why. She briefly closed her eyes to find the courage that she so desperately needed and then softly whispered, "Hello, Angus. You're going to be a good dog…er, wolf and let me pass. Aren't you?"

Against her better judgment, Ravenna lowered her hand. Angus stuck out his cold nose, and as he brushed her fingers, she leaned back against the wall and reached for the door latch with her other hand. Never taking her eyes from the wolf, she slowly pushed open the door. She inched her way with two carefully placed steps along the edge of the wall, then darted inside and threw the door closed in the animal's face.

Ravenna leaned against the chamber wall and scoffed at her predicament. "Damn you, Uncle Walter. You never said there would be dogs—well, a wolf. How many times must I tell you? I. Don't. Like. Dogs," she said through gritted teeth. She sat down on the bed and blew out the breath she held. "If I survive this, it will truly be a miracle." She climbed into bed and closed her eyes, knowing morning would come far too early.

And it did.

When she realized the sun was up and she'd barely slept, she groaned and rubbed her fingers over her tired eyes. If she didn't rise now, she would never hear the end of it from a particular kilted man. Ruairi had more than likely arisen before first light and started his day. He often made a point of insinuating that the English were pampered and the Scots worked much harder. What an idiot.

She lifted the blankets, sat up, and hung her legs over the side of the bed.

"We Highlanders donna lie in bed all day when there is work to be done," she mumbled under her breath in her best Scottish accent.

Ravenna dressed and descended the stairs. Men and women were bustling into the great hall for the morning meal. As she suspected, Ruairi, Fagan, and Torquil were already seated at the table. When she approached the dais, Torquil lifted his eyes and jumped to his feet.

"Good morn, Ravenna." He pulled out her chair for her.

"Very good, Torquil." She sat down and smiled at the boy. "And thank you for being a gentleman."

"Did ye sleep well?" asked Ruairi with a curious expression on his face.

"Yes, thank you." Ravenna took a sip from her tankard before her thoughts gave her away. She wouldn't mention the fact that she'd tossed and turned because her memory was plagued with dangerous animals—the four-legged kind and the two-legged kind.

"Torquil seems to be taking to his studies," said Ruairi.

She swallowed her bite of oatmeal. "Yes, we still have a long way to go, but he's doing well. You should be proud."

He nodded. "I am always proud of him. 'Tis a

nice day and my son has been confined in the library for too long. I want to take him riding this morn. Ye will join us." Ruairi's declaration was more of a command.

"If you wish."

"And will ye need my assistance, my laird?" asked Fagan, as though something unspoken had passed between the men.

A strange look flashed in Ruairi's eyes. "I donna think so. Why donna ye practice your swordplay with the men? *Twice*."

Fagan chuckled. "Och, Ruairi, ye—"

"Twice," he repeated.

"Aye, my laird," said Fagan, trying to mask a smile.

Ruairi rose and Torquil stood, reaching for another piece of bread from the table.

"Torquil."

Torquil's eyebrow rose in surprise at the disapproving tone in his father's voice. "Angus," he replied.

"Angus doesnae need food from the table. He can hunt his own meal." When Torquil paused, Ruairi repeated his words in Gaelic.

The boy nodded reluctantly and put the chunk of bread back on the table. The moment of temporary scolding clearly forgotten, Torquil ran out of the great hall with all the pent-up energy of a young boy.

"Are ye ready?" asked Ruairi, lifting a brow.

His tone of voice implied that Ravenna was being too slow. Granted, she had only eaten half of her oatmeal, but she couldn't help leveling him with a withering stare. Spy or not, she would not let herself be put down by this Highlander. She stood, thinking how weary she was of the man's negative references to the English.

"We English are always ready."

❧

Ruairi looked at Ravenna in surprise as she tossed her fiery locks over her shoulder. He continued to watch her in awe as she left the table, turned around, and placed her hand on her hip. She shot him a cold look and spoke with impatience.

"Well? Are you coming or not? We English do not like to be kept waiting."

He couldn't stay his smile as he followed the lass out into the bailey. The woman never hesitated to show her displeasure when he made certain comments about the English. Although Ruairi spoke the truth, he didn't necessarily mean the words about his son's governess. But he had to admit that he enjoyed seeing her green eyes flash with fury.

After the mounts were saddled, Ruairi watched Torquil as he rode out ahead of them into the field. His son and his governess had been huddled in the library, and he knew Torquil would rather be out in the air. To be truthful, he thought Ravenna could use a brief respite as well. At least that's what he kept telling himself. Surely his actions weren't because he wanted to spend time with her. The mere thought was absurd.

Ruairi followed Ravenna's mount, which gave him time to study the lass without her knowing. Her shiny red tresses looked kissed by the sun. Her skin glowed. Her waist was slim. When she turned, providing a view of her full and rosy lips, he suddenly had a strong urge to taste them. Shifting in the saddle, he discreetly adjusted the front of his kilt.

Her voice broke his impure thoughts.

"Your son enjoys being out in the sun," said Ravenna, watching Torquil run his horse through the grass.

"Aye. He is much like his father. I enjoy the open air."

She laughed. "Being so close to the sea, I imagine so. The air smells...clean. Your home is beautiful."

"I'm glad it suits ye, lass. Come. I will show ye the view from the cliffs."

Ruairi led his mount to the cliffs but placed himself between Ravenna and the edge. He wouldn't chance her horse getting skittish and tossing her into the cold depths of the abyss below. He shook his head and tried to direct his thoughts away from his wife. He'd certainly dwelled on that day long enough. Granted, he should've tried to stop the stubborn lass when she fled in a blind rage, charging her mount carelessly along the steep rocks. But two years had been a long time to be plagued by guilt. He couldn't erase the past, even if he wanted to.

They stopped at the top of the cliffs and Ruairi dismounted. When he glanced over his shoulder, he saw Torquil still riding in the field below. Ruairi walked over to assist Ravenna and she placed her hands on his shoulders, sliding from her mount. When her feet were planted firmly on the ground, he knew he'd held on to her waist longer than he should have.

For a moment he just stood there staring at her. His heart ached in a way he couldn't quite explain.

Only when the scent of lavender spilled into his senses did he pull away. He walked to the edge of the steep rocks without speaking a word and looked down at the waves below.

"I don't think I'd ever tire of that view," she said, walking up beside him.

He placed his arm across her midriff. "Donna come too close to the edge."

"Why? Because I'm English and you'll push me off?"

His eyes narrowed. "If I wanted to kill ye due to your English upbringing, ye would've been dead when ye first set foot on my lands."

"How comforting," she said dryly.

He paused. "I donna want to see ye hurt."

She studied him for a moment and stepped back. "Could you tell me something about your clan?" When he looked at her and hesitated, she added, "Perhaps some history of the Sutherland clan. I don't know much about Scotland and I thought I'd start with you."

He lifted a brow. "Yet ye're here to teach my son," he said dryly. When she didn't respond to his barb, he asked, "Are ye truly interested or only making polite conversation?"

"I wouldn't ask if I didn't want to know."

Ruairi looked out at the sea. "By the early tenth century, Norsemen had conquered the islands of Shetland and Orkney, as well as Caithness and Sutherland on the mainland. The Norse had control over Scotland beyond Moray Firth. The lower portion of the lands was called 'Suderland' because it was south of the Norse islands and Caithness.

"My ancestor was a Flemish nobleman named

Freskin de Moravia. He was given a commission by the king—David the First—to clear the Norse from the lands. My ancestor was a legend in his time, having killed the last breathing Norseman. Some years later, the Sinclairs rebelled against the Bishop of Caithness over tithes he imposed, and once again, the Sutherland clan was charged with restoring law and order. More to the point, these lands have been in the hands of my clan for centuries."

She paused. "I'm not sure what to say to that. I find myself rendered quite speechless. There is so much history in your family. You must be proud." When he didn't respond, Ravenna looked down over the cliff. "I couldn't imagine waking up and having this view every day. Your wife must have loved it here."

He almost chuckled when he thought of the irony.

"My apologies. Lady Sutherland's passing must be painful for you. I hope she didn't suffer long."

"How long have ye been a governess?" Ruairi asked, changing the direction of the conversation.

"Longer than I can remember. I love children."

"I suppose ye'd have to."

"It won't take Torquil long to learn some English, especially if you and Fagan and I continue to speak it to him."

As Ruairi nodded, Ravenna looked over his shoulder and froze.

∾⌘∾

Dear God.

Angus ran across the field from the woods and came straight toward them. If not for the steep drop behind her, Ravenna would have fled. To her dismay, there was nowhere to go. When Ruairi saw the reason for her concern, he smiled patiently.

"Lass, I told ye before. 'Tis only Angus. He will nae harm ye."

They took a few steps away from the cliff, and she was glad they did because when the giant wolf reached Ruairi, two massive paws thumped on his back. The impact of the animal made Ruairi's hard body bump into her. In fact, they were so close that she could practically lay her head on the man's broad chest.

"Please keep him away from me," said Ravenna, trying desperately to hold on to her fragile control.

Ruairi continued to hold back the wolf and then yelled to Torquil. When the boy didn't respond, Ruairi said something again in Gaelic. Torquil finally called for Angus, and the wolf parted company—but not soon enough. At long last, Ravenna was able to breathe a sigh of relief.

"Lass, truly, ye need to calm yourself around Angus. Ye know he is able to sense your fear. Ye are only making matters worse."

"I understand that, but I truly don't like dogs." Her voice was shakier than she would've liked.

"Angus isnae a dog. He's a wolf," Ruairi said with a smile.

"And *that* doesn't make me feel any better." She quickly glanced at Torquil to make sure Angus was staying in the field below. She didn't want to lose sight of the wolf for a single moment. God forbid the animal would jump on her the way he did to Ruairi. She didn't think her poor nerves could take it.

"What happened to ye?"

Ravenna looked at him, puzzled. "What do you mean?"

"What happened to ye that ye're afraid of dogs?"

"Oh, I don't like to talk about it."

He gave her an easy smile. "I've found that fear will always control ye if ye donna speak about it and face it."

She bit her lip and then reluctantly spoke, choosing her words carefully. "I was on an assignment with another family, and a dog bit me brutally in the leg. The wicked beast left quite a nasty scar on my calf, and I haven't gone near anything with four legs since. I don't want to take a chance in case they decide to take a bite out of me for their next meal."

"That must've been painful, but 'twas only one dog. Nae all animals are like that. Angus has been with our clan for years and has ne'er harmed anyone."

"That you know of… I know you think it's a foolish fear, but I see how big Angus is and his teeth—"

"Are only used to eat." When he saw her widened eyes and recognized what she was about to say, he added, "Food. Nae man or woman. Moreover, he knows to stay away from wily lasses." He winked, and she knew he was teasing her affectionately, not maliciously.

She lifted a brow. "And let's not forget that I am English."

"Aye. Angus is smart. He knows nae to touch the English." Laugh lines crinkled around Ruairi's eyes. "Will ye trust me with something?"

"Mmm… I don't know. You look like you're up to something."

"I would ne'er let any harm befall ye."

For some reason, Ravenna believed him. She nodded in consent and he moved to stand behind her. He pressed his entire length against her back and rested his hands at her hips. Leaning back, he let out a loud whistle and Angus came toward them.

He must have felt her tense up because he spoke softly in her ear. "Be calm." He leaned away from her and gestured to the animal. "Angus, come."

Ravenna wasn't sure if she trembled because of the wolf or from the strength of Ruairi's touch. As the wild creature came closer and another stood at her back, she couldn't think clearly about anything. "Ruairi…"

"Shhh… I'm here with ye. Trust me. Angus will nae harm ye," he said in a whispering voice. "Open your eyes, Ravenna."

She wasn't sure how the man knew they were closed. She could hear the blood pounding in her ears, and it was impossible to steady her erratic pulse. "Please don't make me do this. I don't want to do this. I can't."

"Ye're doing fine, lass. Give me your hand." He placed his hand on top of hers and lifted her fingers in front of Angus's nose. "Let him smell your scent."

A cold nose touched her skin and her heart beat faster. She was deathly afraid of the wolf, but all she could think about was Ruairi's touch. He lifted her hand to the top of Angus' head and had her gently pat the animal.

"Ye're doing it, Ravenna. Ye see? 'Tis just Angus. He wouldnae harm ye."

Ravenna closed her eyes again and, against her better judgment, leaned back against Ruairi. She felt his chin lower into her hair. Suddenly, she was so conscious of his body that she almost forgot about Angus—almost. Laird Sutherland certainly had a pleasant way of distracting her from her fear.

For a brief time, neither of them spoke. She realized Angus had walked away a few moments earlier. When Ruairi brushed the tips of his fingers lightly on her arm, she felt like a breathless young girl. He whispered her name in her ear in that alluring Scottish accent and it was almost her undoing—well, until Torquil called to her and the moment was lost.

She promptly stepped away from the man before she lost her mind. God help her. For a moment, she'd wanted Ruairi to crush her against himself in a heated embrace. She briefly wondered what that would be like, then told herself to stop these ridiculous notions. *Now.*

Torquil rode toward them and smiled. "Good, Ravenna." He looked like he was searching for his words. "Umm…Angus."

She approached the boy and tapped his leg in the stirrup. "Thank you, Torquil."

"Would ye like to ride to the village?" asked Ruairi, grabbing their mounts.

"I'd love to."

He assisted her onto her mount and handed her the reins. "Ye took a big step forward with Angus. 'Tis only a matter of time before the two of ye are friends."

"I don't know if I'd go that far, but thank you, Ruairi."

His smile was boyishly affectionate, and then he effortlessly swung his leg up over his mount. He nodded to Torquil and said something in Gaelic.

But when the boy responded, a strange look crossed Ruairi's face, as if he was troubled.

"Does he not want to travel with us to the village?" asked Ravenna.

"Nay, he comes."

Ruairi was quiet and his lightened mood disappeared. He led his horse onto the dirt path and Ravenna followed. Something had definitely changed, and she could not quite put her finger on what that was.

"I get the feeling something is wrong. What did Torquil say?"

There was a heavy silence as she stared at Ruairi's back. She had about given up hope that he was going to respond. But after several uncomfortable moments, he finally spoke.

"Torquil asked if ye were going to be his mother."

Five

RUAIRI'S THOUGHTS SPUN. HE KNEW HE SHOULDN'T have let his manhood rule his mind. But when he pressed up against Ravenna and she trembled in his arms, he couldn't help himself. She felt so damn good. Even though he was hesitant to admit it, the English woman's behavior was astoundingly not so *English*. She was kind toward Torquil and quick to speak her mind. He found she wasn't like most lasses, for that matter.

But his son's question unnerved him. Torquil hadn't had a female presence in his life since the death of his mother, and Ruairi didn't want his son to become too close to his governess. After all, when the lad's studies were complete, Ravenna would take her leave and report back to the king. Scotland was not her home or where she was meant to be. Ruairi needed to remember that and keep things in perspective.

As they rode back from the village, the lass didn't utter a single word. From the expression on her face, Ruairi knew she was deep in thought. He couldn't say that he blamed her. Torquil's question more than likely weighed heavily on her mind. Ruairi tried to break the uncomfortable silence by changing the subject.

"What did ye think of the village?"

Ravenna smiled, but the smile did not reach her eyes. "Oh, it was quite lovely. I see how much everyone adores you."

He shrugged. "They are my people, my responsibility. I merely look after them."

She reined in beside him and lowered her voice. "I hope I didn't give Torquil a reason to think... I am his governess. You only have one mother in this world, and I assure you that I have no intention of taking his mother's place."

For some reason, her words felt like a deep cut to Ruairi's soul, but the feeling made no sense. He knew the lass spoke the truth, but hearing the words from her lips angered him. What was the matter with him? Until he could answer that question, he wouldn't give the lass the satisfaction of knowing how much she unsettled him.

He looked at her, his eyes narrowed, and spoke defensively. "Donna worry your bonny English head upon it. Ye will find I have nay intention of having ye take my wife's place."

He kicked his mount and rode on ahead of her. Once he entered the bailey, which was not soon enough, he released his mount to the stable hand. He stormed off to find Fagan—suddenly having a burning need to practice his swordplay. And Fagan was the perfect object on which to take out all his mounting frustration. Ruairi quickly found his captain standing in the great hall.

"What has happened? Did ye find another animal?" asked Fagan with a sense of urgency.

Ruairi found that his friend's words put things a bit more into perspective. He realized he was behaving as if he was troubled over something of importance. "Nay. I just returned from—"

"Ah, your ride with Ravenna," said Fagan with a wry grin. "And how did ye do with the bonny lass?"

Mixed feelings surged through Ruairi and he was puzzled by his behavior. When the only response he could provide was a scowl, his friend lifted a brow.

"Ye know it has been quite some time since ye attempted to woo a lass. Do ye find yourself needing my instruction after all, my laird? Mayhap I should've come with ye."

"So help me. If ye werenae like my brother, I'd ball my fist into your face right now."

Fagan chuckled, slapping Ruairi on the shoulder. "Let's have ourselves a wee bit of ale and ye can tell me all about your woes."

∽

The man had taken off as though the seat of his Sutherland kilt was on fire. What had made Ravenna think she could find momentary comfort in the arms of a Highland laird? A recently widowed Highland laird at that. He must think of her as some kind of wanton idiot. She shook her head at her stupidity.

Taking advantage of her distracted state, Torquil tried to sneak past her. She tried not to smile because the boy reminded her so much of Kat.

"Torquil…"

He slowly turned around, and an innocent expression crossed his face. "Aye?"

Not fooled for a moment, Ravenna pointed and said, "Library," then gestured him forward. She laughed when the boy groaned, mumbling under his breath and pouting as they walked through the halls. If he slowed his pace any further, it would be time to sup before they reached their destination.

As they finally took their seats in the library, Ravenna struggled with the thought of Torquil's question to his father. She should've known the boy was still in a fragile state after the recent passing of his mother. And her behavior today… Not only were Ravenna's actions inexcusable, but Lady Sutherland was only in the ground a few weeks. And more importantly, Ravenna had forgotten her most sacred rule. Although she was a spy for the Crown, she would never use a child— ever—to suit her purposes. The thought of doing so went against everything she stood for.

"Ravenna…"

She blinked to clear the cobwebs. "Oh, yes. Let us continue." She pulled out her drawings and held up one at a time as Torquil recalled most of the English words. For the remainder of the afternoon, she and Torquil worked hard on putting those words into sentences.

When it was time to sup, Ravenna briefly thought about taking her meal in her chamber. She definitely wanted to choose the coward's way out. But with her luck of late, someone would come looking for her and she'd have to explain her absence. Reluctantly, she made her way to the great hall and sat down at the table.

"How did ye enjoy the village?" asked Fagan as he reached for a piece of bread.

"It was such a lovely day. I was telling Laird Sutherland that I could see how much his people truly care for him. We also traveled to the cliffs. The view—"

"Can be verra dangerous. I donna want ye going there alone," said Ruairi. The man spoke in an odd tone and kept his eyes on his trencher.

"I have no intention of doing so, but the cliffs were beautiful nonetheless."

"Aye, Ruairi wouldnae want ye going there…*alone*. I'm sure my laird would accompany ye whenever ye'd like to go," said Fagan. When he raised his brow at Ruairi, the silence grew tight with tension. She also noticed that Ruairi would not look Fagan directly in the eye.

She said a silent prayer of thanks when two Sutherland guards came into the great hall with their hands on the hilts of their swords, interrupting the uncomfortable moment. They walked forward and bowed their heads to Ruairi.

"My laird, the Munro is at the gates."

Ruairi dropped the meat he held in his hand and stood, while Fagan placed his tankard down and did the same. The men didn't say another word and simply walked out of the great hall with the guards.

Ravenna turned to Torquil. "Mmm…I wonder what that's all about."

When the boy shrugged his shoulders and continued to eat, Ravenna realized Ruairi's son understood more than he acknowledged.

꧂

Why? Why couldn't he have one day of peace? With the bonny English governess who continued to haunt his dreams, the slaughtered cattle, and now the Munro who pounded at his gates, Ruairi needed a drink. Maybe several.

The Munro dismounted from his horse and stood surrounded by his faithful guards. His long, red hair was tapered at the neck, and half his tunic was pulled out at the waist and hung over his kilt. He placed his hand on the hilt of his sword, and when he spotted Ruairi, his expression darkened.

"Sutherland, ye would keep me waiting beyond your gates?"

Ruairi approached the man with Fagan by his side. "Munro, ye are a wee bit far from home, are ye nae?"

"We need to have words."

"And I think ye like to hear the sound of your own."

Munro smiled as he reached out and embraced Ruairi with a slap on the back. "I see ye are still in one piece, Ruairi."

"'Tis good to see ye, Ian. We just sat down to sup. Join us." The men walked into the bailey. "I am pleased to see ye, but what are ye doing here?"

"'Tis a conversation best held behind closed doors."

Ruairi nodded. "Come. Cook made a fine meal."

They entered the great hall, and Ravenna's eyes widened at the sight of Munro's men. Ruairi suddenly realized he hadn't had a chance to explain her presence to his friend. He slowed his pace and turned his head to say something to Ian, but the man was no longer by his side. God's teeth! He was already at the table in front of Ravenna.

Ian gave Ravenna a slight bow. "My lady, I am Laird Ian Munro. A pleasure to make your acquaintance."

She shifted in the chair and looked uncomfortable. "My laird, I am no lady. I am Mistress Denny, governess for Laird Sutherland's son."

"Governess?"

"Yes. Since Lady Sutherland had fallen ill, I was sent by the king to educate their son here and not in the Lowlands."

He stared at her, confused. "Because Lady Sutherland had fallen ill, eh?"

Ruairi slapped Ian on the shoulder, and his friend gave him a puzzled look. "Come and have a drink."

"I daresay I think I need one."

Ian was smart enough to recognize that something was afoot, and Ruairi only prayed the man wasn't daft enough to open his mouth. They took their seats at the table, and Ruairi almost chuckled when Ian took a long drink of ale.

"I think I need another."

Ruairi refilled Ian's tankard and was taking a long swig himself when his worst fear came true. Ian leaned forward and spoke to Ravenna.

"Ye are here on behalf of the king?"

"Yes."

"I have to ask. Have we met before? I cannae help but say ye look familiar, and I verra rarely forget a face."

"I'm sure that I'd remember, Laird Munro. This is my first time in Scotland."

"Mmm…" Ian had an odd look on his face as he took another drink of ale.

They were almost finished with the meal when

Ruairi noticed that Torquil's chair was empty. "Where is Torquil?" he asked Ravenna.

"Off to find *Angus* somewhere for sure." The lass shook her head in apparent disgust. "Pray excuse me as well. I'll be retiring to my chamber. It was a pleasure to meet you, Laird Munro."

"The pleasure was mine." Ian continued to watch Ravenna walk away from the table. "Although I swear I've met that lass before," he said, lowering his voice to Ruairi.

"I donna see how."

"Mmm…it will come to me. It always does. In the meantime, is there something ye want to tell me? For instance, when did your beloved wife return from the grave?"

"Mayhap 'tis best if we take our leave to my study."

"Aye, bring the ale. I have a feeling I'll need it."

Ruairi closed the door to his refuge and sat down in a chair. He poured Ian another tankard of ale and gestured for him to sit. "So tell me the reason for this unexpected visit."

"Have ye heard anything from the Gordon?"

"Naught as of late. Why?"

"Three of my cattle have been killed, and nae by another animal or sickness," said Ian with concern.

"Five of mine as well. I know the Gordon still blames me for Anna's death—although we've ne'er had words on the subject."

"But that doesnae explain why *my* cattle were killed. I donna like it, Ruairi. Ye know the Gordon is attempting to raise arms against the Crown. Even though our men are verra skilled, I donna think we would win if we decide to do battle against the English. Too much blood would be shed, too much lost. I will nae lead my men into slaughter. The last time I spoke with the Gordon, he wasnae pleased that I refused his request for men and weapons. And I've heard whispers that he formed an alliance with the Seton clan. Let me tell you what I think. His men target our cattle to convince us to join their cause."

Ruairi took another drink from his tankard. "Even if what ye say is true, the Gordon cannae hold ground against us if we join as one. Our numbers are too great."

"And I thought the same until the Seton joined him. And now Gordon is trying to engage the other Highland clans to unite as one."

"That will ne'er happen." Ruairi chuckled, shaking his head. "The lairds barely tolerate one another. Do ye think they'd actually work together for one purpose? Nay. And if any of them had any sense, they would see the Gordon for who he is. He has always sought political gain. He cares naught about his people, only himself."

"Ye would know that better than anyone. So what do ye propose?"

Ruairi sighed. "We have nay proof 'tis the Gordon's doing and I will nae be so quick to judge as to start a bloody war with my wife's father. Until we have proof, we keep our eyes and ears open."

"I agree, but I cannae afford to lose any more of my cattle. And before ye say another word, nay, ye have already offered your assistance for last year's crop. I will nae accept your charity again."

"Ye are far too proud, Ian. Ye know I will help ye in any way I can." When he saw Ian's expression, he knew a change of subject was in order. "We need to watch our lands and make certain naught comes in or out. Did ye increase your guards along the border?"

Ian rolled his eyes. "Of course. I'm nae daft."

"We need to catch a man in the act to question him. And please try to make sure your men donna kill him. I know it will be difficult, but we need the bastard alive. If another attempt is made, we will both be ready. If we find out 'tis the Gordon's doing, ye leave the man to me. Send a messenger should anything else happen."

Ian nodded and then reached for another drink. His eyes grew amused. "Ye know King James demands we send our sons to learn the ways of the English. Clearly, ye didnae send Torquil. I donna understand ye. Ye dare to nae follow our liege's command?"

Ruairi mentally readied himself for the verbal sparring that would surely follow. "Hell, Ian. I am nae going to send my son to learn their ways. Torquil will one day take my place and be a fine Highland laird. He needs to know our ways of survival and chieftainship, nae theirs."

"And the king sent the lass here because ye didnae send your son, didnae follow his command."

He sighed. "King James still doesnae know of Anna's passing two years ago. I used that to my advantage and told him that she had fallen ill so that I wouldnae have to send Torquil to the Lowlands. Howbeit I didnae expect the king to send someone to my home to teach the lad."

"What did ye expect, Ruairi? Ye didnae do as commanded. If the lass discovers ye lied about Anna, she'll report back to the king and your bollocks will nay longer be your own. What did ye tell her when she realized ye nay longer had a wife?"

"I told the lass Anna died shortly before she arrived."

Ian's voice went up a notch. "And she believed ye?"

"Aye, until the truth almost spewed from your mouth, ye bastard."

Ian laughed. "Have ye bedded her yet?"

⁂

Ravenna had a task to complete. She had been sent here on a mission. She had to keep reminding herself of that until it sunk in or until she could find a way to somehow banish Ruairi from her thoughts. Choosing to not pay any heed to the ceaseless inner questions that were hammering away at her, she made her way to his study. When she reached the closed door, she looked around the hall to make certain she was alone. Quietly, she placed her ear to the door.

Ruairi and Laird Munro were talking about catching a man in the act in order to question him. She heard the name Gordon, but she wasn't sure who he was. She would need to find out. She understood that Ruairi and Laird Munro were working together, but were they conspiring to raise arms against the Crown? When the subject quickly changed to Torquil's education, Ravenna almost pulled away, but then something warned her to stay. And she was glad she did.

Praise the saints.

Ruairi lied to King James and to her. His wife had

died two years ago! When she heard Laird Munro's final question to Ruairi, her blood boiled. She realized she'd heard enough. Why did men have to behave like swine? If you gathered two or more of them in a room, the subject always turned to coupling.

She promptly turned on her heel and fled to her bedchamber. She may have even growled under her breath. The man was trying to play her for a fool. She shut the door to her chamber and sat in the chair. In spite of herself, she chuckled. Wasn't she doing the same thing to Ruairi? She was a spy for the king, planted in his home to discover machinations against the realm. She was so tired of lies. Frankly, she wasn't sure if anyone spoke the truth anymore. After a few moments, she realized she wanted to clear her head. The parapet was just what she needed.

Ravenna stood, but as soon as she opened her bed-chamber door, Angus rose from the floor outside it. She gasped and whipped the door shut in the animal's face. Why couldn't the beast leave her be? She refused to be trapped in her own room by a wolf.

"Angus, go away! Now!" she yelled through the door. She placed her ear to the door, and when she didn't hear anything, she slowly cracked it open.

Angus stood there, merely staring at her. The animal cocked his head and his expression, if there was such a thing, was clearly one of "what the hell are you doing?" She kept the door cracked with her body pressed against it. Who knew if Angus would try to enter *her* sacred domain?

"Go on. Off with you! Shoo…Angus. Will you *please* get out of here?" she asked in desperation.

To her surprise, Angus lowered his head and slowly walked toward the other end of the hall. Thank God for small favors. Finally, Ravenna opened the door and stuck her head out to make certain the animal was gone. The giant wolf was nowhere in sight, so she walked out quickly and shut the door.

She managed to avoid the beast and found herself safely at the parapet door. Turning, she closed the latch firmly to make sure the door was shut securely behind her. She couldn't imagine being trapped on the roof of the castle with Angus. Then again, she'd sooner jump to her death than be eaten alive by a wolf's sharp fangs.

As she stood on the parapet and enjoyed the cool breeze that blew through her hair, she relished the view. She looked out at the vast ocean, stretching as far as she could see. The amber hues of the setting sun reflected off the water. She turned to her left, appreciating the green trees with their different shades of foliage and, of course, the beautiful mossy field that lay ahead. She had placed her hand on the cool stone wall and closed her eyes when a voice cut through the silence.

"What are ye doing up here, Ravenna?"

She jumped at the sound of Fagan's voice. "You startled me."

He stood beside her. "My apologies."

"I found myself in need of some air. And what about you?"

"Much the same." Fagan paused. "How is Torquil doing with his studies?"

She smiled. "He's doing extremely well. Although I think he favors the sun more than the library."

Fagan chuckled. "A lad after my own heart. How are ye finding our Highlands? 'Tis much different than London, is it nae?"

"Oh, very much so. Laird Sutherland's home is very lovely, and I find myself drawn to the sea. The water is so incredibly peaceful. You must love it here."

"Aye. Did Ruairi take ye to the beach?"

Her eyes lit up. "No. I didn't know there was one. He mentioned that the cliffs are dangerous, so I just watch the waves from the safety of the garden wall or here on the parapet."

"Then ye donna know what ye're missing. I'll mention it to Ruairi. Mayhap he will take ye on the morrow."

After her last encounter with Ruairi at the cliffs, the last thing Ravenna wanted was to spend time alone with him. "Please don't mention it. Laird Munro—"

He waved her off. "Donna worry about Laird Munro. He will be gone by the morrow."

"Does he come here often?"

"Nae too often. Munro is the neighboring clan. He and Ruairi have known each other since they were bairns. Ian's father, Laird Munro's sire," he clarified, "and Ruairi's father were verra close."

"It's wonderful that their sons still follow in their footsteps." She gazed out at the ocean waves, trying to keep her expression composed. "So do you have any neighboring clans other than Laird Munro's?"

"We have the Gunns, Sinclairs, and MacKays."

That was not the list she had expected to hear. Ravenna needed to broach the subject carefully as to not draw suspicion. "I thought I heard some of the

men mention Gordon. Are they a neighboring clan?"
she asked with an air of indifference.

"Nay."

How could she to find out who this man was?
Perhaps one of the servants would know. Maybe
they'd open up to her a little more since she's been
here several weeks. She'd most likely get more out of
them than the laird's henchman anyway, even though
they weren't very forthcoming with the small bits of
information she'd already asked them for. She'd have
to find another way. Her woolgathering was abruptly
interrupted by Fagan's words.

"The Gordon is the father of Ruairi's wife."

Six

AFTER BECOMING KNEE-DEEP IN HIS CUPS WITH IAN, Ruairi stumbled toward his own chamber. As he made his way around a corner, he paused when the door to the parapet swung wide open. Ravenna entered the hall, stopping to place an errant curl behind her ear. He had just taken a step forward to greet her when Fagan appeared and closed the door behind her.

She turned around and faced the captain of Ruairi's guard. "Thank you for the company."

"The pleasure was mine, lass."

Something deep within Ruairi stirred at the sight of their private moment together. He certainly wasn't a jealous man, but he felt something attuned to regret that his friend had shared Ravenna's company. Once Fagan had departed, Ruairi stepped from the shadows.

"And what brings ye out so late wandering the castle alone? I thought ye'd retired to your chamber some time ago."

Ravenna jumped and placed her hand over her heart. "I was not alone. I found myself in need of some fresh air and discovered Fagan sought the same." She approached Ruairi and smiled. "Do you perhaps have a moment to escort me back to my chamber?" When his eyes widened, she quickly added, "Angus seems to have developed a sudden fondness for stalking me."

Ruairi couldn't help it. His smile deepened to laughter. "Come. I will make sure Angus isnae troublesome."

She smiled her thanks as he escorted her through the halls. "Has Laird Munro departed?" she asked.

"Nay. He sleeps off his drink and will take his leave in the morn."

"I must offer you my sincere apologies. It was apparent Laird Munro didn't know of your wife's passing, and he shouldn't have heard the words from me. I'm truly sorry."

When he took too long to respond, Ravenna reached out. The touch of her hand on his arm was almost unbearable in its tenderness. He stopped and looked down at her, seeing something in her eyes that he could not quite put his finger on. She was so damn beautiful.

Lightly, he fingered a loose tendril of hair on her cheek. When her lips parted in surprise, he knew he should have pulled away. But at that moment, his hand instinctively came down on her shoulder in a possessive gesture.

Without looking away, she backed out of his grasp. "Ruairi…"

"Ravenna, before I change my mind, I verra much want to kiss ye right now."

&cҩ

God help her. His words would be her undoing.

Ravenna wondered what it would be like to

feel the warmth of Ruairi's lips, the strength of his touch. She forced herself to settle down. She needed to stop thinking—now. Because no matter how much she tried to deny it, she wanted him to kiss her, too.

His hands slipped up her arms, bringing her closer. Ravenna vowed not to become too involved with him. She couldn't. She shouldn't.

Oh, bloody hell.

He lowered his mouth to hers, and his lips were more persuasive than she cared to admit. The sweet taste of ale lingered on his breath. His kiss was urgent, and she was shocked at her own response to his touch. He seared a path down her neck, her shoulders, and then his lips recaptured hers.

Ruairi took her mouth with savage intensity, forcing her lips open with his thrusting tongue. Her knees weakened, and if not for the support of his hand at her back, she would have fallen.

She wrapped her arms around his waist and drew him closer. The corded muscles she felt under his tunic quickened her pulse. When he pulled back and appraised her with more than a mild interest, her curiosity was aroused as well as her vanity. Her mind told her to resist, but her body refused to listen. She knew such an attraction would be perilous, but she couldn't find the strength to pull away.

She caressed the strong tendons in the back of his neck, realizing he felt as good in her arms as she'd known he would. His head was lowered and his long hair brushed her cheek. His eyes burned with tenderness and passion she had never seen in another.

"I will take ye to your bed lest I take ye standing against the wall." His voice was thick and unsteady.

He took her by the hand and led her silently to her chamber. Lifting the latch, he pushed open the door. He had just stepped through the entrance and closed the door behind him when Ravenna turned around and placed her hand on his chest.

"Wait. There is something you should know."

His face clouded with uneasiness, and he briefly closed his eyes. She could see a muscle ticking at his jaw. He looked pained, as if he was struggling to compose himself. "Please accept my apologies, lass. I shouldnae have been so forward. Ye have my word that I am an honorable man. Although 'tis verra difficult to remember that right now. I would ne'er ruin ye. I only wanted to taste your sweet lips." When he lowered his head to kiss her, she pulled away.

"I appreciate your honesty, but that's not what I was going to say."

He gave her a gentle smile. "Ye donna have to tell me anything. We all have a past. 'Tis better left that way. And I am nae so callous as to have ye say the words aloud, lass."

"I am not chaste."

Ruairi paused. She hadn't noticed the strained tone in her voice, but an inner torment began to gnaw at her. The harder she tried to suppress the truth, the more it persisted. She lowered her eyes and waited to be judged.

He lifted her chin with his finger and his eyes captured hers. "Then ye are in luck…because neither am I."

He kissed the hollow at the base of her throat, and the touch of his lips was a delicious sensation. "Ruairi, I can't replace your wife."

Without lifting his head, he murmured, "I didnae ask ye to. Did anyone ever tell ye that ye talk too much?"

As though his words released her, she flung herself against him. The warmth of his arms was so male, so bracing. She had no desire to back out of his embrace.

Ruairi swept her, weightless, into his arms. He walked to the bed and gently eased her down onto the soft mattress. He buried his hands in her hair, kissing her relentlessly. She suddenly realized that his feelings toward the Crown were utterly insignificant at the moment. The only thing that mattered was his tongue in her mouth because the world had ceased to exist.

He nibbled, sucked, devoured. He kissed her like no man had ever kissed her. She was hot, swollen, achy, wanting more. There was something about him—rawness, strength, something she'd never be able to explain to someone else. They'd think her mad. A woman would have to be kissed by Laird Ruairi Sutherland to simply understand how the man could bring her to her knees. But truth be told, there was nothing simple about it.

His hands moved from her hair to her breasts, cupping and plumping. When his thumbs grazed her nipples, they peaked instantly. She felt as if she was drowning and Ruairi was the only man who could save her.

She clung to him, arching against him, reveling in the sensation of his big, strong hands sliding over her body. She burned with fever.

He pulled her gown from her shoulders and lowered his head. His tongue tantalized the buds, which had swollen to their fullest. When one of his hands seared a path down her abdomen and onto her thigh, she thought she was going to die.

She wrapped her legs around his powerful hips. She couldn't help but whimper into his mouth when he shifted, fitting the two of them together so perfectly that his ridge was cradled against her womanly heat.

He ground himself against her, driving her crazy with need. She lifted his tunic, and it was flesh against flesh, man against woman. His touch became light and painfully teasing.

She wound her fingers through his thick hair, delirious with need. She tugged on his kilt, which fell to the ground in a single swoop. Her eyes lowered and she realized that everything about him was too much man. He was a Highlander—rugged, untamed, and for the moment...*hers*.

Someone pounded furiously on her door.

This could not be happening. She did not want to stop. If she did, she would think. And she didn't want to do that now. She fought to control her swirling emotions.

"Ravenna, is Ruairi with ye?" asked someone through the door.

"Is that Fagan?" she whispered. Her voice was hoarse with frustration.

She heard Ruairi grind his teeth, and a muscle ticked in his jaw. *"Dè tha ceàrr ort?"* What is wrong with you?

Resuming his purpose, Fagan again pounded on the door. *"Dùisg! Eirich!"* Wake up! Get up!

With much reluctance, Ruairi rose from the bed and hastily donned his kilt from the floor. *"Dè th'ann?"* What is it?

"Duine." A man.

Ruairi turned back toward the bed. "This is far from over, lass. Donna even think about denying me. There is nay turning back now. I will be with ye again, and next time, I will have ye in my own bed." He put on his boots, grabbed his tunic from the floor and quickly walked out, closing the door behind him.

Ravenna flung herself back on the bed and blew the loose hair away from her lips.

What had she done now?

❦

"Ye better have a damn good reason for interrupting me."

Fagan smirked. "I'm glad ye took my advice, my laird." When Fagan saw that Ruairi wasn't amused, he changed the subject to the matter at hand. "Our guards found two men making their way across our border. Both were armed with swords and knives. If I were to render a guess, I'd say they were making another attempt on our cattle. Our men hold them in the bailey."

"We will finally have some answers. Have someone rouse Ian."

Ruairi entered the bailey and walked toward the two men. Their features were difficult to discern at first in the glowing torchlight. With each approaching step, Ruairi's eyes narrowed. He had to look twice to make certain he was not mistaken. To his surprise, he wasn't. The men wore kilts of red, green, and blue.

The same colors as the Munro.

"What are ye doing on my lands?" he asked one of the men.

The man smiled a toothless grin. "I donna answer to ye. *Thalla gu taigh na galla.*" *Go to hell.*

Ruairi balled his fist into the man's face and heard something crunch under the forceful blow. If the bastard continued with his sharp tongue, his nose would not be the only thing broken. Ruairi promptly turned his attention to the man's comrade, but when he repeated the question, the man visibly trembled and chose to remain silent. He was clearly the wiser of the two.

"I see I didnae miss all the excitement after all. I made it just in time," said Ian. His eyes widened when he noticed that the men's kilts mirrored his own. "Who the hell are ye?"

The daft man with the sharp tongue spit blood in Ian's face.

Ian wiped his hand over his cheek and then cocked his head at the vagrant. The man cried out when Ian grabbed him by the bollocks and gave a wry smile. "I am in nay mood for games, my friend. Ye arenae a Munro. From which clan do ye hail? I will nae ask ye again."

The man shot him a wicked smile and spoke between clenched teeth. "Mayhap lost cattle isnae the only thing ye should be worried upon, aye?"

Without warning, Ian stepped back, unsheathed his

sword, and shoved the blade right into the man's gut. Blood poured from the wound as the man toppled to the ground, lifeless. Ian turned and smiled at the man who still stood as he wiped the blood that stained his sword on the dead man's kilt. "Your friend wasnae so lucky and didnae give me the answers I sought. I cannae help but wonder if ye will follow his path."

"We were offered coin," the man blurted out.

"Who made ye such an offer?" Ruairi demanded.

"I donna know. We ne'er knew his name. He gave us this tartan to wear in case we were captured and told us there would be more coin for every cow we slaughtered."

"My cattle as well as those of the Munro?"

"Aye."

"Why?" asked Ian. When the man hesitated, Ian placed his sword to the man's throat.

"I donna know! I swear it upon my life."

Ruairi smirked. "'Tis quite a shame really, but your life will serve to repay the debt owed to my clan." He nodded to Ian and made a dismissive gesture with his hand as the man yelled out.

"Wait! We are to meet him on the morrow. I can take ye to him if ye spare my life."

"And why would we believe ye?" asked Ian.

"I donna want to die."

"Ye should've thought of that before ye set foot on our lands. Ye took food away from our people, slaughtered our animals. I should kill ye right where ye stand." Ruairi rubbed his fingers over his chin. "In truth, I havenae yet made up my mind what to do with ye."

The front of the man's kilt suddenly became very wet and Ian's eyes widened in surprise. "Did he just piss in a Munro kilt?"

Ruairi smiled. "I think he did."

"The bastard has nay respect."

The man shook with fear. "Please donna kill me."

Ruairi gestured to Fagan. "Throw his arse in the dungeon." He turned his head toward Ian. "Unless ye want to kill him now."

Ian sheathed his weapon. "Nay, I would like to meet the arse who ordered my cattle butchered." He turned and snarled, and the man jumped. "But if ye're lying…"

"I swear I am nae!"

Fagan shoved the man forward, escorting him to the room Ruairi held vacant for all his enemies. The Sutherland dungeon was feared by many, but this poor bastard should be thankful his head wasn't currently stuck on a pike.

"Do ye think he'll lead us to the man?" asked Ian.

"Did ye nae see the bastard piss himself? Aye, I think he'll lead us, but ye know the Gordon wouldnae leave things to chance. We'll have to use caution to get close enough to capture the man who paid the coin. Is your head clear enough for thought? We need to devise something clever."

"Aye. Naught wakes up a man more than by killing his enemy in the darkened hours of the night."

⤜⤏

Ravenna dressed quickly, her breathing still labored. While her mind burned with the memory of being held in Ruairi's arms, she was stunned by the idea of leaving her chamber to spy on him. What kind of person had she become? She knew she was unable to give herself completely to any man because of her duties for the Crown. She promptly shook off the feeling. There'd be time for such thoughts later, because right now she needed to discover what was afoot under Laird Sutherland's roof.

She'd known something was wrong by the tone of Fagan's voice when he came to her door to summon Ruairi. She'd wanted desperately to understand what Fagan said and wished the men would've stopped speaking Gaelic. What did *duine* mean, anyway? There was only one way to find out.

She wandered through the halls in search of the men.

As Ravenna walked into the great hall, she heard a commotion out in the bailey and paused just inside the door. She was as careful as she could be to remain partially hidden, but she had to see what was happening. She decided to take a necessary risk by stealing a peek around the corner, praying she wouldn't be seen.

Laird Munro was pulling his sword from the belly of a man. Even in the shadows of the night, she could see the dark liquid pooling on the ground from the man's wound. She'd seen death before, but she was startled by the images before her eyes. She didn't think she'd ever get used to seeing someone die.

One man remained standing before Ruairi and Laird Munro. She continued to watch as the man trembled before the fearsome Highland lairds. From her angle, she wasn't close enough to hear their words. She was about to move closer, but Fagan suddenly led the man away. Her eyes widened when Ruairi and Laird Munro turned and walked straight toward her.

Ravenna lifted her skirts and darted to the top of the stairs as Ruairi entered the great hall with Laird Munro. She hesitated, out of sight, until she was certain they had departed. When no voices were heard from below, she quickly descended the stairs and followed the men as they made their way to Ruairi's study. The hour was late, and Ravenna prayed that Angus didn't suddenly get the urge to have a midnight hunt. She was careful not to be seen, ducking into a nook a time or two to avoid Ruairi's men.

When she reached the study, she was surprised that the door remained ajar. Then again, who would be wandering around the castle in the middle of the night? She stood silently against the stone wall.

"I cannae believe the bastard had the nerve to wear a Munro kilt. What the hell was he thinking?" asked Laird Munro.

Ruairi sighed. "If 'twas the Gordon, I bet he didnae expect ye to be here. Think about it. If ye werenae under my roof and I caught the men on my lands wearing the Munro tartan... I bet the arse wanted me to think ye had a hand in slaughtering my cattle, as if I would be foolish enough to believe that. But he would think that way, always conniving and plotting. I swear the man is daft."

"Bastard."

"Aye."

There was a heavy silence.

"On the morrow, we'll follow the daft fool in

the dungeon, but I think we should take less than a handful of men. I donna want to chance discovery before we're able to find the man responsible. If we're somehow spotted, the bastard will run, and this is the best chance we have to uncover who is behind the attacks on our cattle or confirm 'tis the Gordon's doing. This has been happening for too long now. I've had enough of foolish games," said Ruairi.

"Ye've been dealing with the Gordon for some time now. When was the last ye spoke to him?"

"When he asked me to give him men and arms against the Crown."

Ravenna jumped when lips brushed against her ear and a hard body pressed tightly against her back.

"Ye wouldnae be spying on my laird now, would ye, Ravenna? I thought ye better than that," said Fagan in a whisper.

She spun around and led him away from the door by the arm. "I was not spying," she blurted out. "When Ruairi left my... When you came to... I wanted to make certain everything was all right. When I heard he was in his study with Laird Munro, I decided not to intrude." She paused. "Please don't disturb him."

His eyes narrowed. "Mmm... Were ye in the bailey a moment ago?"

"The bailey? No. Why?"

"Listen to me," he said in a harsh, raw voice. "Ye need to return to your chamber and leave the men to their business. Nay matter what your intent, lurking in the hall by Ruairi's study door is nay place for ye to be. Take your leave."

"My apologies, but I assure you, I wasn't lurking. I only wanted to make certain he was all right. I—"

"Care for him," said Fagan with a knowing smile.

God help her. She thought she did.

Seven

RUAIRI RUBBED HIS HAND ACROSS HIS BROW. HE HAD spent almost the entire night with Ian dealing with the latest pain in his arse when he should've been enjoying sins of the flesh with Ravenna. He would never forget a single detail, a single curve. She set him aflame with her touch. He had been watching her with Torquil for weeks and knew she was gentle and caring, everything he could possibly want in a woman and more. And for the first time since she'd arrived in the Highlands, he realized "English" never came to mind.

When she had initially stopped him inside her bedchamber, Ruairi was aware he had to fight a battle of personal restraint because he wanted nothing more than to remove her clothes and ravish her until the early hours of the morn. Unfortunately, that moment was one of those times when his honor and chivalry intervened and drove him nearly to the point of madness.

Ravenna's face still haunted him, serious, thoughtful. That's why he was pleasantly surprised when she said she was not chaste, especially the way she trembled beneath his touch. But her innocence or lack thereof didn't trouble him. Why should it? He was thankful he wouldn't have to deal with the virginal uncertainties of a young lass. His woolgathering halted abruptly when Fagan approached him in the great hall, a worried expression crossing his brow.

"Ye are ne'er going to believe this."

Ruairi folded his arms across his chest. "Tell me the man still lives in the dungeon because I do believe my instructions were perfectly clear."

"Aye, but we have more pressing matters upon us. The Gordon is at the gate."

His jaw dropped. "Why the hell would the man be at my gates now?"

"Aye, so soon after the men were discovered trying to butcher our cattle. I thought the same. 'Tis almost too convenient."

"How many are with him?"

"Only a handful."

"Are ye ready?" asked Ian, walking into the great hall.

"It seems we may have our answers sooner than expected, and we donna even have to wander verra far from home to get them."

Ian gave Ruairi a puzzled look. "What do ye mean?"

"The Gordon is at my gates."

"Now that is verra curious," said Ian with a wry grin.

Ruairi turned to Fagan. "Escort the Gordon and his men to my study and then make certain Torquil and Ravenna remain in the library."

While Ruairi sat in his study with Ian and waited for the Gordon to grace them with his presence, Ruairi showed an ease that he didn't necessarily feel.

He remembered the last time he had spoken with his wife's father. Granted, the Gordon wasn't pleased with Ruairi's refusal of his request for men and arms, but even then, the man's behavior had been somewhat odd.

Ruairi continued to struggle with the fact that the Gordon hadn't been distraught over his daughter's death. He also was amazed that the purpose of the Gordon's visit that day had been to discuss politics. That's when he knew his father-in-law was a coldhearted bastard, an opinion Ruairi held toward most of his wife's clan.

Fagan walked into the study with the Gordon while two Gordon guards remained out in the hall. Fagan gave Ruairi a knowing look and then closed the door on his way out. Ruairi knew his captain would remain close by. He shifted his attention to the Gordon, whose bulbous nose only accented the arrogant look on his face. His gray hair was ruffled by the wind.

"Sutherland…" Gordon nodded to Ian. "And what a surprise to see Laird Munro here as well."

"Aye. I'm sure ye're verra surprised," said Ian under his breath with a heavy dose of sarcasm. If the Gordon heard Ian's words, he didn't acknowledge them.

"And what brings ye to my gates?" asked Ruairi, gesturing for the man to sit.

"King James interferes too much in our ways."

Ruairi had to suppress a sigh. Leave it to the bastard to move straight to the matter at hand. As if the Gordon heard Ruairi's silent thoughts, his eyes narrowed, and he studied Ruairi and Ian with heavy scrutiny.

"I need both of ye to hear what I have to say. I've

received word the king has imprisoned the Earl of Orkney, his own cousin, because the man resisted the king's laws on Iona. Orkney has since been forfeited to the realm." The Gordon hesitated and tapped his fingers on his thigh. "How long do ye think it will be before our own lands are seized by the bloody English? The king is a fool if he thinks we'll bend to his authority. He has nay right bringing his laws into the Highlands."

"And saying as much will get ye killed," said Ruairi.

"Nay one is removed from following King James' ridiculous commands, nae even ye, Sutherland. I took ye for a wise man and hope I am nae mistaken. I only pray that ye and Munro arenae too foolish or stubborn to see that. 'Tis nay great secret that I've made an alliance with the Seton clan. Together, we join Patrick Stewart's son, Robert, to gather arms against the realm. We *will* fight to protect what is ours, as we have done for centuries."

Ruairi chuckled. "Ye've joined forces with the Earl of Orkney's son? The same earl who was just imprisoned by the king for nae following orders? And a man known for his lavish spending and cruelty to his people? Are ye completely mad?"

"Determined," said the Gordon through clenched teeth. "King James wants naught more than to bring the Highland lairds to heel. How dare he bring *English* laws to our lands? We arenae England and ne'er will be."

"What do ye want?" asked Ian. "I grow tired of games."

"Ye were ne'er one for subtlety, Munro." Hastily dismissing Ian, the Gordon turned his attention to

Ruairi. "I propose an alliance between our clans. The men of clans Gordon, Seton, Sutherland, and Munro will join forces with Stewart's men. There is strength in our numbers, and we will bring the realm and those who support it to their knees. The Highland lairds will demand that the king and his laws stay out of the Highlands, and we will show him once and for all that we Highlanders donna sit upon command."

Ruairi gave Ian a look to keep his mouth shut. "We need time."

"How long?"

"A fortnight."

"Ye have a sennight to give me an answer," said the Gordon in a clipped tone.

There was a heavy moment of silence.

"Ye have been verra blunt with your purpose. Now I will be blunt with mine. Five of my cattle and three of Munro's have been slaughtered on our lands. I donna need to tell ye those animals were meant to feed our people during the winter months," said Ruairi with no inflection.

A sparkle twinkled in the Gordon's eye. "How verra…unfortunate."

"Unfortunate, aye, until we found two men encroaching on my lands last eve in an attempt to make another move on my cattle."

"Good for ye. I should hope ye showed them as much mercy as they showed your cattle."

Ruairi was about to reply to the arrogant arse when a warning voice whispered in his head. The only thing he permitted was the curse that fell from his mouth and the distrust that continued to chill his

eyes. That's why he was surprised when Ian spoke for
them both.

"One of the bastards is nay longer of this world."
Ian paused for added impact. "The other is verra much
alive. Nevertheless, it seems one eve in the Sutherland's
dungeon will make any man loosen his tongue."

When the Gordon paled, the truth was finally
revealed. Ruairi clenched his fists to keep from reaching over and killing the man who sat across from him.

"Is there anything ye wish to say?" asked Ruairi, his
accusing voice stabbing the air.

"Why would I wish to say anything?" asked the
Gordon with a vague hint of displeasure.

"Ian, leave us for a moment and shut the door on
your way out." When the door finally closed, Ruairi's
eyes darkened with fury. "Are ye telling me ye know
naught of these men?" The Gordon was about to
speak when Ruairi cut off his words with a hostile
glare. "Donna even think of insulting me by denying
your hand in this."

Ruairi sat forward and continued. "I want ye to
listen to me verra carefully. Ye sit here under my roof
and ask me to raise arms against the Crown. Ye ask me
to form an alliance, but know this… I donna take to
threats, nor will I stand by and watch as my clan suffers
for the likes of political gain. Ye made a grave error in
judgment by killing my cattle, and your actions in nay
way gained my or Munro's trust. In truth, if ye werenae
my late wife's father, I'd run ye through right now."

The Gordon continued to give Ruairi a blank stare,
keeping his features composed with purpose.

"I want to hear the truth from your own mouth,

but I'd think verra carefully before ye let the next words escape it. Did ye actually believe for one moment that by killing our cattle ye would force us to join ye?"

The Gordon shrugged with indifference. "When ye think about the words I have spoken, ye will realize they serve but a higher purpose. I hope that within a sennight ye and Munro see reason. It would be most unfortunate nae to have ye join us. Besides, how many more cattle can ye and Munro afford to lose?"

Ruairi smirked. "Make nay mistake, should your men make another attempt, we will defend what is ours."

"I must admit I'm rather disappointed by your response. I thought when ye wed my daughter that ye'd support our clan, but ye've fought my political decisions at every turn. My daughter, on the other hand, always knew her place and when to support her father. Although Anna was merely a lass, her ambition was as passionate as my own. Howbeit it seems neither one of us were verra good at convincing ye to feel the same."

Ruairi paused, wanting to ask the question that weighed heavily on his mind. "Do ye blame me for Anna's death?"

The Gordon's eyes grew amused and his smile deepened to laughter. "Is that what ye think, Sutherland? God's teeth, lad, I can see ye think as much." He wiped his hand over his face and then shook his head. He sat forward and his expression lightened. There was actually a twinkle in his eye. "Tell me. Should I blame ye for my daughter's death?"

⤮

Ravenna spent hours in the library with Torquil. When he gave up and laid his head on the table, she realized she'd given the boy more than enough instruction for today. Frankly, she'd had enough too.

"I think the men have forgotten about us."

When Torquil lifted his head, his eyes were heavy. "Done? Go?"

"Yes. We're finished for today. You did very well."

The boy didn't hesitate and made a mad dash out of the library. She gathered her drawings and cleaned off the table. When she stood, her back cracked under protest or relief—she wasn't quite sure which. She walked through the halls toward the bailey for some much-needed air. At least she didn't need to worry about Angus because the beast ordinarily chased God knew what during the day, out in the woods far away from her. She felt some relief at not having to constantly look over her shoulder. But as soon as she set foot out into the courtyard, she froze at the sight before her.

An older man with gray hair stood towering over Torquil. The man was flanked by two men, clearly not Sutherland guards. He wore a kilt of blue and green, and Ravenna suddenly realized that she needed to brush up on the tartan colors of the Highland clans.

She quickly glanced at Ruairi and he glared at her. She was wondering what she had done wrong when Fagan approached her.

"Did I nae tell ye to remain in the library?" he asked in an odd tone.

Her eyes widened. "I thought you had forgotten about us."

Ravenna heard Fagan growl at her, but then he hastily looked away. She turned her attention back to the man in the blue and green kilt as he reached out and placed his hand on Torquil's shoulder. Ruairi stiffened at the gesture.

"Torquil, I havenae laid eyes upon ye for quite some time. My, how ye have grown. Ye are a strapping young lad," said the man.

The boy stood before him and didn't move.

"Do ye remember me? I am your mother's father. I am your *seanair*." *Grandfather.*

When Torquil looked over his shoulder to Ruairi, Ravenna realized she was looking at Laird Gordon. What was he doing here?

"Do ye know ye have your mother's eyes? I can see her in your face."

"Torquil, take your leave with Ravenna. Your *seanair* was just leaving."

The Gordon frowned. "Truly, Sutherland. Give me but a moment with my *ogha*." *Grandchild.* "Perhaps ye will come to visit me one day soon, eh?"

"Torquil...now," repeated Ruairi, his tone more commanding.

The boy pulled away from his grandfather and approached Ravenna. She wrapped her arm around him and promptly escorted him to his chamber. When they reached the door, she ushered him in and held up her hand. "I want you to stay here until I come for you. Do you understand?"

He nodded. "Aye."

Ravenna spun around and practically ran to the parapet. She may not be able to hear the men below, but she wasn't going to miss what was happening in the bailey.

◈

He could have killed her.

As if Ruairi didn't have enough problems, the last thing he needed was a lass who didn't know how to follow commands. He had told Fagan to have Ravenna stay in the library with Torquil until he or Fagan came to release them. And did she listen? *No.* He wanted his son to avoid the Gordon. The man might be Anna's father, but he held only one purpose, and Anna and Torquil were never of concern. Why would they be now? Ruairi made a mental note to talk with his son later to make sure the boy was all right, but for right now, his main task was to get the Gordon out of here.

"I will wait a sennight for your answer. Until then, I hope ye and Munro both have enough sense to see reason." He lifted his head high, standing at his full height. "We are Highlanders," he said with pride. "We do what we must."

"Aye, on that we agree. We do whatever it takes to protect our people—and our lands." Ruairi's words were meant as a warning to the Gordon, but the man merely gazed around as if he was unaffected by the remark.

"Your stable hands leave a lot to be desired, Sutherland. It seems they are ill equipped to even bring me my mount."

Ian walked toward Ruairi with an arrogant grin. With a quick nod that Ruairi didn't miss, Ian stepped to the side. Ruairi wasn't foolish enough to start a war, but he would make sure the Gordon knew that his poor choice of judgment held consequences.

The stable hands brought the guards their mounts, and then a path was cleared as the Gordon was brought his horse. The prisoner from the dungeon stumbled behind in order to keep up with the horse's gait. The man's wrists were bound with a long rope that was tied to the saddle of the Gordon's mount. When a foul stench wafted through the air, Ian plugged his nose and Ruairi tried not to breathe. The man was covered in muck.

"What the hell is this?"

"Have a pleasant trip home," said Ian.

Ruairi approached his father-in-law and slapped him on the back in a friendly gesture. "I leave it to ye to take charge of your hired ruffian. 'Tis the least ye can do." He lowered his voice. "And if I find another one of your men or someone ye have hired setting foot my lands, I will nae be so merciful. I hope ye have enough sense to see reason." He held his head high, standing tall. "'Tis exactly like ye said. We are Highlanders. We do what we must."

The Gordon's expression clouded with anger. "Mount up. As the Sutherland said, we'll take charge of this man."

The prisoner yelled and struggled against his bindings. "Nay! Ye send me to my death!"

Ruairi's voice hardened ruthlessly. "Ye were already dead the moment ye set foot on my lands."

⁂

If Ravenna hadn't seen it with her own eyes, she would never have believed it. She recognized the disheveled man in the bailey from the previous night. Did Ruairi actually give the man to Laird Gordon? Why? She wished she could've heard the conversation, but another appearance in the bailey would be too obvious.

The dust billowed in the wind as the men rode through the gates and departed. Ravenna quickly descended the stairs from the parapet and made her way back through the halls to Torquil's chamber. No sooner had she walked through the boy's door than a deep voice spoke from behind her.

"Ravenna, we will have words. Torquil…" said Ruairi, continuing to speak in Gaelic.

The boy nodded, and Ruairi turned, pulling her along behind him. She knew better than to utter any protest because he did not look pleased. He led her to the bailey where two mounts stood ready and waiting. Wordlessly, he lifted her onto her horse and then he mounted his own.

They rode through the bailey and turned south. As they walked their horses through the mossy fields, Ravenna glanced over her shoulder toward the trees. She couldn't help it. She prayed the wicked wolf with the massive jaws would stay wherever he was and was thankful when he wasn't in sight.

She had just started to wonder where Ruairi was taking her when the sight before her suddenly made her lose all thought. They led the horses down a path that led to a white sandy beach extending as far as the eye could see. The blue waters of the ocean crashed onto the shore, and the sound of the waves was serene. She briefly closed her eyes, and when she opened them, she was so enthralled at the sight before her that she didn't realize Ruairi had dismounted.

"Would ye like to come down now, or will ye just sit there on your mount?"

She looked down to see Ruairi standing beside her with his hand extended. "Of course. I was admiring the view."

"Aye. Fagan told me ye wanted to see the beach."

Of course he did.

Ruairi led her to the edge of the water and then stood silently. He definitely had something on his mind, but Ravenna decided that when he was ready to speak, he would. He finally turned to face her, but then his eyes narrowed. "When Fagan gives ye an order, he is speaking on my behalf. Ye arenae to disobey a command again. Do ye understand?"

Her body stiffened. "Disobey a command? You cannot treat me as though I am one of your men," she blurted out. Ravenna bit her lip before anything else came out. If he was surprised by her demeanor, he didn't say so. At the moment, she was taken aback by her words because they almost sounded like something Grace would've said.

"I must know something. Do ye think ye'll be able to finish Torquil's studies by a sennight?"

She paused briefly because of the abrupt change of subject. "A sennight? Torquil is making progress, but I don't think—"

"Can ye make it happen? For me?"

She gave him a compassionate smile. "What has happened?" He looked out at the sea and a muscle ticked in his jaw. "Tell me. Does your request have something to do with Torquil's grandfather paying you a visit?"

There was a heavy moment of silence.

"The matter isnae easy to explain. My son hasnae seen the Gordon for some time. I didnae want him to. That was why I asked ye to remain in the library. Ye should've listened." She waited for him to continue. "I donna expect ye to understand." He turned and waved her off.

"Then explain it to me."

Ruairi smirked. "Lass, there is far too much to tell."

"I'm not going anywhere. We're alone. I would hope that after our…" She gestured with her hand and smiled. She didn't think she needed to finish the sentence. "You convinced me to tell you about my fear. I believe your exact words were: 'Fear will always control you if you don't speak upon it and face it.' You will continue to be troubled unless you let someone share the burden. I may not have Fagan's wise words of battle, but I've been told I'm a good listener." When he still hesitated, she added, "Why don't you tell me from the beginning? Tell me about your wife." She had to admit that she was a little curious to see if he would tell her the truth.

"Why would ye want to hear about Anna?"

"Because I care." When his eyes lit up, she quickly added, "I care what happens to your son." She was a little unnerved when the words came out faster than she could stay them.

He took a step forward and brushed the back of his hand across her cheek. "It has been a long time since I confided in a lass."

She smiled. "It's been a long time since I confided in a man."

"Can I trust ye, Ravenna?"

She hesitated, and for the first time since she could remember, she was uncertain how to answer.

"God help me if I'm wrong." He closed his eyes and paused, and then he looked at her intently. "I didnae exactly tell ye the whole truth about my wife."

"What do you mean?" When he hesitated, she gave him an encouraging smile. "Ruairi…"

"Verra well. I didnae want to send Torquil to the Lowlands so I told the king my wife was ill. She did actually die, but her death was two years ago."

Ravenna tried to look surprised. "Why would you do that?"

He shrugged. "I'm stubborn—the same as my father before me. My son will be a Highland laird someday. I didnae necessarily want him to learn the ways of the English."

"In a way, I understand how you feel." She couldn't imagine being told she could no longer speak English and had to embrace the Gaelic language and Highland culture. At that moment, she realized how difficult this must be for him.

"Torquil hasnae had an easy life. His mother was a difficult woman to love and, truth be told, even to like. 'Tisnae an easy thing for me to say, but my wife despised me and everything about me. She hated living here. When she gave birth to our son, I was foolish enough to think she'd change. But Torquil's birth only made things worse. I could never understand how a woman could resent her own son and her own husband. Granted, Anna and I were ne'er a love match, but I think our life together fell apart even more when I managed to ruin the alliance with her clan by not siding with her father's political aspirations."

Ruairi let out a heavy sigh. "But she was my wife, and she was the Gordon's blood. The man was ne'er interested in his daughter. His only purpose was political gain."

"I'm sorry. I know some families aren't as close as others. But what I don't understand is why Laird Gordon was here now, after all this time."

He rolled his head from side to side and reached up to rub his neck as if it ached. "Five of my cattle have been slaughtered on my lands as well as three of Munro's. The Gordon was responsible."

"Why would Laird Gordon kill your cattle?"

"To provoke us."

"Provoke you? Into doing what?" When he shifted his weight, Ravenna knew there was far more to the story than he actually told or was willing to tell. "Ruairi…"

"This isnae a conversation to be held with—"

"An English woman?"

"I wasnae going to say that," he said defensively.

She folded her arms over her chest. "Then what? You will not talk to me because I am only a lowly governess far beneath your station?"

"Ravenna, ye are a governess who holds the king's ear. I have already told ye too much. I could be hung for disobeying the king's command."

"My report is given to one of the men in the king's service. I do not meet with King James. When I am no longer needed, I will report back on your *son's* progress. I have no intention of speaking about your wife."

The conversation was not flowing in the right direction. Ravenna needed to do something fast. She had to find out once and for all if Ruairi conspired against the realm, and now was the perfect opportunity to get him to trust her. She briefly closed her eyes and prayed to God that He and the man in front of her would forgive her.

She threw herself into Ruairi's arms and lowered his head to hers.

Eight

Ruairi's mouth covered Ravenna's, and her lips were soft and searching. Reluctantly, he pulled back, his breathing labored. He placed his forehead against hers, stopping before he lost all sense of reason.

"I told ye. I will have ye in my bed where we will nae be interrupted."

A dim flush raced like a fever across her pale and beautiful face. She pulled away and then uncertainty crept into her expression. "Why did you ask me if I could finish Torquil's studies within a sennight? Am I so unbearable that you'd want to get rid of me so soon?" The expression in her eyes suddenly changed from passionate to openly amused.

"Och, lass, ye arenae *that* unbearable. I may find ye a wee bit tolerable, even if ye are English."

They shared a smile, and he reached out and took her hand in his. He walked with her along the beach.

"Why donna ye tell me of your clan…er, family."

Her eyes lit up with surprise. "There is not much to tell. I'm afraid my life is not nearly as captivating as that of a Highland·laird."

"I'll tell ye a little secret." He lowered his head and whispered, "'Tisnae that captivating."

"Now I don't know about that," she said with a trace of laughter in her voice.

"Ye seem to have me at a disadvantage, lass. Ye know much of my life and I know naught of yours. I understand ye've been a governess for some time, but I have to admit, I am somewhat surprised." When she raised her brow, puzzled, he added, "Ye are a bonny woman. I'd have thought ye'd be wed. Or mayhap ye were wed before?"

She shook her head and looked down at the sand. "I was in love once—a long time ago—but no, I've never been wed."

Ruairi sensed an odd twinge of disappointment coming from her.

"Please don't feel sorry for me. My assignments do not grant me that privilege. I understand the price I pay for such responsibility. I simply can't afford to get too close."

He briefly wondered if her words were meant for him. He was about to ask her, but then decided against it. "Do ye have family waiting for ye in England?"

She smirked. "I have three unruly younger sisters."

"Three?"

"Yes. My mother and father passed away, and now we have only each other."

"And ye work as a governess to support them?"

"I try my best. Kat and Elizabeth are the youngest. My sister, Grace, is almost ready for marriage, but she wants no part of a man."

Ruairi chuckled. "Aye. I cannae say that I blame

her. Most of us are rogues. At least your sister has enough sense to see that."

"I suppose, but Grace is very headstrong and always gets into trouble. She does whatever she pleases and doesn't listen at all."

He gave her a wry grin. "She is verra much like her sister, then."

Ravenna slapped him playfully on the arm. "Now that wasn't very nice, Laird Sutherland. I am not headstrong and don't get into trouble...much."

He nodded in amusement. "Four women under the same roof. Frankly, I cannae even imagine. Is it difficult for ye?"

"At times."

"I've ne'er had any siblings, but I do have Fagan. Sometimes I find he can be verra annoying."

"It's easy to see that the two of you are like brothers."

"Aye. I guess ye could say that. I consider Fagan and Ian both my brothers, even though we arenae bound by blood."

"When Fagan and I spoke on the parapet, he mentioned that your father and Laird Munro's father were lifelong friends. I see you carry on the same tradition with his son. I'm sure your fathers would be proud of the two of you."

"I would like to think so. My father was a great man who believed heavily in honor and tradition. I hope to instill the same in Torquil." He stopped and turned, placing his hands on her shoulders. "Ravenna, the Highlands can be a verra dangerous place, especially for a lass who doesnae know our ways."

"I know. I've seen Angus, remember?"

He chuckled. "Be that as it may, there are others who are far more vicious than Angus. Nay matter how much I enjoy having ye under my roof, I would be indebted to ye if there was anything ye could do to move along Torquil's studies."

"I don't understand. Why this sudden sense of urgency?"

He paused. "The Gordon asked something of me, and he wants my answer within a sennight. I'd like to see ye safe and away from here before it comes to that."

Ravenna lifted her chin in the air. "You don't have to worry about me. I can take care of myself."

"Lass, the man killed my cattle to make his point, and I donna know if he will stop there. Now I will ultimately refuse his request, but the Gordon will be verra cross with me. I cannae say what he'll do once he hears an answer he will nae be happy with."

Her eyes became searching. "Ruairi, what did he ask of you? You said Laird Gordon was concerned with politics. I can only assume the reason for his visit was to get you to do something for his own political gain."

Ruairi smirked. "For a governess, ye certainly have a keen sense for political matters."

"What will you do?"

He hesitated. "I told ye. I will refuse his request."

"And he will not take your refusal lightly," she simply stated.

He sighed. "For many years I've tried to keep peace with the Gordon, if only for my wife's sake. I think I can nay longer postpone the inevitable. I've tried to keep our clans from warring, but I will protect what is mine if the Gordon doesnae see reason."

❧

As they rode back to the castle, Ravenna was silent. From what she could interpret from Ruairi's vague responses to her questions, this was nothing more than another battle between the Highland lairds over clan politics. She didn't have any proof that the men conspired against the realm.

Perhaps Uncle Walter was right and the Highland lairds were completely out of control. All they seemed to do was battle with one another. Now she knew why King James required these men to report to Edinburgh to stand for their actions. The king's laws were difficult to administer in the Highlands because the men were so far removed. Apparently, Highland justice was the only law present in northern Scotland.

Ruairi dismounted in the bailey and assisted Ravenna from her horse.

"I think I'll be able to give Torquil a good start in the time you've requested." She gave him a warm smile. "And you don't have to worry. I'll report back to the king's man that all is in order here, but I will have to tell him of your wife's passing. Nevertheless, he doesn't have to know the time of her death. You have my word."

"Thank ye, Ravenna."

She nodded in response and walked to her chamber. At least she'd be able to journey home faster than she'd initially anticipated. Grace and her insolent behavior were undoubtedly driving Uncle Walter mad. He was more than likely praying every night for Ravenna's safe return. She hoped her uncle had learned his lesson, and she smirked when she thought that Grace's willfulness was indubitably punishment enough for the man. But Ravenna would gladly refresh her uncle's memory of keeping watch over her sisters the next time he decided to send her so far from home.

She closed the door to her chamber and sat down to pen a letter telling Uncle Walter she was coming home. She also asked him to send Grace to meet her in Edinburgh to give the poor man a much-needed break.

If Ravenna was being truthful, she couldn't overlook the fact that a part of her would miss the Highlands. She didn't have a single regret about meeting Laird Ruairi Sutherland or the time she spent with him, contrary to what most English lords thought about the Highland *barbarians*. She'd be sure to tell the men their interpretation was completely wrong—at least about one laird in particular.

Ravenna sealed the missive and then approached the washbowl. She splashed cool water on her face as her mind drifted to Torquil. The boy would be thankful he no longer had to be trapped in the library with her. And she had to admit, she was relieved that she no longer needed to vie for his attention. The last thing she wanted to do was hurt Torquil by giving him false hope that his mother had been replaced.

She picked up a cloth and patted her face dry. Even though she couldn't wait to see her sisters, she felt a sudden, inexplicable sourness in the pit of her stomach. But she refused to dwell on these ridiculous notions any longer. When it was time to sup, she made her way to the great hall and noticed that Laird Munro and his men were not in attendance.

She took her seat as Fagan looked up from his

meal. "How did ye enjoy the beach?" he asked with a wry grin.

"It was quite lovely."

"Aye. I told Ruairi ye would enjoy it." He tossed a piece of bread in his mouth and wiped the crumbs from his hands.

"Where are Laird Sutherland and Laird Munro?"

Fagan swallowed his bread and took a drink from his tankard. "Ian took his leave after the Gordon departed."

She nodded. "I suppose you've heard that I'll be leaving in a few days."

His eyes shot up in surprise. "Truly? Nay, I hadnae heard." A strange look crossed his face and he paused. "Ye've completed Torquil's studies, then?"

"For now." She wouldn't mention the fact that next year Ruairi would need to make certain Torquil was sent to the Lowlands to continue his studies, especially since Ruairi's wife had now "officially" passed away.

"Well, have nay doubt ye will be missed around here, Ravenna. Ye've livened up the place with your presence. And 'tis quite obvious Torquil has developed a certain fondness for ye…and so has Ruairi." His eyes caught and held hers.

She promptly lowered her gaze to her trencher. "He's developed as much fondness for me as Angus, I'm afraid."

Fagan's voice deepened. "Now I wouldnae say that, lass. Know this… Ruairi doesnae let just any lass close to his heart."

Ravenna raised her eyes to find Fagan watching her. "And how would Ruairi feel about the captain of his guard saying such words to his son's governess?" she asked in a scolding tone.

"Ye should know me well enough to recognize that I am nae just Ruairi's captain. I'm his friend, his brother, and sometimes the one who kicks him in the arse because he doesnae know what's best for him."

She immediately felt a sense of guilt. "Come now. You barely know me."

"'Tis my responsibility to look out for Ruairi. I've been watching ye for weeks. I've noticed how kind ye are to everyone around ye, except mayhap Angus."

"With good reason."

He waved her off. "A blind fool can see that ye care for my laird."

She lowered her voice and feigned indifference. "My duty is to... In England, I have family, other people who depend on me. And you can't overlook the fact that Ruairi has responsibilities here to his lands and his people." When Fagan seemed disappointed by her response, she added, "You have a kind heart, but don't look for something that isn't there. Ruairi and I live in and are from two completely different worlds. Nothing would ever work between us."

He looked as if he was weighing his response. "Mayhap, but if ye loved him, ye'd find a way." He paused and lowered his voice. "Do ye love him?"

Ravenna's mouth dropped open, and she found herself suddenly irked by Fagan's prodding. She knew he meant well, but the question was like a double-edged sword. Of course she cared for Ruairi. But *love*? She didn't love him. She couldn't. It was impossible. She hadn't even known him that long. No matter what she felt, she couldn't think any more about Fagan's question because she'd be gone by the end of the week.

Fagan continued to watch her with the eyes of a hawk. He studied her as she was struggling to collect herself. When she realized he was still waiting for her response, she wondered what he would say if she told him that her feelings or lack thereof were none of his concern.

She felt as though she was speaking with Grace because her sister also had a way of hounding her to the point of madness. That's when she had a revelation. Fagan actually reminded her of Grace. The two of them were from the same mold, never knowing when to hold their tongue. She needed to change the direction of this conversation.

"I always find you to be so interested in Ruairi's life. What of your own?"

His eyes narrowed. "What do ye mean?"

"I think you know exactly what I mean."

Fagan shifted uncomfortably in the chair. "Many lasses have captured my heart, but nae one of them has held it."

"Mmm...I can't help but wonder why that is." She tapped her finger to her chin. "And why do *you* think that is?"

"We were speaking of ye. I'm nae sure when ye made the switch, but that was verra clever of ye, lass."

"What did she do now?" asked Ruairi, pulling out his chair.

"It was naught," said Fagan, turning his attention back to his meal.

Ravenna felt someone pull on the sleeve of her day dress. She turned her head to see a grim expression crossing Torquil's face.

"I nay want ye to leave."

She pulled the boy close and embraced him. "You are doing so well, Torquil." He lifted his head and she brushed back the hair from his face. "I will miss you too, but I must return to England." When he lifted his brow, Ruairi repeated her words in Gaelic.

The boy nodded and pulled away from her, taking his seat with hastened purpose. Her eyes met Ruairi's and he offered her a smile.

"I was surprised when Ravenna told me she was taking her leave," said Fagan to Ruairi. Something unspoken passed between the two men, and Ruairi's eyes narrowed.

"Ye know there are pressing matters upon us."

"Aye, but I didnae think ye would make her—"

Ruairi silenced Fagan with a glare, and Ravenna suddenly had a strong desire to simply disappear.

She stood. "If you will both excuse me..."

As she walked away, she heard Ruairi say, "Now look what ye have done."

⁂

"What did I do?" asked Fagan with widened eyes.

Ruairi lowered his voice. "Do ye honestly think I would want Ravenna here when I refuse the Gordon men and arms?"

"I guess nae. I just didnae think ye'd send her away so soon. I know ye favor her. I thought ye'd keep her around for a wee bit longer."

Ruairi shook his head. "Ye do remember she is a governess who was sent here by King James. Whether she takes her leave within a sennight or remains for several months, she will eventually take her leave. Ravenna cannae stay here, and if ye thought as much, ye are a fool."

Fagan grabbed his tankard, an amused look crossing his face. "Are ye telling me those words for a reason, or are ye only saying them aloud to reassure yourself?"

"Ye're an arse."

"Admit it. Ye love me for it."

Ruairi smirked. "I'd rather ye worry about yourself and let me worry about me."

"But if I didnae interfere—"

"My life would be so much easier."

"Believe what ye will, my laird."

Ruairi sought a much-needed respite from Fagan by retiring to his chamber. He'd thought of luring Ravenna to his bed, but he needed time to clear his head. He didn't even bother to undress as he lay across the bed, waiting. The lass had lowered her defenses on the beach earlier in the afternoon, and he'd tried to convince her to talk about herself. She never did. Her life must be hard, losing her mother and father and now having to care for her younger siblings. Ruairi didn't like to see anyone struggle, especially someone as kind as Ravenna. He would be sure to line her purse with coin before she departed. That was the least he could do.

He stood and looked out the small window in his chamber. As he studied the moon, he realized it was almost time for low tide. Now was the perfect time to gather coin, because after tonight, he would make certain the lass shared his bed every eve until she left. And there was no way he was leaving the comfort of her warm embrace to wander the cold, dark tunnels alone.

Ruairi walked through the halls and entered the kitchens, hesitating when he reached the pantry. The room was silent and no one was about. As he had done so many times before, he pushed back the cloth and entered the pantry. He approached the shelved wall and lifted the false shelf to pull the lever. When the wall creaked open, he paused to make certain he was alone, as he had done before. When he didn't hear anything, he pushed open the partition and walked through. He lit the candle and closed the wall behind him.

As always, the air in the passageways was cold and damp. He descended several hundred feet through the tunnels and turned east. The sound of the ocean waves crashed in the distance. He had just set foot in the natural room when he thought he'd heard something behind him.

He walked back out and held up the candle. He looked left, then right. There was no sign of anyone. He reentered the room and placed the candle on the ground. Bending over, he once again encircled the giant rock with his arms. When the hole in the floor was revealed, Ruairi removed the pouch from his sporran and lowered himself to the wet stone floor. His fingers reached around in the hole, but something didn't feel quite right.

He grabbed the candle and lowered it into the

hole. He knew he had recently added the rents, but the amount of coin was less than before. How was that possible? He shook off the thought—he had to be mistaken. He reached in and tossed a couple handfuls of coin into the bag.

Ruairi replaced the rock and stood, wiping the grit from his hands onto his kilt. He had grabbed the candle and was walking out of the cavern when he heard a loud banging from the opposite end of the tunnels. He turned around and followed the noise he had definitely heard this time. When he reached the end of the tunnel that entered into the hidden glade, he stopped. There were no signs of anyone or anything, but he was certain he'd heard something. As he turned, his foot scraped something on the dirt floor.

Lowering the candle, the light reflected from a steely blade. He lifted the dagger and studied the shiny surface. The weapon had not been here long. It was far too clean. Perhaps it was simply his own uneasiness, but something about the size and shape of the dagger troubled him. Ruairi stood and listened for any sound of an intruder. After a few moments of complete silence, he was starting to make his way back toward the castle when he stopped mid-stride.

As if he were struck over the head, the shock of discovery hit him full force. No wonder the weapon appeared to be different. Ruairi lifted the dagger closer to the light. His sudden revelation was now confirmed. The object was indeed a woman's dagger.

And he only knew one woman who carried a blade.

Nine

RAVENNA FINISHED TORQUIL'S LESSON EARLY. HIS demeanor had definitely changed since he found out she would be gone in a few days. The usual smile that crossed his face was sorely missed. When she dismissed the boy from the library, he didn't bolt out of the room like he always did. He only lowered his head and quietly walked out the door. She gathered her things and stepped into the hall where Ruairi waited for her.

"Why donna we take a ride to the cliffs? Only the two of us."

She intertwined her arm with his. "I'd love to. I think I'm going to miss the view and the sound of the sea very much."

The mounts were saddled, and Ravenna followed Ruairi out the gates. As she studied his strong back and his long hair whipping in the wind, she realized she meant what she said. The view would most definitely be missed. She tried to study him and learn him by heart. Although his physical attributes were obvious, she'd actually grown quite fond of the Highland laird, the man himself.

When they reached the steep rocks, Ruairi dismounted and walked over. She didn't miss the slight touch of his hand as he assisted her from her mount. She closed her eyes as his fingers slowly slid up her outer thigh. When he suddenly stopped, Ravenna opened her eyes to find him reaching for her waist and lowering her to the ground.

"Thank you."

His arm draped across her shoulders as they walked to the edge of the cliff. She leaned her cheek into his broad chest and sighed. She inhaled deeply, loving the smell of the sea and Ruairi's spicy scent. Both were very comforting. She and Ruairi continued to stare down at the rolling waves in silence, each comfortable enough to leave the other alone with their thoughts.

"May I ask ye something?" he asked, breaking the quiet moment.

She looked up at him. "Yes."

"Why do ye carry a dagger?" An inexplicable look of something she could not quite identify came over Ruairi's face. He stared back, waiting in silence.

Ravenna shrugged to hide her confusion. "Why would you ask me that?" When his eyes narrowed, she quickly added, "My apologies. Your question was just unexpected. The answer is simply my father."

"What do ye mean?"

"Since my parents were blessed or cursed—well, it depends on how you look at it—with only daughters, my father insisted we know how to defend ourselves. Grace carries a blade also, although she's not very skilled at using it. When Elizabeth and Katherine are old enough, I'll make certain they know how to wield one as well. Why?"

"When I saw ye threaten Angus with the dagger, I wanted to take a look at what ye carried. May I see it?"

She nodded, not mentioning that she had lost the one her father gave her somewhere in the tunnels. "I don't see why not, as long as you give it back. I really don't want to find myself alone and cornered by your *pet* without a weapon." She bent down and turned slightly away from him, blocking his view.

Ruairi chuckled. "I've seen much more of ye, lass. There is nay need to hide your bare leg from me."

"Be that as it may, one of us has to at least maintain some sense of reason." She lifted her skirts to the side and pulled out the dagger.

There was a trace of laughter in his voice. "Mmm... some sense of reason? That is a rather peculiar choice of words. I seem to remember nae long ago standing with ye by the wall in the garden." Without warning, he raised his hand and fanned himself like a woman who was far too warm. His voice became higher, feminine, as he continued to speak. "Praise the saints. I donna know what's wrong with me. I'm only standing here, so handsome, sporting my kilt." His eyes lit up as he jested with her, and his mouth lifted with a subtle tenderness. "I still cannae believe ye said those words."

"Oh, I know you *think* you're very amusing." She handed Ruairi the blade, hilt first. "But keep that up and you may find the pointy end sticking in your gut, my laird."

"That's one thing I will definitely miss about ye, Ravenna. Ye do make me laugh. I can honestly say I've ne'er known a lass to be so forthcoming with what's on her mind."

She folded her arms across her chest. "Then let me strongly suggest that it would be wise for you to change the subject if you know what's good for you. I don't need to be reminded of my foolish words."

Not that she'd ever forget. She still shuddered when she remembered that day when Ruairi had confessed he understood every word she said.

She was an idiot.

⁂

Ruairi had deliberately rubbed his hand over Ravenna's skirts before he had assisted her from her horse. At the time, he had felt some relief when he found the weapon still sheathed underneath her dress. Now that he had an opportunity to openly study the blade, he saw that it didn't look anything like the dagger he'd found in the tunnel. The weight, the shape—nothing was the same. Although Ravenna was the only woman he knew who carried a dagger, the two weapons were not alike. But now he had another problem. Someone other than him had trod around in the tunnels.

"What's the matter? You look troubled."

He tapped the blade in his hand. "Nay. I was only wondering if ye knew how to use it."

"Of course I know how to use it." She lifted an eyebrow. "If you stand over there and remain perfectly still, I'll be more than happy to demonstrate."

He chuckled. "I donna think so, but I would like to see what ye can do with it. Follow me."

"Where are we going?"

"Do ye always have to ask so many questions? Grab your mount."

They walked their horses through the field, the only sound the clomping hoofbeats. Ruairi felt a certain gnawing in his gut now that his time with Ravenna was coming to an end. Although he had told her in a jesting manner that he would miss her, he'd meant it.

When they reached the tree line, he tied off their mounts. He shook his head when he noticed Ravenna's odd behavior yet again. She was turning her head from side to side, her eyes searching through the brush. There was usually only one reason for her total lack of comportment.

"Do you know where Angus is?"

And there it was.

"Now that's the one thing I will nae miss hearing from ye. How many times must I tell ye? Angus will nae harm ye."

She placed her hands on her hips in a defiant gesture. "And how many times must I tell you that—"

Ruairi walked into the trees and didn't hear the rest of her words. Well, he did, but he chose to not pay them any heed. After all, the lass had been saying the same thing for weeks. He found a thick log and pulled it back through the foliage.

"What are you doing?"

He propped the piece of wood up against a tree. "I am testing your skill with your weapon."

"You doubt my word?"

"Nay. I merely want to see ye…" He didn't need to finish his words because he heard the blade whiz behind him and land with a thump. He turned around and approached the log. Fingering the hilt, he shook his head. The dagger had landed dead center in the piece of wood. "That was verra impressive, but luck was on your side."

Ravenna huffed and brushed past him. "Luck had nothing to do with it. It's skill, I assure you." She reached over and pulled the weapon from the target. When she looked up at him, he winked at her. She didn't seem to care if he was jesting because she quickly added, "Then why don't you pick where you'd like me to throw it from?"

"Verra well." He walked a couple of feet back to where she had initially thrown the dagger, and then he stepped to the left—far to the left. "Right here. I wouldnae want to make it *too* easy for ye."

"Of course you wouldn't." She stepped up beside him and briefly studied the target. She raised her hand and was about to throw the blade when he spoke.

"Now donna let your nerves get the best of ye, lass."

She lowered her hand. "Truly, Ruairi. No wonder you irritate Fagan."

He chuckled in response. Without hesitation, Ravenna hurled the dagger at the target. A smug look crossed her face and she raised her brow, folding her arms over her chest.

"From that shot, I don't think you can say that luck was on my side. I told you it was skill."

Ruairi pulled the blade from the piece of wood. "Mayhap."

"Mayhap?" Her voice went up a notch.

"All right. I will admit that ye have a fine aim."

Ravenna smiled. "That must've hurt, my laird."

"It wasnae nearly as painful as I thought it would be."

As she glanced over his shoulder, her eyes widened, her jaw dropped, and all color drained from her face.

～✤～

Ravenna stared at the dark hooded figure in the woods. She could not make out a face. If she didn't know better, she'd swear the still mass was a specter. She'd heard tales of strange occurrences in the Highlands. Perhaps this was one of them. She refused to blink, thinking she was mad. Just when she started to think she'd lost her faculties, the figure disappeared as quickly as she'd spotted it. Her mind had to be playing tricks on her. At least that's what she believed until she spotted Angus as he turned and retreated through the woods.

She lowered her voice. "Ruairi, there was someone in the trees, watching us."

He turned around and his eyes searched the woods. "Where?"

"Over there." She pointed.

His hand reached for the hilt of his sword. "Stay here."

She grabbed his arm to stay him. "It's too late. I hesitated too long. He's already gone."

"What did he look like?"

"I couldn't see his face. He wore a dark cloak that covered him from head to toe. I thought I'd imagined someone standing there until I saw Angus. I think he followed the man."

Ruairi looked at her doubtfully. "I'm nae saying ye didnae see something, but Angus wouldnae be so friendly toward a person he doesnae know. He would've growled and wouldnae walk away with the man. Are ye sure of what ye saw?"

She hesitated, already knowing the answer. "Yes. I'm sure."

As they rode back to the castle, she wondered if Laird Gordon had sent another of his men to spy on Ruairi. Although one would've thought that after Ruairi and Laird Munro threatened the man in the bailey, Laird Gordon would've left well enough alone.

Ruairi's thoughts must have been racing because she didn't think he realized that he had been increasing his pace the whole way home. They arrived in the bailey and she barely had time to dismount before he called to his captain and the men quickly rode back out the gate.

Ravenna walked to her chamber to wash up before it was time to sup. There was a knock at the door, and she knew it was too soon to be Ruairi. She placed the drying cloth on the table, and when she swung open the door, the boy smiled.

"Hello, Torquil."

He spoke slowly, clearly thinking of every word he said. "Da nae back. I go ye sup?"

"Of course. He should be back soon."

Ravenna walked out, closing the door behind her. As she walked with Torquil down the hall, she felt a small hand clasp hers. She instinctively felt her mouth lifting with tenderness. She'd known there was something special about the boy from the beginning. All those weeks of being confined with him in the library only confirmed what she already knew. She looked down into those beautiful green eyes and felt her heart fill with love.

❧

"And ye say he wore a cloak from head to toe. In this heat?" asked Fagan.

Ruairi shrugged. "I know there is a chance that Ravenna is mistaken, but I'm sure she saw something or thinks she did. Since I found that dagger in the tunnels, I am nae leaving anything to chance."

Fagan studied the brush, looking for any signs of a cloaked figure. He circled the area and then bent down to touch the ground.

"The grass is pushed down in this spot, but it could've been from Angus. 'Tis hard to tell. If it was a man, he's gone. I will keep an eye on the tunnels from the glade. I assure ye that if someone goes in, they will nae come out. And our men still watch the border. Do ye think the Gordon would be foolish enough to send another man after our cattle?"

"Dressed in a cloak? I donna know. His actions would be unwise since I havenae yet refused his request for us to join Stewart's son. And ye know I told the arse there would be nay mercy if I found someone else on my lands. I donna understand it, but until we catch this bastard, there is naught we can do but watch the tunnels and make certain the men stay alert at the border. I grow weary of this."

"Aye."

They walked back through the brush and grabbed their mounts. As they rode back to the castle, Ruairi felt Fagan's eyes on him. He knew his captain had something else to say, but he wasn't sure if Fagan's words were about the Gordon or another topic so he wisely decided not to ask. When Fagan cleared his throat, Ruairi knew to prepare himself for the battle of wills that was sure to come.

"Do ye still intend to send Ravenna back in a few days?"

Ruairi dropped his chin to his chest and sighed. "Didnae we already have this discussion? But I will tell ye this…" He turned and gave his captain a wry smile. "I leave it to ye to keep up the guard."

His *friend* regarded him with amusement.

"What? Why are ye looking at me like that now?" asked Ruairi.

"Och, nay reason." Fagan shook his head. "Ye just spend every eve with your bonny lass, and I'll be curious to see if ye let her go."

By the time they returned to the castle, the meal was already over. They went to the kitchens and raided what was left of the eve's food. Fagan sat with Ruairi at the small kitchen table and poured them some mulled wine.

"I think I'll take Angus to the glade with me this eve. He may hear something I am nae able to."

Ruairi nodded. "'Tis a good idea because if he is with ye, he cannae be stalking Ravenna's door."

"He does seem to have taken a certain fancy to the lass like someone else I know. I'm sure ye'll be taking over watch for Angus and stalking Ravenna's door yourself this eve."

"Arse."

"Aye." Fagan stood. "Have a pleasant eve, m'laird. If ye'll excuse me, I'll be taking watch while ye'll be taking Rav—"

"If ye know what's good for ye, ye will nae finish those words," Ruairi warned.

Fagan held up his hands in mock defense and Ruairi heard his captain chuckling as he walked out into the great hall.

Bastard.

Ruairi finished his meal and made his way to Ravenna's chamber. He knocked on the door, and when she opened it, he was relieved to see that she hadn't settled in for the night.

"May I come in?"

"Yes, please." She gestured him through the door and closed it behind him. "Did you see any signs of the man?"

"There were signs of something, but Fagan wasnae sure if the marks were left by Angus or someone else."

She nodded. "I see."

He placed his hands on her shoulders. "I believe that ye saw something."

"I know I did."

"Howbeit there is naught we can do until we see him again." He looked around her chamber. "Do ye have all your belongings in your trunk?"

Her gaze became puzzled. "Yes. Why do you ask?"

Ruairi grabbed her by the hand and opened the door. "While ye are under my roof, ye are my responsibility. I will see ye safe. Ye'll stay in the bedchamber next to mine."

❧

Ravenna couldn't say whether she was irked by Ruairi's blatant command or angry with herself because she wanted to be closer to him. Either way, she wouldn't give in that easily.

"Do you think that's wise since I'll be leav—"

He looked at her and she felt the eager affection coming from him. "I told ye. Donna even think about denying me. Ye want this as much as I do. I dare ye to deny it."

She remained silent as he led her to his chamber. Once inside, she realized that this was where she'd wanted to be all along. The room was large with a huge bed with four corner posts and a golden coverlet, a fireplace, and a sitting area. Broadswords hung on the wall behind the bed and shields on the opposite wall. She supposed if he wanted to cause her harm, she could grab a sword from the wall in defense—well, from any wall in the castle.

Ruairi pulled back the blankets from the bed.

"What are you doing?" She knew exactly what he was doing. She could see and practically feel the lust coming from him. Being carried away by her own response, she'd failed to notice the look of impatience that crossed over his face.

"What do ye think I'm doing, lass?"

He casually walked in a slow circle around her. She was strangely flattered by his interest. He stopped and fisted a hand in his tunic behind his neck, pulled the garment over his head, and flung it to the floor.

The air suddenly left Ravenna's lungs. The man was dressed in nothing but his kilt. His long hair fell around his face, and he was so incredibly handsome. As he bent to take off his boots, the muscles in his strong back and wide shoulders reminded her that he was a lot bigger than she was. Dangerous. Captivating.

He stood there, legs splayed, and she licked her dry

lips. This beautiful man before her was going to love her, if only for a night or two.

He walked another silent circle around her and then took her hand. Her heart jolted and her pulse pounded. He regarded her with possessive amusement, as if he could sense her unease. He took his other hand and loosened his belt, his kilt falling to the floor.

"Rua…" She cleared her throat. "Ruairi…"

"Hush."

Ravenna snapped her mouth shut. There was an air of command about him that fascinated her. The sight of this…*Highlander* with his hard body and erection that pushed hungrily toward her would forever be engraved in her memory. The man was so big, so hard, and so very tempting.

She suddenly found herself unable to perform the simplest of tasks—like breathing, talking, and even blinking. She didn't want to blink and miss a single heated moment. His gaze raked boldly over her, inch by inch, as if he was contemplating which part of her to taste first. It was too easy to get lost in the way he looked at her.

His ravenous gaze made her knees quiver. The prolonged anticipation was almost unbearable. He turned her around and loosened her gown. When the material pooled at her feet, he stripped her of all remaining clothing—slowly. There was a hint of arrogance about him that she liked.

He gently eased her down on the bed and growled, "Ravenna," as he stretched his body over the full length of hers. He felt heavy and warm. God, how she tingled when he said her name. She buried her hands in his thick hair. The magnificent man in her arms made her tremble.

His kiss was slow, thoughtful. His lips demanded a response, and she was more than happy to oblige. When he lowered his head, he left her mouth burning with fire. His tongue explored the rosy peaks of her breasts.

He rubbed himself back and forth between her legs and then spoke in a language she didn't understand. He slid a hand down her body to the vee at her thighs. She instinctively cried out at the warmth of his touch. Muscles deep inside her begged to be filled and sated.

When his lips grazed the hollow of her neck, she whimpered. When he sucked her earlobe, she cried out. She was most definitely aroused. Hot, achy, swollen. He raised his hand to her cheek, and she turned her head and sucked his finger. She wanted any part of him she could get.

He was nudging his thick manhood against her soft folds, and she was pushing wildly back against him.

"Please, Ruairi." She couldn't stand it any longer. How much longer would she be made to suffer?

"Is this what ye want, lass?" His voice was deep next to her ear.

She cried out and he pushed himself in gradually, easing inside while torturing her with a teasing touch. He withdrew slowly and filled her again as she nearly sobbed with frustrated desire. With thrust after blessed thrust she arched against him, trying to take more of him to gain her release. But his big hands were on her hips and prevented her from controlling the pace or gaining what she sought.

"Do ye want me, Ravenna?" he whispered in a sultry voice.

"Yes," she cried out.

"Then ye will have me."

His lips came crashing down on hers at the same moment he thrust deep and held. She deepened the kiss, and his tongue mirrored the motion of her lower body. The tension that gripped her body exploded, flooding her to her very core.

She called out his name, and he continued thrusting until she went limp beneath him. He wrapped his arms around her so tightly that she could barely breathe. Then he said her name through gritted teeth and spilled his seed within her, sighing with pleased exhaustion.

Ten

Ruairi stirred, remembering the smoldering passion that he had shared with Ravenna only hours earlier. He rolled onto his side and draped his arm across her slender waist. The scent of lavender filled his senses. Until last eve, he hadn't realized how much he'd missed savoring a lass's touch. And not just any lass...Ravenna. He knew she would always hold a tender place in his heart.

Red tendrils of hair hung loosely down her back in total disarray. Soft ivory shoulders beckoned to him, begging to be kissed. He lowered his gaze to her bare bottom nestled into his groin, which immediately tightened at the thought of taking her again. The melting softness of her luscious body would surely be his undoing.

She wiped unruly strands of hair away from her eyes. "Are you awake?" she asked in a sleepy daze.

"Aye."

She opened her eyes to find him staring at her, then shut her lids again and groaned. "What are you doing?"

"Watching ye." He kissed her on the shoulder.

"While I sleep?" She rolled over, pulling the blanket up around her shoulders. "That's a little unnerving, my laird."

"Why? Ye're a bonny lass. Ye look so peaceful when ye slumber."

She smirked. "I don't know about that. My pillow is more than likely wet with slobber, but I wouldn't know because I slept like the dead."

"I'm glad I satisfied ye."

She turned and faced him, giving him a knowing smile. "Thoroughly." She giggled, and then her expression turned serious. She lifted her fingers and brushed his cheek in a gentle gesture. "I enjoyed being with you, Ruairi."

He kissed the palm of her hand. "Oh, I'm nae quite done with ye yet, lass. We still have a few more days, and I intend to sate your needs—every last one of them—many times."

Her face reddened. "And what of you? Did you enjoy last eve?"

He chuckled in response. "Ye couldnae tell?" He lowered his head and gave her a tender kiss. He rubbed his thumb over her chin. "Nay matter how much I'd like to keep ye chained in my bed all day, I must meet Fagan this morn."

"And Torquil will be expecting me to break my fast with him."

Ruairi rose from the bed and donned his kilt. "Before I forget, I have something for ye." He picked up a flower from the table and then sat on the bed. Lightly, he traced the soft petals over her cheek, her jaw, and her lips. He lowered his head and brushed a soft kiss to her forehead. "A rose…for the bonniest lass who ever graced the Highlands."

✺

Ravenna never felt so much the fool as she did right now. No matter how much she believed that sharing Ruairi's bed had brought them closer, there would always be a wall between them. He could never know her true purpose. If he did, he would never look at her the same way again. She had to deceive him at every turn. Granted, that was part of being a spy, but this was the first time since she could remember that her masquerade had actually angered her. Ruairi was a good man. She didn't like lying to him.

"Thank you. The flower is beautiful."

"My pleasure, lass. Your trunk has been brought up, and ye can find it through the adjoining door." He bent and kissed her on the top of her head and then walked out the door.

Ravenna rose from the bed, her body protesting. Last eve's bed sport had been exhausting. She'd used muscles that she hadn't used in a long time. Still, she couldn't seem to stay the smile that crossed her face at the memory of Ruairi's touch. She gathered the dress that was still pooled on the floor and walked over to open the adjoining door. Her trunk was placed on the floor at the foot of the bed. She stood beside it, holding her bunched-up gown to her chest.

She gazed around the room, which she had presumed was Anna's old bedchamber. Feminine touches were evident throughout the chamber. A blue coverlet was draped over the bed, which had tall, wooden corner posts. To the far left, a large sitting area had fresh flowers on the table. The room was made up as if someone had expected Ravenna to stay here. For a brief moment, she yearned for a life that she knew she could never have. She wondered what her world would be like if Ruairi was in it and this was her home, and then reality crept back in.

"Stop it, Ravenna. You're a fool for even thinking that way," she said aloud.

She opened her trunk and pulled out another day dress. While she donned her clothing, all she could think of was her time with Ruairi. Once she'd made herself presentable, she walked to the great hall where Torquil was already seated at the table.

"Good morning, Torquil."

He nodded. "Good morning, Ravenna." He continued to pick at his food.

"Aren't you hungry this morning?"

"I nae hungry. I take walk. Ye come?" he asked hopefully.

She ruffled his hair. "All right. I'll come along, but you'll have to do your studies after our walk."

He rolled his eyes.

"Torquil…"

"Aye, Ravenna," he said in an appeasing tone.

Ravenna laughed at the way he said the words. He was already learning to be a good husband. She thought she'd groomed him well and hoped he'd remember her lessons long after she had departed. When they finished their meal, they walked out into the bailey. She held up her hand to shield her eyes from the blazing sun.

"It's a beautiful day. Where do you want to walk?"

"Ye nay want Angus to come?"

She raised her brow. "I think it would be better if Angus stays wherever he is at the moment. Is that all right with you?"

He nodded in response.

They walked out into the field, and it didn't take long for Torquil to leave her side. As always, he ran ahead of her, throwing tiny rocks. She turned and looked back at the castle. She'd thought at first that she'd find Ruairi's vast home a bit staggering since she was used to her much-smaller manor house, but the warmth of the castle was more than she'd expected it to be.

Ravenna continued to follow the boy as his attention shifted from rocks to whipping sticks. When she noticed a slight movement out of the corner of her eye, she discreetly glanced toward the tree line.

The hooded figure stood perfectly still in the shadows among the trees. Ravenna couldn't see his face, but she could make out the shape of the man who watched her. When Torquil started to wander closer to the forest, she knew she had to get him away from there.

"Torquil, wait." When she caught up to him, she leaned over and placed one hand on the boy's shoulder while the other fumbled under her skirts and reached for her dagger. "Listen to me. I want you to run as fast as you can and seek your father. When you find him, you bring him here. Do *not* follow me. Do you understand?"

"Aye, but what wrong? Angus?"

She smiled and rubbed her hand over his head. "No, it's not Angus. You must listen to me and run. Find your father and bring him here."

He nodded.

"Go. Run now!"

Ravenna spun on her heel and darted toward the hooded figure with her dagger in hand. She heard Torquil calling for his father in the distance and knew he'd be safe. When the man turned and ran, Ravenna increased her speed into the forest in pursuit. If this was the Gordon's man, at least Ruairi would know for sure which enemy was close at hand.

Sticks snapped under her feet. Branches slapped her in the face. She looked ahead and saw the cloak whip to the right. She was only a few yards behind. Her uncle's men had trained her well. Not only was she proficient at throwing her dagger, but she could easily defend herself and generally run as fast as any man. But her skirts had started to slow her down. With one hand, Ravenna lifted her dress as the material started to become tangled in the brush again. She couldn't lose this man. She refused.

She heard something coming toward her from the side. She turned her head to see Angus running straight for her, trampling branches underneath his paws.

Oh, God.

"Angus, no!"

The wolf's heavy paws leaped from the ground and pounded Ravenna's hip, knocking her down with a heavy thump. The dagger flew from her hand and landed somewhere in the brush. She found herself pinned in the dirt beneath the eyes of a killer.

❧

Ruairi met Fagan as he returned from the glade. His captain looked tired and worn, as if he'd been up all night. Once they caught this miscreant, he'd make certain Fagan had some days of much-needed rest. Until then, he needed to keep all his men alert.

"I assume ye didnae see anyone."

Fagan shook his head wearily. "Nay. I watched all eve. Angus didnae even stir. Naught moved except the damn midges." He reached down and scratched his leg.

"Seek your bed. The men are still watching the border, and we will try the glade again this eve." Ruairi slapped him on the shoulder. "I should've known the bastard wouldnae make another appearance so soon. Of course that would be far too easy for us."

"But we'll be ready when he decides to come again." Fagan paused, studying Ruairi intently. "I have to say that ye donna look at all well rested, my laird. Mayhap ye were up past your bedtime last eve?"

Ruairi chuckled. "I didnae get much sleep last night."

"I assume Ravenna looks much the same."

He shrugged. "Let's just say that I donna think she'll be doing much sleeping for the next few days. She can sleep on her way home."

"Da! Da! *Thig an seo! Thig an seo!*" *Come here! Come here!*

Ruairi was halted by the tone of Torquil's voice. He turned and his eyes widened at the sight of his son running toward him. By the time Torquil reached his side, the boy could barely speak. He hunched over, placing his hands to his knees and gasping for breath.

"Calm yourself, lad." He patted Torquil's back. "Ravenna…"

When Torquil hesitated and seemed to be thinking of the English word, Ruairi shook his head. *"Sput a-mach e! Gàidhlig againn." Spit it out! Speak Gaelic.*

Once the words flew from his son's mouth, it took Ruairi a moment to grasp that the daft lass had actually given chase to the man. A chill ran down his spine. "Ye stay here," he ordered.

Ruairi and Fagan made a lightning dash out the gates and into the field. As they thundered toward the tree line, Ruairi's battle-hardened senses came into full awareness.

"Ravenna!" he shouted, his eyes searching frantically through the trees.

When no one responded, he gestured to Fagan to widen the search. They continued to call for her and made their way deeper into the forest. God's teeth! He was mad with worry. What woman in her right mind would decide to give chase to someone who could potentially cause her harm? He knew one thing for certain. The lass had better be all right because he sure as hell was going to kill her when he found her.

He gazed over at Fagan, who shook his head, a grim expression crossing his face. If anything happened to her…Ruairi didn't want to finish the thought.

Leaves rustled beneath his feet, and he knew with every inch he took that he was one step closer to finding Ravenna. He was not a religious man, but he suddenly had a strong desire to say a silent prayer for her safety. He looked in front of him, behind him, to the side. He wouldn't forgive himself if something happened to her. She was a guest in his home. He was supposed to be her sworn protector.

"Do ye want me to go back and gather some horses?" asked Fagan as he walked toward Ruairi through the brush.

A desperate cry pierced the air.

He thought at first he'd imagined the sound, but when Fagan's eyes widened, Ruairi's heart leaped in his throat.

❧

Sheer black fright swept through Ravenna as she tried to keep her fragile control. It no longer mattered that she'd lost the man. She didn't care if he'd long since fled Ruairi's lands. She tried to slow her heart. She dared not move. The wicked beast had her pinned facedown to the ground with massive paws. She felt his breath on the back of her neck.

Her poor sisters would never know what happened to her. Her body would never be found—or parts of her body would—but she didn't want to think about that. Her mind strayed to Elizabeth and Kat. Now that Ravenna was about to meet her untimely demise, her sisters would be raised by Grace. God help them all. This was not how she wanted to die. This was not how she wanted to be remembered.

She changed the position of her neck with the slightest of movements and felt the wolf's muzzle brush her skin. Her face was wet with tears. She tried not to make a sound. The tension increased with frightening intensity, and for a moment,

Ravenna tried to lay there like she was dead. As if the wily creature sensed her cunning act, he refused to budge.

"Ravenna!"

Praise the saints. Ruairi had come for her. At the time, she wasn't sure Torquil had understood her command, but Ruairi would be here any moment now and that's all that mattered. Her savior. Her hero.

The moments passed as she lay pinned to the cool ground. To her surprise and mounting dismay, no one came for her. Where was the dastardly man?

"Ravenna!"

She heard Fagan and Ruairi's voices moving farther away from her. If she didn't call to them now, they'd be too far gone and would never be able to find her.

"I'm here," she said quietly.

Angus pawed at her back, and she closed her eyes and shuddered. The scar on her leg started to ache. Whether the pain was real or from the memories that she'd tried to bury long ago, she couldn't say. When she realized Ruairi or Fagan were no longer close, she knew what she had to do. Either way, Angus was going to bite her. But there was a slim chance that if Ruairi reached her quickly, he'd be able to stay Angus' sharp jaws from tearing further into her soft flesh.

Ravenna willed her lips to open and finally screamed for help. The men shouted in the distance, but she heard them coming closer. She remained perfectly still as tears streamed down her face. She yelled again to make certain they knew where she was.

Ruairi and Fagan ran to her side, swords drawn. Ruairi's eyes were sharp and assessing.

"Angus, move!" Ruairi commanded.

She felt the animal leave her back as Ruairi knelt beside her. He pushed back the hair from her face. "Are ye all right? Are ye injured?"

She rolled onto her side and sat up abruptly, her wide eyes staring at Angus.

"Ravenna, ye must answer me. Are ye injur—"

Turning her head, she threw herself into Ruairi's arms. She gulped hard, hot tears slipping down her cheeks. Suddenly yielding to the compulsive sobs that shook her, she couldn't believe she was alive. Strong arms encircled her as a wet nose touched her cheek. Ravenna whimpered, burying her face deeper into Ruairi's chest.

"Angus, go!" ordered Ruairi. "Shhh… *Sèimhich*, lass." *Calm*. "Angus hears your cry. He only makes certain ye are all right. He has taken his leave now." With her in his arms, Ruairi gently ran his hand over her hair in a soothing gesture. "Can ye stand?"

She nodded as he assisted her to her feet. He kept his arm firmly wrapped around her.

"What happened?" asked Fagan.

Ravenna wiped the tears from her eyes. "I was walking with Torquil when I spotted the man from last eve standing in the shadows watching us." She noticed the frown that crossed Ruairi's face.

"So ye gave chase to him?" asked Ruairi.

She looked away swiftly at the sight of his scowl. "I made certain Torquil was safe, and then yes, I ran after him." She lowered her voice, hoping Ruairi would follow suit. She didn't appreciate being scolded in front of Fagan.

"God's teeth, lass, what were ye thinking?" Ruairi asked in a raised voice. "Ne'er mind because clearly ye werenae. What made ye believe ye could chase down this man? Hell, Ravenna, what would ye had done had ye caught up with him? He could've killed ye."

"I didn't want him to get away. By the time I would've sought you or Fagan, he would've been long gone. I had an opportunity. I took it. I also had my dagger, and you know I am perfectly capable of protecting myself."

He smirked and lifted a brow. "And where is your dagger?"

She glanced around. "I don't know. I dropped it somewhere when Angus attacked me."

Ruairi picked up the blade from a nearby bush and shook his head when he handed it to her. "Angus didnae attack ye. He thought ye were playing with him. If he jumped on ye, his actions were only because he believed ye were running from him. 'Tis a game to him. And he licked your cheek when he heard ye cry." When she was about to protest, he added, "Angus is the only one who had sense. Had he nae knocked ye on your arse, ye'd be dead. Ye donna know what kind of man this was. Ye were foolish."

She placed her hands on her hips in a defiant gesture. "I will not apologize for trying to keep your family safe. Had your *pet* not knocked me on my arse," she repeated with her best imitation, "I would've caught the man and you'd be thanking me right now instead of lecturing me."

Fagan started to walk away. At least one man in the Sutherland clan had some sense. Ruairi made her so angry. She hated when men thought of her as faint. If they only knew… She only had one weakness and that wolf was it. The animal had made her lose the man.

Ravenna knew Ruairi was seething with mounting rage. That's why she didn't say one word on the way back to the castle. He needed to cool his temper. When they were almost at the gates, she reached out a hand to stay him.

"I know you are somewhat angry with me."

He turned and his nostrils flared with fury. "'Somewhat angry' doesnae begin to describe what I feel."

"Would you put that aside for one moment? Please?"

He took a deep breath and she knew he was trying to be patient with her.

"Even though I couldn't see the man's face, his form was similar to my own and he was about my height. From what I could see, the cloak he wore was of fine quality, not one a servant would wear. He might have been a growing boy or a small man. That's all I saw."

He paused for a moment.

"Ye are a governess. Yet, ye know how to wield a dagger, donna hesitate to give chase, and now even give me a wee description of the man." His eyes narrowed.

"Don't look too much into things, my laird. I told you. My father taught me how to wield a dagger, and my mother insisted that I read a lot of books. You'd be surprised what you can learn from a good book."

Ravenna slapped him playfully in the chest and walked away. She closed her eyes and prayed he believed her words.

Eleven

RUAIRI SAT BACK IN THE CHAIR IN HIS STUDY AND took another drink from his tankard. His blood boiled. He'd lost count of how many times he had cursed Ravenna and her foolishness. What lass in her right mind would have attempted such a feat?

"I'm surprised ye didnae ask me to throw her in the dungeon," said Fagan with a wry grin.

"Aye, well, donna give me any ideas. The day isnae over yet. The lass was completely daft to chase after the man." When he saw the look on Fagan's face, he sighed. "Donna even say it."

"I didnae say anything, but I think ye'll agree that Ravenna has some bollocks. Mayhap the English lass has some Scottish blood in her after all."

"Be that as it may, she wasnae thinking. She's only a woman." He threw up his hands in exasperation. "She sent Torquil to find me and then ran down the bastard on her own. And the lass says she's afraid of Angus," he said with a smirk. "She was the one who hunted the man like she was a damn wolf on the prowl."

Fagan rubbed his brow and spoke dryly. "So ye have said several times, my laird."

Ruairi's eyes widened in surprise. "I didnae realize I said the words *that* many times."

"And then some."

"Arse."

Fagan grinned mischievously. "Aye."

Ruairi pulled the dagger he'd found in the tunnels from the desk drawer. "I thought this was a woman's dagger, but now that Ravenna has told us what she saw, 'tis possible the blade belongs to a lad. Mayhap the Gordon paid someone to keep watch on us." He tapped his finger on the weapon. "But as I said before, I cannae figure out why. Why would he risk discovery before my answer was given? And how would a lad know about the tunnels?

"That entrance hasnae been used for some time. I need answers to my questions. I donna like the fact that this *spy* has kept to the shadows, watching my son and Ravenna so closely. And yet he is somehow slipping through our guard. Make certain the men stay alert. Ravenna and Torquil will nay longer be permitted outside the gates without an escort."

"I will keep watch on the tunnels myself. Donna worry. Our men will catch this bastard the same as the last two. I will leave it to ye to speak with Ravenna and Torquil."

"Try to keep Angus with ye while ye stand watch."

"Aye." Fagan slapped his hands on his thighs and then stood. "I've been up all eve and I'm weary. I'm seeking my bed now for a few hours of rest." He started to walk away and then turned back, a flash of humor crossing his face. "I already heard ye've moved Ravenna's chamber to a more...*convenient* location. Let me, being the only voice of reason here, be the first to remind ye that 'tis still too early to seek your bed." There was a trace of laughter in his voice and Ruairi promptly waved him off.

"*Tha farmad agad. Mach à seo.*" *You are jealous. Get out of here.*

A chuckle answered him. "As ye wish, my laird."

When Fagan closed the door, Ruairi wanted nothing more than to wipe that grin from his captain's face. The man thought he knew everything. Who knew? Maybe he did. Ruairi wasn't going to admit to his friend that the thought had crossed his mind to summon Ravenna back to his bed right after their conversation.

～

Since Ruairi had disappeared for about an hour with Fagan, Ravenna walked into the great hall. She spotted Torquil sitting on a bench at the table, drawing. He looked up when she approached him.

"Are you all right? I didn't mean to frighten you." She sat down beside him. "I also wanted to thank you for listening like you did." She brushed her hand over Torquil's locks, and he looked at her with concern.

"What ye saw?"

"What did I see?"

He nodded. "Aye."

She wasn't sure if Ruairi wanted Torquil to know about the hooded man in the woods, and she didn't think it was her place to tell him. She also didn't want to frighten the boy because he should feel safe in his own home.

"Umm…" Ravenna turned when she felt a hand on her shoulder.

"I'd like to speak with the two of ye in my study," said Ruairi.

She and Torquil stood and followed Ruairi to the study. When the door closed, she realized her first instinct was correct. Why did she suddenly get the feeling she was being scolded by her father? She stood tall and wrung her hands in front of her, awaiting punishment for her actions.

"Please sit." Ruairi gestured to the chair next to Torquil while he took his seat behind the desk.

Ravenna glanced nervously around the room and felt like a young girl again. All that was missing was her sisters cowering behind her, like in the days when their actions landed them in a heap of trouble.

"From now on, I donna want either of ye to wander beyond the gates without an escort."

Torquil's voice went up a notch. "Why? *Chan eil mi 'tuigsinn.*" *I do not understand.*

Ruairi spoke in Gaelic, and his son nodded with every word. Torquil suddenly turned to Ravenna with a wide-eyed stare, and his mouth dropped open.

"A' bhana-ghaisgeach." *Female warrior.*

"Donna encourage her," said Ruairi. "She was naught more than a foolish *sealgair* without a weapon." *Hunter.*

"Pardon?"

The boy stood and bent to kiss Ravenna on the cheek. He placed his small hand on her shoulder and smiled. *"Neart carraig làidir."* The might of a strong rock to you.

She watched Torquil walk out of the study, and when she looked back at Ruairi, he shook his head.

"What did he say?"

"He doesnae know of what he speaks. He thinks ye're some kind of warrior."

She smiled and lifted her brow. "At least your son doesn't scold me and is able to admit the truth."

He paid her no heed. "I told him about the man in the forest. For the remainder of your stay, ye and Torquil will nae leave the castle alone. Do ye understand?"

"Just because I chased that man, you don't have to punish me by—"

"I am keeping ye safe. I am nae punishing ye."

"I'm surprised you don't chain *me* in the dungeon," she said, her expression holding a note of mockery.

Ravenna jumped when he stood abruptly and rounded the table. He pulled her to her feet and his lips met hers. What were they talking about? She couldn't remember. When he pulled back, he gave her a roguish grin.

"Chaining ye in the dungeon wasnae exactly what I had in mind, but if I have to chain ye to my bed to keep ye safe…now there's a thought."

She knew her face had reddened under his heated gaze and she looked away.

He brushed a curl behind her ear. "Ye're staying in my home and are under my protection. I donna want ye meddling with things that are dangerous. Surely ye can do this for me for the few days ye have left. 'Tisnae much to ask of ye."

She raised her eyes to find him watching her. "Of course."

He looked up at the ceiling as if he briefly thanked God that she was in agreement, and then he lowered his eyes to hers. "My men are watching the border. Torquil is now within the castle walls, and Angus is with Fagan." He raised his brow. "Everything is once again under control. Whatever shall we do to pass the time, Mistress Denny?"

"What do you propose, my laird?"

⤝⤞

Ruairi gave her body a raking gaze, the meaning of his look made perfectly clear. God how he wanted her. He craved sliding his hand along her soft flesh. At that moment, nothing else mattered. There was no vagrant trespassing on Sutherland lands, no impending war with the Gordon, and Ravenna wasn't leaving today.

Desire stretched between them, and every muscle in his body tensed with restraint. He refused to make her feel uncomfortable. The choice was hers.

He stood perfectly still as he waited for her decision. One nod, one move was all it would take before his mouth captured hers. When she stepped forward and brushed a soft kiss to his lips, that little response was all the approval he needed. With a primal growl, he returned her kiss with fervor.

"I cannae get enough of ye."

"Then take all you need." She pulled back slightly and smiled with passion-glazed eyes. "But first, please bolt the door."

Without hesitation, he walked over to the door and

slid the latch closed. "Nay one will disturb us. I will nae let them."

Every inch of his body felt as though it was aflame as he approached her. She matched his kiss and the thrust and parry of his tongue stroke for stroke. The harder and deeper he kissed her, the more he wanted.

Ravenna felt so good in his arms, too damn good. He never thought he'd crave a woman's touch the way he craved hers. He had a burning desire, an aching need to hold her, kiss her, make her his.

She slid her hands up and explored his wide shoulders. When she clenched him harder, he intensified the kiss.

He lifted his head, breathing hard, and she stared with longing at him. The depth of emotion in her eyes took his breath away. Of course there was desire, but he noticed something deeper. Something that he wanted to believe with every fiber of his being.

He watched her expression as he loosened her bodice and tugged the fabric down below her stays. Her breath was heavy between her slightly parted lips. Never had he seen her so beautiful.

His lips trailed a path down her neck, and his fingers dipped below the edges of her stays. He outlined the swell of her breast with his finger and she was so soft. He moved to cup her.

"Ye are so verra beautiful."

He lifted her closer to his mouth and his tongue flicked her nipple.

"And ye taste so verra sweet."

She moaned as he continued to tease her taut nipples, rubbing the rough pads of his fingers over the sensitive buds. He sucked her, hard, and she pressed against him. He lowered his hand to her bottom as he nipped and sucked, driving her wild.

When she grabbed his shoulders for support, he knew she was coming apart. It was time. He pressed his lips to hers, kissing her relentlessly. His hand slid under the edge of her skirts as he leaned her back on the desk. His fingers worked their way up along her calf, then higher still.

"Ruairi, please. I…need…you."

She didn't need to tell him twice. Ravenna's passion was like everything else about her, refreshingly honest and open. She was just as hot and desperate as he was.

He lifted his kilt and entered her with a single thrust. He nibbled her lip with his teeth as she gasped with desire. He wanted to devour her, to explore every inch of her body slowly and carefully. She drove him wild.

Her breathing was coming hard and fast.

"Ruairi…"

"Come for me, my sweet Ravenna."

His need for this woman was too strong. She was so wet, so ready. Blood pounded in his loins, his desire close to spilling over. He thrust up high and hard inside her, filling her with the hot burst of his seed.

No woman had ever done this to him, and he knew the need to be inside her wasn't only from lust. He wasn't sure what the feeling was, but it was definitely far more than senseless tupping on his desk in the study in the middle of the day.

All he knew was that she was his.

Ravenna brushed down her skirts and pulled up her bodice. She smoothed back her hair and smiled at Ruairi. Her mind was muddled, and she couldn't believe the way she had given herself to him. On. His. Desk. She wondered when the two of them had lost all sense of reason, but she was also astonished by the sense of fulfillment she felt.

"Your men are watching the border, Torquil is now within the castle walls, and Angus is with Fagan." She raised her brow. "Everything is once again under control. I think we passed the time quite nicely. Wouldn't you say, Laird Sutherland?"

Ruairi chuckled as he fastened his kilt. "I would think so. I have to admit, I've ne'er had so much fun in my study before."

"I would certainly hope not." She ran her hand over the top of his desk. "I daresay, I don't think you'll ever be able to think of your desk the same way again."

He approached her and cupped her chin with his hand. "I would have to agree."

She reached up and took his hand. When she looked into the depths of his green eyes, her heart called to her, demanding she speak the truth. "I'll truly miss you, Ruairi." Her lips lightly brushed his hand.

"Da! Da!" Torquil called from behind the door, followed by a loud pounding.

Ruairi smiled at her as though he was apologizing for the interruption. He swung open the door and Torquil walked in. When the boy spotted Ravenna, he visibly relaxed.

"What's the matter?" asked Ruairi with concern.

"I go Ravenna's chamber and she nae there. 'Tis empty. Naught is there. I thought she leave."

Her heart sank.

She approached Torquil and knelt beside him. "I would never leave you without saying good-bye." She pulled him close and wrapped her arms around him. Ruairi stood and watched as her eyes welled with tears. She quickly closed them to hide her emotions. "Are you all right?"

Torquil pulled back. "Aye. But where are your trunk?"

"Where is my trunk?" She looked for help from a certain Highland laird.

Ruairi stepped forward and spoke in Gaelic, placing his hand on Torquil's shoulder as he escorted his son out the door. She was too embarrassed to stick around and find out what Ruairi had said. She didn't want Torquil to think poorly of her and didn't want his last memories of her to be unfavorable ones. He was still young and innocent. Even though Torquil knew of the man in the forest, she hoped that Ruairi would continue to shelter the boy from the harsh realities of the world. He was too young to be plagued by adult situations. And he certainly didn't need to know about the time she'd spent with his father.

Ravenna walked back to her new chamber and sighed when she closed the door. This was becoming much more complicated than she cared to admit. There was something about this Highland warrior, this man that she found—well, she wasn't exactly sure what.

She sat on the bed and pressed both hands over her

eyes as if they burned with weariness. Every time her mind drifted to Ruairi, her sisters' names kept slipping through her thoughts. She felt guilty for the pleasure she had found with him, a Highland laird of all things. At least the missive she'd sent would reach Uncle Walter soon. She could only imagine the look on her sister's face when they met in Edinburgh and Grace saw Ravenna was not with child. How did her sister ever come up with such things?

The adjoining door opened and Ruairi knocked briefly before he entered. "I figured ye were in here."

"Cowering."

"Now there isnae a need for that. My son cares for ye. I think he mumbled some words about a warrior being rewarded for their bravery." He sat on the bed beside her. "He'll miss ye."

"And I'll miss him. You are truly blessed with Torquil."

"I'm reminded of that every day. To be honest, I havenae seen him that happy for a long time."

She tapped him on the arm. "Oh, Ruairi. I can't say I'm responsible for that, but I thank you just the same."

He raised his hand and softly brushed his thumb over her cheek. "Ye brought the light back into his eyes." For a long moment, he looked back at her. "And mine as well, lass."

Twelve

TIME WAS RUNNING OUT AND HE DIDN'T LIKE IT AT ALL. He'd do anything to stop it. Ruairi walked to the court-yard to see if Fagan had returned from his nightly watch, but his actions were more an attempt to dodge thinking about Ravenna's departure. He tried not to dwell on how he would spend his last eve with her, but he could no longer avoid the inevitable. By this time tomorrow, Ravenna would be gone, on her way back to England.

He needed to make certain Torquil recovered quickly from her absence. He'd already decided to spend more time with his son, hoping to somewhat fill the hole he knew he couldn't possibly fill. Torquil had grown close to his governess, and without her presence… Not that Ruairi would handle the situation any better than Torquil, but one thing was certain: Ravenna would be missed.

Fagan approached with a worn look on his face. "Nae a thing." He scratched his arm. "Only the damn midges again. I think Angus had a better time than me. He fed his belly on some animal and gnawed on that thing all night long. He wasnae verra good company."

"Have something to eat and then seek your bed. I'll ride out to the border and make sure everything is as it should be."

"Ye're certain ye donna want me to ride along?"

"Nay, ye've been up all night. Get some rest." He slapped his friend on the shoulder and then made his way toward the stables. He was looking forward to a long ride to clear his head.

Ruairi waved off the stable hand and saddled his mount, reveling in the smell of leather and hay. As he led his horse out of the stall, he patted the magnificent animal on the neck. The sun was shining and a cool breeze blew through the bailey. He swung his leg up over his mount and galloped hard out the gates.

Hooves pounded the ground beneath him, wind whipped through his hair, and he encouraged his mount to accelerate even further. He had high hopes that he could somehow outrun his demons. Reaching the border of his lands faster than he would've liked, Ruairi slowed his mount. He led his horse along the edge of the brush and let out a whistle.

"My laird," said Calum, stepping out from the trees.

"What have ye found?"

"Angus paid us a wee visit last eve, but everything else has been quiet. I'm afraid we havenae seen or heard anything, and naught has moved."

"That's what I like to hear. Stay at your post. Additional men will be sent to relieve ye soon."

Calum slightly bowed his head. "Aye, my laird."

Unfortunately, Ruairi knew there was nothing further he could do until something else happened. He briefly said a silent prayer that Ravenna's last night would be marked with no noteworthy incidents. He turned his mount for home and decided to go to the cliffs. He wasn't sure why, but he knew he wasn't ready to return to the castle. When he reached the grassy knoll, he stopped and dismounted. He walked up the small grade to the edge of the cliff and let out a heavy sigh.

The rolling billows of the sea were a grand sight as the waves crashed onto the rocks below. He knew he needed to travel home—but not right now. He needed to savor this quiet moment alone. He kept telling himself that the situation with Ravenna was easier to accept because they were from two different worlds. At least they were completely honest with each other and knew where the other stood. He was aware of that, but that didn't explain why he was so troubled about it.

Ruairi unsheathed his sword and sat at the cliff, dangling his feet off the edge. How odd that he found comfort in the same place where his wife had died. Granted, Anna was not the most pleasant of women, but he wouldn't have wished her fate on anyone. He would rather die by his own sword than by meeting his maker on the rocks below.

～

Ravenna promptly stood from the bed and bundled her daggers. She needed to keep busy. There was no sense thinking about what could never be. God, Ruairi didn't know who she really was, not even her true name. All the man knew about her was her Christian name and that she had three sisters. If she'd had a flicker of hope that he would one day find her again, she quickly stayed the thought. Before long, she'd be given another assignment and be back to her ordinary life. But she didn't want to think about that right now or how she'd feel returning to her lonely bed in the manor house.

There was a knock at her door and she opened it to find Torquil. He cast a wry grin and had his hands behind his back. He was definitely up to something.

"Close eyes," he said.

"All right, my eyes are closed."

"Ye open now."

She opened her eyes to find red and yellow roses from the garden. "Oh, Torquil, the flowers are beautiful. Thank you." The boy smiled from ear to ear and handed her the blooms.

"I pick them for ye remember me."

"I don't need flowers to remember you. I'll always remember you. Would you like to take a walk with me in the garden?"

"Aye."

Ravenna placed the flowers in some water and then walked down the hall with Torquil. As they descended the stairs to the great hall, Fagan stood on the last step. His exhausted eyes smiled at her.

"Torquil, have ye seen Angus?"

The boy shook his head. "Nay."

"Is there something wrong?" asked Ravenna.

"I hadnae seen him from this morn. I'm seeking my bed for a few hours of sleep."

"I take it you've had no luck, then."

"Nay."

Torquil grabbed her hand and started to pull her away. "Will I see you later?"

"Aye," Fagan responded.

As he turned and walked up the steps, she asked, "Have you seen Ruairi?"

"He went to check on the men at the border. He should be back soon," he said over his shoulder.

"Sleep well." When Torquil tugged on her hand again, she pivoted on her heel. "All right, I'm coming. I'm coming."

Ravenna walked the garden path and wanted to savor every moment. She rested her hands on the cool stone wall and closed her eyes, lifting her face to the sun. There was great serenity to be had in the Highlands. If she hadn't experienced it herself, she would never have believed it. If anyone asked, she'd have a difficult time describing the feeling that washed over her. The land, the sea, everything seemed to call to her. And God help her, for a brief moment she wanted to answer.

She glanced over at Torquil, who stood perfectly still. The boy had his back to her and was studying something on the ground.

"What are you doing?" she asked in a raised voice.

He turned and gestured her over, pointing to the ground. "Look."

She walked toward him and stopped when she saw some poor mutilated animal lying on the path. She wrinkled her nose. "What is that? Or perhaps I should ask what it was."

He shrugged.

As Torquil bent over to touch the creature,

Ravenna hastily pulled him back by the tunic. "Don't touch it!"

His eyes widened. "Why? 'Tis only animal."

"Why don't we go to the stable and have someone remove the poor thing? We shouldn't be touching it." She wrapped her arm around Torquil's shoulders and urged him away.

"Ye afraid?" asked Torquil with a wry grin. The boy was suddenly the mirror image of his father.

"No," she said defensively. "I just don't think the animal was left there for us to poke at it."

❧

Ruairi rode through the gates and thought he'd take Ravenna to the beach again since she enjoyed it so much the first time. He realized he didn't need to look too far because she stood in the bailey with her arms folded across her chest. She looked uneasy, and he certainly hoped he was not the cause of her discomfiture. He handed his horse to the stable hand and approached her.

"What are ye doing standing in the middle of the bailey?"

Her expression was bleak. "I'm waiting for Torquil to return. We had a man from the stable gather up the remains of a dead animal on the garden path. Do you think Angus left it there?"

Ruairi rubbed his hand over his brow. "'Tis possible. Fagan told me Angus chewed on something all eve. I guess that was it."

She reached out and touched his arm. "I have to tell you what Torquil did. He knocked on my door this morning and handed me roses. He picked them himself. You're raising him to be a fine young man, Ruairi. He's such a thoughtful boy."

"Aye."

Ruairi silently cursed. Roses? He couldn't believe he'd been outshone by his only son. He discreetly tapped the bundle of heather stems that were gathered at his waist under his tunic. He could not give them to her now. Damn. Now he'd have to think of a gift that was better than roses. He suddenly had an idea.

"I thought mayhap I would take ye to the beach. I could have the cook prepare us a basket."

"What about Torquil? I know he really wanted to spend some time with me before…" She looked down at the ground.

"If ye donna mind, he can come too. But remember this, I will have ye all to myself this eve." When his eyes darkened and her face reddened, he knew he made his point perfectly clear.

Ruairi walked to the kitchens to have the cook arrange a basket and then made his way to his chamber. He approached the dark wooden trunk in the corner of the room and lifted the lid. Kilts and tunics lined the top. He reached in and pushed around the clothing until he found what he was looking for. He pulled out the plaid and folded it, then stuffed the material into a small satchel. When he was about to leave, something drew him to the adjoining door.

He walked into Ravenna's chamber and glanced around the perfectly kept room. Not a single piece of clothing, not a comb or ribbon remained. Ravenna was all packed. He spotted her trunk at the foot of the bed and couldn't resist the urge to peek inside. He wanted to remember what she wore the first time his eyes met hers in the great hall. He needed to smell her lavender scent. God help him.

He wasn't ready to let her go.

Ruairi lifted the lid to see some kind of bundle lying on top of Ravenna's clothing. He picked up the cloth and slowly unwrapped four identical daggers.

❦

Ravenna waited for Ruairi at the stables. She watched as Torquil's mount was saddled and jumped when she heard his voice behind her.

"Cuine a tha a'falbh? Cuine a chì mi a-ris thu?"

She looked at the boy and raised her brow. "Pardon?"

"When ye leave? When I see ye…again?"

She paused a moment to gather her words. Since Torquil had spent all this time learning English, her language, she wanted to surprise him and show him what Ruairi had taught her. She spoke slowly to make certain she'd get the words right.

"Ionnlaidh mise m' aodann."

Torquil only stared at her, his eyes widening, and then he burst out laughing.

"And what do you find so amusing?" The boy stopped laughing only when he tried to speak, but her annoyance increased when he started to giggle and point his finger at her. "Did I not say the words correctly?"

"Ye tell me ye wash face."

"Truly? Now you know that's not what I was trying to say." Perhaps she should apologize for ripping the Gaelic language to shreds. At least she knew how to say she was sorry. She'd heard Ruairi mumble the foreign words so many times to Fagan that she'd asked him for the meaning.

She turned around and Ruairi stood there, holding the basket in his hands. His face split into a wide grin. "Mayhap ye shouldnae be attempting to speak *Gàidhlig* in front of Torquil." *Gaelic.* "It might be best for us all if ye donna try again."

"Perhaps you're right. I apparently told him that I needed to wash my face. At least I know how to say I'm sorry." She turned and smiled at the boy. "*Mo chreach*, Torquil." *Damn.*

Torquil bent over and his body trembled. She touched his shoulder, and when he straightened, tears welled in his eyes—from laughter. "Ravenna, ye know ye say—"

"Grab your mount, Torquil," ordered Ruairi.

Not heeding his father's command, Torquil grabbed Ravenna's hand and shook it. *"An can thu sin a-rithist? An can thu sin a-rithist?"* Can you say that again? Can you say that again?

"Torquil!"

"Aye, Da."

She lifted a brow to Ruairi. "Did I not say that correctly, either?"

"Nay, lass, the words ye said were perfectly clear."

They mounted their horses and rode casually out the gate. The three of them were on their way to the beach to have the noon meal on a blanket. The image before her made her long for family. Her family. Of course that's what she meant because she couldn't possibly imagine anything else.

Ravenna kicked her mount to speed up and reined in next to Ruairi. "Are the Highland winters very harsh?"

He stared at her for a brief moment and then shrugged. "As compared to what? England?"

"Yes."

"'Tis much colder in the Highlands than even the Lowlands. Aye, my lands are much colder than your own."

"Do you wear your kilt during the winter solstice?"

He smirked. "Nay, I donna wear anything." When her mouth dropped, he gave her a roguish grin. "What do ye think? We do wear trews, too."

"Of course."

"Why do ye ask?"

All she wanted to do was talk to get her mind off leaving. And how did she accomplish that? Oh, yes, by asking the man daft questions. She was starting to sound like Grace, of all things.

When she turned her head, she realized Ruairi still waited for her answer. "I was only wondering how cold the winters were here. I can imagine there's quite a chill in the air being so close to the sea."

"Aye, but ye get used to it."

They reached the sandy shore, and Ravenna watched while Ruairi spread the blanket and Torquil grabbed the basket from his saddle. They were being quite the gentlemen. As she stood there, the sound of the waves could have lulled her to sleep. She sat down on the blanket with Ruairi while Torquil collected shells on the beach, wandering here and there.

"I want to thank ye for all ye have done for my

son. I also want to thank ye for understanding about my wife."

"I promise to keep my word, and your secret is safe with me. But *please* make certain you send Torquil to Edinburgh next time to avoid His Majesty's wrath."

He chuckled. "I will. I nay longer have a choice. I donna know if 'tis your English blood or what, but I've ne'er enjoyed talking to a lass as much as I enjoy talking to ye."

"Laird Sutherland, it must be your *Scottish* blood because I've never quite met a man like you, I must say. Your love for your son is evident and you are a fine laird."

"Och, lass. Ye swell my head. Fagan will quickly remind me of that too." He turned away from her and opened a satchel. He shifted his body on the blanket and blocked her view. When he faced her, he kept one hand placed behind his back and sat very still.

Her eyes became sharp and assessing. "What are you doing?"

"I wanted to give ye something to remember your time here…with me. I thought this might be appropriate." He handed her material that looked like his kilt. "'Tis the Sutherland plaid. I know ye donna wear our Highland dress in England, but I thought you could wear this as a wrap or *arisaid*. Ye could even use it as a blanket if ye wanted."

"Ruairi, I don't know what to say. I'm honored to receive such a gift." She bent forward and kissed him on the cheek.

"I take it the gift has pleased ye."

"Yes, but I certainly don't need the Sutherland plaid to remember you."

"There is something else." He reached behind him and handed her a pouch.

"What's this?"

"Donna be too proud to take it. 'Tis coin. I know it must be difficult for ye to care for your sisters, and your position as a governess cannae pay verra well. Take it to support your clan...er, family." When he saw that she was hesitant to accept his gift, he added, "Let me help ye because I can."

Thirteen

When they arrived in the bailey, Torquil went to his chamber to change his clothes. Ruairi couldn't remember the last time he'd had so much fun with his son. He'd never forget the surprised look that crossed the lad's face when he'd repaid Torquil's actions in a way the boy had not anticipated.

Ruairi dismounted and assisted Ravenna from her mount. When her feet were planted on the ground and she graced him with a smile, he felt like he'd been punched in the gut.

"What a lovely day. Thank you for taking the time to spend it with me."

"'Twas my pleasure, lass. I'm pleased ye enjoyed yourself. I think Torquil did, too."

She laughed. "If I were you, I'd definitely sleep with one eye open. You know he's determined to repay your kindness for throwing him in the water."

"Aye, so he said. If I know my son as well as I think I do, mayhap I should be worried."

He handed her the bundled plaid from her saddle and she held the material against her breast in a protective embrace. He was glad to see she appreciated his gift—well, at least one of them. Even though she refused to take the coin, he'd be sure to place it in her trunk before she left. She was a stubborn English lass, but he was a clever Scot.

They stood there for a moment in silence, and he wasn't sure what to say. He lifted his hand and his fingertips gently brushed her cheek. When Ravenna's lips parted, Ruairi couldn't help himself. He lowered his head to kiss her.

"My laird! My laird!"

Ruairi whipped his head around and walked toward the guard with hastened purpose. "What is it?"

"'Tis Angus. Ye must come."

"Where is he?"

"In the great hall. He isnae well."

When Ruairi followed the guard and entered the great hall, he instantly spotted Angus. Two of his men were trying to approach the animal and Angus's teeth were bared.

"Stop! Back away from him," ordered Ruairi, holding up his hand to stay his men.

Angus let out a low growl, and black fur stood up on the back of the wolf's neck. Ruairi heard someone gasp from behind him and immediately knew that the frightened sound came from Ravenna. As she cowered behind him, he didn't need to warn her to stay back. The lass wouldn't take one step near the wolf.

Slowly, Ruairi knelt and extended his hand. "Angus, come," he said in a soothing tone. "'Tis all right. Come here. Ye're all right."

Angus looked as though he could barely lift his

head. He turned toward Ruairi and moved one paw forward, letting out a loud yelp. With a bowed head that now practically touched the ground, Angus crept forward with unsteady steps. The animal's cries were unbearable to hear. As Angus came closer, Ruairi leaned to the side and studied the wolf's body. The animal was most definitely in pain, but there was no apparent injury and nothing appeared to be broken. He didn't know what was wrong.

With step after arduous step, Angus finally reached Ruairi's arms and buckled to the ground.

⤝⤞

As Ravenna stood behind Ruairi in the great hall, she caught something move out of the corner of her eye. She glanced to her left and saw Torquil standing at the top of the stairs. His eyes darkened with pain and worry. She was about to call to him so he would not watch his beloved pet who was in terrible agony, but it was too late. What happened next would be engraved in her mind forever.

Torquil darted down the stone steps, two at a time. She had opened her mouth to tell him to slow his pace when his foot caught halfway down the steps. He tripped, fell face-first, and slid down the stairs. Near the bottom, his body flipped and his back landed with a thump, his head smacking hard against the stone floor. The sound—like an egg cracked on a table— sent a shiver up Ravenna's spine. The boy didn't move, and his body lay perfectly still in a pool of blood that fanned out around his head.

"Mo chridhe!" cried Ruairi. *My heart!*

Ravenna reached Torquil, and Ruairi rushed to her side as he continued to shout orders to everyone around him. He knelt down and placed his hand briefly under Torquil's head. Then he gently shifted his son and put pressure on the wound, attempting to stop the relentless bleeding.

As Torquil lay unresponsive, Ravenna realized she had never been so afraid in her life. Biting her lip, she looked away. Torquil didn't move. She wasn't even sure if the boy still breathed. She moved around Ruairi and knelt on Torquil's other side. As she brushed back the hair from the boy's closed eyes, she spoke through her tears.

"Tor…Torquil, can you hear me?" He showed no sign that he heard her words. She lowered her ear to the boy's mouth and tried to listen for any sound of breath that escaped him. The smell of blood engulfed her senses.

"Ravenna, donna smother him. He needs air."

Some of Ruairi's clan members had gathered closer to the boy, and now they froze. Two maids ran with lightning speed to Ruairi's side and handed him several pieces of cloth. He applied the material to his son's head, and within minutes, it darkened with Torquil's lifeblood.

"Hand me another one," said Ruairi, his voice tight with strain.

Guards, maids, and clansmen stood around the great hall with grave expressions on their faces, praying for Torquil to be all right. There were so many people that Ravenna couldn't see out the door to the courtyard.

When Ruairi lifted the cloth from Torquil's head,

she choked back a cry. She'd never seen so much
blood. She heard whimpering and looked at Angus,
who still lay sprawled on the floor. John, the stable
hand, crouched beside the wolf, running his hand
over the animal with a soothing gesture. He was an
older gentleman with a warm smile. With all the
chaos that surrounded them, Ravenna had almost
forgotten about the wolf. The creature looked pitiful
as he too watched Torquil, almost as if he understood
what had happened.

The healer came into the great hall and Ruairi
spoke in a choked voice. "We need to move him."

Ruairi lifted his son in his arms while the healer
continued to hold the material to Torquil's bloodied
head. Ravenna almost wept aloud when she saw the
tenderness that Ruairi held in his eyes for his injured
son. But she knew that under the calm lay a raging
storm filled with worry and heartbreak.

As she followed the healer and Ruairi up the stairs
to Torquil's chamber, men and women started to
gather in the hall outside his room. Ravenna closed
the door as Ruairi laid his son on the bed and the
healer moved to the other side. While the healer
bandaged Torquil's head, Ravenna pulled up a blanket
to the boy's waist.

Although she was sick with worry, she leaned back
against the wall. She didn't want to be in the way.
Her mind was a crazy mixture of hope and fear. The
boy she had grown to love had to be all right. When
Ruairi's eyes met hers, he spoke in a soothing tone.

"'Tis a lot of blood, but that's what happens with
a head injury. In all my years, I've ne'er seen one that

didnae bleed like a raging river. Isnae that right?" he asked the healer.

"Aye, my laird. We'll keep the bandages wrapped up tight, which will help to stop or slow the bleeding."

Ravenna knew Ruairi's words were meant to be reassuring. She wasn't surprised that in the face of tragedy, the man stood strong. Ruairi was a natural leader. She was sure he noticed the grim expression on her face because he started speaking in Gaelic to the healer.

"He hit his head. 'Tis the body's way of healing. He will wake up soon," said the healer.

Ruairi approached Ravenna, his massive frame blocking her view. He placed his hands gently on her arms. "Ye have nay color in your face and ye look as though ye're about to faint. Torquil will be fine. Ye'll see as much when he wakes up." He led her to the door and opened it. "Now I want ye to go below stairs and have yourself a wee drink or get something to eat." He addressed the men and women who had gathered in the hall. "Please go below stairs. I will let ye all know when he awakens."

As the crowd dispersed, Ravenna touched his arm. "Please, Ruairi, I can't leave him."

"Please do as I ask. I insist."

Reluctantly, she nodded. She didn't want to be a hindrance, especially to him at a time like this. Turning on her heel, she walked back to the great hall.

A tense silence enveloped the room.

When she passed the maids scrubbing Torquil's lifeblood from the floor, her stomach churned with anxiety and tension. If she didn't do something, she'd go mad with worry. She noticed Angus was no longer on the floor and figured John had taken the animal out to the stable. There was nothing she could do to help Torquil, but perhaps she could make certain the family's beloved pet was not suffering.

Ravenna opened the wooden door to the stable and saw Angus alone on the straw floor in the front stall. For a moment, she pitied him. Realizing this was more than likely not one of her best ideas, she opened the stall door and slowly approached the wolf. With every step closer, Angus merely stared at her and did not move. When he let out another whimper, she felt helpless. She didn't know anything about caring for an animal, but she knew Ruairi wouldn't want Angus to be by himself, especially in the wolf's poor condition. So she did what she told herself she'd never do.

Very carefully, Ravenna lowered herself to the ground within an arm's reach of the animal's back. She leaned forward and stretched her arm so that her fingers could just about touch the black fur.

"It's all right, Angus." When Angus didn't move, Ravenna inched—a very small inch—closer. She was able to place her entire hand on the wolf's back and gently brushed his fur with her fingers. "There, there, Angus. You're going to be just fine. You have"—she wiped the tears that she didn't know had fallen with her other hand—"you have to be well because Torquil will want to see you when he wakes up."

❧

Ruairi stood beside the bed and watched his son lay perfectly still. If not for the bindings that the healer had wrapped around Torquil's head, one would think the boy merely slept. Torquil had lost a lot of blood, and Ruairi knew his son's head was undoubtedly swollen. But he also knew the dangers of Torquil remaining in this state for too long. The chances of recovery would decrease with every passing hour.

"My laird, there is naught further we can do but watch him," said the healer. "Ye know his injuries are severe."

Ruairi nodded. "I will call upon ye if anything changes."

"I can stay with the lad, my laird."

"Nay. He is my son and I will be with him. Take your leave, and thank ye for all ye have done."

"As ye wish... He'll be in our prayers, my laird."

The door closed and Ruairi placed a chair by Torquil's bed. This is where he would stay until his son opened his eyes or was no longer of this world. The bedside candle was the only light that illuminated the room. He sat and watched the flame flicker as shadows danced across the wall. The dim light suited him just fine because he felt as though it matched his darkened mood rather nicely.

Why Torquil? Why did this have to happen to his son? They had jested at the beach, been like father and son, family. And now it was if their precious time together had been stripped away, parting before the real memories had even begun.

Even though he wasn't a religious man, he would certainly take whatever help he could get. Grabbing Torquil's hand, Ruairi closed his eyes. *"Dia is gràs,* Torquil." *Bless you.* "If there is a God, I pray ye watch over my son and let him live. I will do anything ye ask of me. I have done many things in my life I am nae proud of, but I try to be a good and honorable man. That's why I ask ye to take my life and spare his."

Ruairi opened his eyes and squeezed Torquil's hand. "We will come through this. *Tha thu treun.* Ye are a Sutherland." *You are brave.* "Ye mean everything to me. Ye are my blood, my son. I am naught without ye. I beg ye to wake up now and make me whole again."

Ruairi lowered his head to Torquil's chest.

⁂

Ravenna never thought she'd see the day when she held Angus in her lap. She only wished she could do something to help the wolf. She wasn't sure the last time he drank, but she had a good idea the last time he gnawed on something.

A sudden thought came to mind.

She wondered if Angus was sick over something he'd eaten. Ravenna cupped some water into her hand from the bucket that was left in the stall. She held it fairly close to Angus' muzzle, but he moved his head away slightly. He continued to be lethargic, and that's what scared her the most. The wolf was always on the prowl, forever stalking, and no one ever knew where he'd turn up next. To have him so still… This did not look good.

"Please, Angus, you must drink." When he refused again, she closed her eyes and prayed the wolf wouldn't take a chunk out of her hand. Slowly, she turned his head up with her arm and cupped another handful of water with her other hand. Wiggling the tips of her fingers into his mouth, she quickly released the water and pulled out her hand.

Droplets ran down Angus's fur and most of the water ran out of his mouth, but she thought he managed to swallow some. She repeated her actions three times until she was sure he drank.

"Mistress Denny, whatever are ye doing?" asked John, the stable hand.

She looked up and shrugged. "Is he going to be all right?"

He opened the stall door and knelt beside her. "I can have another look at him." John scratched Angus behind the ears and then felt the animal's body for any sign of injury. "What's the matter with ye, eh? There are nay cuts or bruises that I can see."

"When Laird Sutherland called to Angus, the wolf's head was low to the ground and he let out a yelp with every step. He did not walk right and looked as though he were dizzy. Is that possible for a wolf?"

"Aye, 'tis possible."

"Could he be sick from something he ate? Perhaps you can take a look at the dead animal you recovered in the garden. Maybe the meat was rotten."

"Nae if Angus just killed it. But aye, I will have another look."

"I've tried to get some water down his throat, but I have not tried any food."

"Donna give him anything else. Wolves donna eat every day. He can usually go a few days, even a sennight, without something in his belly. Why donna ye let me take care of him and ye go back inside now? This is nay place for ye to be."

"Of course. That would be best." Ravenna gently lifted Angus' head from her lap and John assisted her to stand. She wiped the straw from her skirts and shook her head at the sight of the poor animal.

"Donna worry. He'll be in good hands, lass."

❧

The door opened and Ruairi lifted his head. He wiped his eyes and turned his head away from Fagan. His friend approached the bed and placed his hand on Torquil's shoulder. A glazed look of despair spread over Fagan's face.

"How is he?"

"The same. He doesnae move," replied Ruairi in a low, tormented voice.

"Ye know 'tis common for this type of injury to the head, Ruairi."

He knew Fagan meant well, but he also knew what would happen if Torquil did not awaken soon. Ruairi could feel his throat closing up. He didn't want to talk and wasn't in the mood for Fagan's company, but apparently his captain had other ideas.

Fagan moved a chair from across the room and sat down next to Ruairi. "How are ye?"

"Trying to keep myself together and nae weep like some feebleminded lass."

"Why donna ye let me watch over him for a while? Ye get some rest. I'll call ye if—"

"Nay. I will stay with him. I need ye to watch the tunnels. We cannae lower our defenses when we donna know what is afoot. I will nae risk it."

There was a heavy moment of silence.

Fagan stood. "I'll see to my post, but send word if ye need me here. Ravenna is out in the stables caring for Angus. I'd like to send her up to sit with ye. She's worried about ye both."

He nodded, and Fagan walked out the door.

Ruairi's entire body was engulfed in tides of weariness and despair. His mind kept returning to its tortured thinking. Remembering the sound of Torquil's head cracking against the stone floor made him shudder. The memory of his son's spilled lifeblood placed a stain on Ruairi's soul that could never be removed.

The knock on the door interrupted Ruairi's dire thoughts.

"Come in."

Ravenna opened the door and closed it behind her.

She approached Torquil and gently rubbed her fingers over his head. She closed her eyes, but Ruairi knew the gesture was only to hold back her tears. She walked around the side of the bed and sat down.

"Fagan told me ye cared for Angus. I'm nae sure how ye managed that, but thank ye. I couldnae leave Torquil."

She nodded. "John took him out to the stable. He will keep a close eye on him." She looked at Torquil. "He's still the same?"

"Aye."

"I'm sure it will only be a matter of time before he wakes up and runs through the fields again with Angus." Ravenna felt the need to return the kind gesture that Ruairi had offered earlier. She reached out and squeezed his hand, her eyes welling with tears.

He bowed his head and murmured, "I'm sure ye're

right." He leaned forward and faced her. "Ravenna, I'm sorry our last eve wasnae as I had intended. I hope ye know how much our time together has meant to me. I have arranged for my men to escort ye on the morrow."

Her eyes darkened with emotion and her body stiffened. "Ruairi, what kind of woman do you think I am?" she asked in a whisper.

"What do ye mean?"

"How could you possibly think that I would leave you now when Torquil—"

"Ye know why."

"Damn the Gordon." When his eyes widened, she quickly added, "If you think I'm going to travel back to England while Torquil fights for his life…" She sat back in the chair and folded her arms over her chest. "I'm not leaving until he wakes up, my laird." He was about to speak when she held up her hand to stay him. "I refuse to have this discussion with you. And unless you intend to throw me over your shoulder and carry me back to England, I'm not leaving."

He stood and pulled Ravenna to her feet. His arms encircled her, and she held him in a tight embrace. When her hand rubbed his back in a gentle gesture, he lowered his head onto her shoulder.

"Everything's going to be all right, Ruairi. Torquil will make it through this. We'll make it so. He's a strong boy…just like his father."

And that's when he wept in Ravenna's arms like a newborn bairn.

Fourteen

RAVENNA STAYED BY RUAIRI'S SIDE AND WATCHED Torquil well into the night. The boy didn't move. She held his hand, talked to him, stroked his hair, and he didn't respond to any of her efforts. She approached the washbowl and wet a cloth.

"He doesnae know ye're there, and I donna think he knows the difference."

"I didn't know you were awake."

Ruairi sat back in the chair and rolled his head. "My eyes were closed, but I wasnae sleeping."

When Ravenna sat down on the bed next to Torquil, the boy looked like he was in a deep slumber, peaceful and rested. She lifted the cloth and bathed his face. "No matter, my efforts make me feel better," she said in a solemn tone.

She placed the cloth on the bedside table. "There will be a time when I will insist that you rest, my laird." She walked behind him and placed her hands on his broad shoulders. Ruairi's body was tight with strain. Her fingers dug into the strong tendons in the back of his neck, and he turned his head to the side.

"That feels wonderful."

After a few moments, he placed his large hand over hers and stilled her. He pulled her around onto his lap while his tired, worn eyes looked back at her. She supposed his troubled expression mirrored her own.

"I want to thank ye again for staying here and being with Torquil, especially when ye could verra well have taken your leave and returned home. I'm sure ye miss your sisters. Ye know I wanted to see ye home before I talked to the Gordon, yet ye stayed."

She rubbed her fingers over the stubble on his jaw. "How could I go? I couldn't leave you and Torquil like this. And don't forget, I can take care of myself."

He chuckled. "With five daggers in your possession, I suppose ye certainly have enough to prepare for battle."

She stiffened. "How do you know I have five daggers?" She wouldn't mention the fact that she actually had six, but she had to admit, this was the first time she'd ever seen Ruairi at a loss for words.

"If ye must know, I saw your trunk was packed and—"

"You spied on me."

"I wouldnae say *spy* exactly."

Ravenna tried to compose herself because she was surprised Ruairi had pried into her things. Thank God the only questionable items in her trunk were her daggers. Although she knew he still held the one she had lost somewhere in the darkened tunnels, the loss was a small price to pay for not being discovered. Fortunately for her, the man who encroached on

Ruairi's lands was a happy coincidence that couldn't have come at a better time.

"I'm not angry." She placed her head on his shoulder and he held her. "Do you think he'll wake up soon?" she asked in a softened tone. "Be truthful. Please."

He rubbed his hand gently on her arm. "I donna know. I truly donna know."

"Well, he is a young and healthy boy. And one thing I've discovered through the years is that the young recover much faster than the old. We must have faith that God will watch over him and make him well again. And there is no way we'll give up in battle before the war is over."

"Ye're a wise woman. Nay wonder ye're a governess for young minds."

❧

Ruairi was mentally exhausted, but Ravenna had stayed with him when he needed her most. That was something he'd never forget. He watched her as she sat with his son. She was kind and giving, and he knew she loved Torquil.

He hadn't moved from Torquil's side since the accident, but he knew he needed to keep things in perspective. Curtailing his duties wouldn't benefit anyone. How else would he be able to make certain the walls didn't crumble, intruders were kept at bay, and Torquil was safe? He also couldn't overlook something else that weighed heavily on his mind.

He wondered how Angus fared.

When he thought about the day's events, he

contemplated how he could've almost lost his son and Angus within a breath apart.

"Will ye stay with him? I want to step out for a moment and see to Angus. Ye said John took him to the stable?"

"Yes, he did. And of course, Ruairi, take your time. I'll be sure to call you when Torquil wakes up."

She gave him a warm smile and he knew she was being kind. He didn't think she'd be calling him any time soon. He pulled himself to his feet and gazed at Torquil. Lightly, he brushed his son's cheek with the back of his hand.

Ruairi made his way to the great hall and paused when he reached the last step. A few hours ago, he watched his son's lifeblood spill all over the floor in this very spot. A shiver ran down his spine as he remembered the sound of the crack when Torquil... He closed his eyes. This type of thinking was not doing either one of them any good. He tried to shake off the feeling and his foul mood.

When he walked out into the bailey, he realized there were still a few hours before the sun rose. That was all right with him because there was no way he'd be able to sleep now anyway. He opened the door to the stable and saw the stable hands sleeping on the floor. Not wanting to wake them, Ruairi found the wolf in the front stall.

Angus lay in a tight black ball. His tail lifted once and thumped the ground in greeting.

"How are ye, Angus?" Ruairi opened the stall door and sat on the floor. "What happened to ye, eh?" He patted the wolf on the head and scratched him behind the ears.

"My laird, I thought that was ye. Angus is doing much better than he was. He brought up whatever he ate in the garden. Once he did, he wasnae in so much pain."

Ruairi ran his hand through Angus' thick fur. "I'll leave him here in your care until he is well again."

"Aye, my laird. I'm sure he'll be up and about in nay time."

Ruairi stood and Angus turned his head, not lifting his muzzle from the ground. The wolf's pitiful eyes looked up at him.

"Ye stay here with John and ye'll be all right." As if the wolf understood Ruairi's words, Angus' tail moved only once in response. At least the animal looked as though he was getting better. Ruairi only prayed his son would follow suit.

He left the stables and walked through the darkened fields. He didn't take the time to light a torch since he knew his lands well. When he reached the clearing, he let out a whistle that only he and his men knew. He waited a moment for his captain's response, and when no one answered, Ruairi approached with caution.

As he reached the entrance to the tunnels, he looked around for Fagan and saw no one. Where the hell was he?

Ruairi walked along the outer edge of the tree line and stealthily entered the brush where he thought Fagan kept watch on the tunnel entrance. The foliage was so thick that he couldn't see a damn thing. He heard someone moan and unsheathed his sword. As he walked toward the sound, he made certain his footsteps were carefully placed as to not alert anyone of his presence.

When he lost track of where the noise came from, he stopped. Everything fell silent and he could hear the sound of his own breath. Someone cursed and he moved toward the voice, tripping over something and falling quickly to the ground. He scrambled for his sword and received a hard kick in the side.

"I'll kill ye, ye bastard!"

"Fagan?"

There was a brief silence.

"Ruairi, what the hell are ye doing? Och, ne'er mind. Help me to my feet."

He grabbed Fagan under the arm. "What happened?"

"Ne'er mind me. Why are ye out here? God's teeth, is it Torquil? How is he?"

"The same. Now tell me why ye are on your arse."

Fagan staggered into the clearing, barely able to stand. "Someone knocked me on the back of the head is what the hell happened. I'm nae sure how long ago."

"Will ye be all right?"

"Aye."

"I'm going in the tunnels. Nay matter what ye do, donna let anyone come out. We'll get this man once and for all."

"Aye."

Ruairi took off with purpose and thundered into the dark tunnel with his sword drawn. He quickly realized the narrow passage was too small to properly carry a sword. He turned to the side and sheathed his weapon, then pulled his dagger from his boot. He placed his hand on the cool stone walls that guided his way farther into the darkness. Up ahead, a faint light flickered and he slowed his pace. Shadows danced on the walls, and he wasn't sure how many men he'd soon be facing. At least Fagan would make certain no man escaped.

He peeked around the stone wall of the tunnel and two men stood in the natural room, their faces hidden by their cloaks. The men had to have known the schedule of the tides and when the caves were flooded. But how? Even as he tried to figure out the answer, another thought came to mind—surely they didn't know where he kept his coin. How could they? No one knew.

Ruairi was about to enter the cavern and put an end to all this madness when one of the men bent over, his arms encircling the giant rock. When the hole in the floor was revealed, the man grasped a handful of coins and tossed them into his companion's bag.

"Is that enough?"

When the arse nodded, the man replaced the rock while Ruairi sheathed his dagger and pulled out his sword. He would strike down one of the men and force the other to talk. And once and for all, he would know if the Gordon was responsible for far more than he was willing to admit.

Ruairi stood perfectly still, the sound of the sea making it difficult to hear the approaching men. He had taken another step forward and was looking around the edge of the wall when the men came upon him. The bigger bastard unsheathed his sword, and Ruairi hastily shoved the man back.

The ringing sound of metal upon metal clanked through the cave. The torchlight reflected from their swords as Ruairi looked into the eyes of the man he would kill this night. He didn't recognize the arse, not that it mattered. When the smaller man backed up against the wall and held the torch out in front of him in a cowardly gesture, Ruairi couldn't help but smirk. Nothing stirred his blood like a good fight, and frankly, this was just what he needed.

He pointed his sword briefly at the smaller man. "Ye'll have to wait your turn. I'm a wee bit busy right now."

Ruairi swung his gaze back to the man before him.

The bigger bastard was able to ward off every one of Ruairi's blows. Little did the man realize that Ruairi was only testing his opponent's skill with a sword. He wanted to kill the man slowly, taking his time and actually savoring the moment. No one stole Sutherland coin. And this man wouldn't be the first.

Ruairi sliced the man on the upper arm and then lifted his brow. "Och, that had to hurt."

The man growled and became enraged, lifting his sword high into the air. Ruairi turned out of the way and elbowed the man in the gut.

"Who are ye?" asked Ruairi.

When the man didn't respond, Ruairi gave his opponent another matching slice on the other arm. The man grunted, and Ruairi repeated his question in a tone that was more of a warning.

"Mo mhallachd ort!" My curse on you.

Ruairi laughed. *"Cha bhrist mhallachd cnàimh."* A curse breaks no bones.

He easily deflected another blow when the man struck at him again. Something suddenly moved, and

Ruairi saw it out the corner of his eye. The other man was trying to retreat along the wall, edging his way closer to the tunnels.

"And where do ye think ye're going? Donna even think about it because after I'm through with your friend here, ye and I will have words."

Ruairi wasn't surprised when the man didn't heed his warning and continued to make his way out of the cave with the bag full of coin. When he spotted the man slipping into the tunnel passage, he realized the time for swordplay had swiftly come to an end. Besides, this bastard wasn't telling him anything he wanted to know. He turned to face his opponent one last time, and the man's eyes widened when a smile crossed Ruairi's face. He could have easily brought this man to his knees some time ago.

"Apologies, I nay longer have time for play." Ruairi pulled his sword out of the man's gut, knowing the incoming tide would sweep the bastard out to sea. Let the fish have at him because Ruairi was done with him.

With a quick swipe on the man's cloak, Ruairi wiped the blood from his sword. He sheathed his weapon and pulled his dagger out of his boot. Hastily grabbing the other torch, he ran after the man in the tunnel, following the faint light ahead. The man didn't get much of a head start and even if he did, Ruairi knew Fagan would hold him at the end. The bastard had nowhere to go. Praise the saints. At least something now worked in Ruairi's favor.

Increasing his speed, he saw the whipping tails of the cloak not far in front of him. He quickly reached his target and dropped the torch. With a heavy thump, Ruairi tackled the man to the ground. The torch flew out of the man's hands as he continued to struggle beneath Ruairi's firm grasp. He noticed this man was a lot smaller than the one he'd just sent to his maker. Even though he could easily restrain the bastard, he wanted the man punished—to feel the wrath of what happened when anyone crossed a Sutherland laird.

Ruairi lifted his hand, ready to land a forceful blow, when hands reached out and touched his arm.

"Please, Ruairi."

She pulled the cloak back from her face, and Ruairi had never felt so betrayed in his life.

Fifteen

RUAIRI WAS ENTIRELY SPEECHLESS BECAUSE NOTHING IN the world could have readied him for this moment. How could she be so deceitful? He quickly realized that was a daft question because he knew why.

She wasn't a Sutherland.

He stood and then reached down and pulled her to her feet by the cloak. She brushed off the dirt and had the nerve to simply look up at him with an innocent gaze. The lively twinkle in her green eyes incensed him even more. Neither one of them spoke as Ruairi's angry gaze swung over her and fury continued to choke him. When he found he could no longer restrain himself, he shook her into gasping silence.

"Why? Why would ye do this?" he said with disgust, pushing her away from him.

Ruairi took a step farther away and ran his hand through his hair. If he moved any closer, he'd kill her. He didn't expect her to answer his question. After all, what reason could she possibly give? But he needed a moment to think. Did the woman truly have no conscience?

She simply stood there, her mouth set in annoyance. The fact that she was caught stealing his coin didn't even trouble her. She looked as though she was merely inconvenienced by his presence. When she turned away from him and picked up the torch, Ruairi wanted nothing more than to reach out and strangle his sister-by-marriage with his bare hands.

"I take it ye're surprised to see me, then," she said over her shoulder.

"Surprised?" His voice went up a notch. "Surprised doesnae begin to express what I feel. And since when did ye learn to speak English, Cotrìona?"

"'Tis quite amazing what one can accomplish in two years' time. Donna ye agree? Although I must say, naught has changed around here. I see ye still have Fagan wearing the skirts."

Ruairi grabbed her roughly by the arm. "Ye overstep."

Cotrìona looked down at his restraining arm and her eyes narrowed. "Remove your hand from my arm, *Brother*."

"I assure ye, my hand is the least of your worries." He grabbed the torch and his body brushed up against hers as he passed her in the narrow tunnel. When she gave his body a raking gaze, he pulled her along behind him and she practically had to run to keep up with him.

"And just where do ye think ye're taking me?"

"When your father arrives, I'm sure he'll love to see I've captured his beloved daughter."

She laughed, and blood pounded in his ears. Taken aback at seeing Cotrìona, he hadn't considered that the Gordon more than likely knew his daughter was stealing Ruairi's coin. Of course the man did—like father, like daughter. Ruairi led his sister-in-law out of the tunnel, and she pulled up her cloak around her head. He was so furious he didn't even notice the rush of cool wind that brushed his cheek. With a firm grip, he led her into the clearing as Fagan stepped out of the shadows.

"Ye caught the bastard."

"If ye mean my sister-in-law, then aye."

Fagan held up his hand to stay them. "What did ye say?"

Cotrìona pulled back the cloak and Fagan's reaction amused her. "Fagan, Ruairi's right hand and ever the obedient dog. 'Tis been quite a long time. Have ye missed me?"

Fagan's eyes widened. *"Cha tugadh an donas an car asad." The devil could not get the best of you.*

"Aye," said Ruairi. "Isnae that the truth? Take her to my study and have someone stand guard. She isnae to leave. Nay one goes in or out without my permission."

Fagan grabbed Cotrìona by the arm as she turned and spoke over her shoulder. "Ye look well, Ruairi. I'm glad to see my sister's death hasnae changed ye. Ye're still a verra handsome man. More's the pity that ye donna love your country as much as ye love yourself."

"If ye know what's good for ye, ye'll stop talking," snarled Fagan.

"Ye ne'er liked me. Did ye, Fagan?"

Fagan led Cotrìona away as Ruairi stood alone in the clearing. The sun had started to rise and cast its golden hues above. He needed a moment to clear his head. Never had he imagined that his wife's sister was behind the missing coin. Cotrìona was a venomous lass who never knew when to hold her tongue. She was completely reckless, always vying for her father's attention, even more than his wife had.

In addition, Cotrìona was the last living progeny of the Gordon and could be just as deadly as any man. He didn't think there was anything she wouldn't do for her father. She'd slept with many men to get what she wanted, but something about her unsettled him and Fagan. His captain had always said the woman was the devil herself.

Ruairi rubbed his hand over his brow. He was furious, yet there was no way he could speak to Cotrìona right now. There would be no words, only curses and a lot of screaming. More to the point, his son came first. He would see how Torquil and Ravenna fared, and then he'd decide how to deal with the latest catastrophe.

When he opened Torquil's door and saw Ravenna sleeping, he was thankful the lass had fallen into a deep slumber. She didn't even stir when he covered her with a blanket. Now that he knew Torquil remained the same, Ruairi felt calm enough to seek some answers. Cotrìona may not have spoken to him in two years, but she was going to talk to him now.

He grudgingly walked to his study and relieved the guard at the door.

"Where are your manners, Brother? Ye donna even offer me anything to drink?" She sat in a chair and picked an imaginary piece of lint from her day dress. Her brown hair was pulled back into a bun, and her oval face was something he'd sooner forget.

Ruairi closed the door. "Nae until ye and I have a wee chat." He sat down behind his desk. "Ye're going to answer every question I ask of ye, and I will accept naught but the truth. Do ye understand?"

Cotrìona smirked. "And what if I donna? What are ye going to do, Ruairi? Throw me over the cliffs as ye did my sister?"

He sat back and placed his hands behind his head. "I have all the time in the world. We will simply sit here until ye do."

Her eyes grew openly amused. "And what, pray tell, do ye want to know?"

"Why?"

"Why, what?" she asked in an innocent tone.

"Donna play games with me, Cotrìona."

"But I'm so verra good at them." She looked around the room, studying the furnishings. "'Tis nay great secret that my sister couldnae bear being wed to ye, especially after the way ye dishonored her and my father."

"How the hell did I dishonor them?" he asked in a raised voice.

Her eyes narrowed. "When Anna wed ye, ye made an alliance with my clan. Ye were to support my father, but ye went about doing things your own way. Ye always have. What ye fail to realize is that my father is a great man. He always was and he deserves your respect."

"And as I told ye and my wife before, I cannae side with a man who has nay regard for the lives and safety of his clan. He looks after only himself. I wouldnae send my men to be slaughtered then, and I will nae now."

"Ye're a damn fool."

Ruairi spoke through clenched teeth. "I give ye fair warning that I have ne'er raised my hand to a woman, but ye know ye're making this extremely difficult."

Cotrìona didn't seem to hear his words, continuing to speak as if she talked about the weather. "Orkney has been forfeited to the realm. King James brings *English* laws to our lands while he wants us to sit here like dogs on command. The only way to keep our ways, protect what is ours, is to fight. My father and the Seton clan have joined forces with Robert Stewart. If ye were wise, ye'd join us. And ye know if ye do, Munro will follow suit. We'd finally have enough men to be able to defend what's ours and keep the king and his henchmen out of the Highlands."

Ruairi chuckled. "Ye do know the Earl of Orkney was imprisoned by King James for nae following orders." He shook his head in awe. "And now ye actually follow his son. Have ye learned naught? Ye're just like your father."

She lifted a brow. "Thank ye."

"That wasnae a compliment." He leaned forward in the chair. "Let me make something perfectly clear. Ye are a lass. Ye hold nay lands or title to your name. In truth, ye have naught. So why do ye insist on meddling in the business of men? Ye should have ne'er been involved with your father's political aspirations—yet ye always placed yourself in the middle of his conquests. Ye and my wife. She was to stand by my side."

Cotrìona waved him off. "Please, Ruairi. Anna was nay longer the dutiful wife ye so desperately desired once ye refused to give my father men and arms. Anna and I are Gordons. I will forever be a Gordon. And as ye said, I am my father's daughter."

"Anna was a Sutherland, my wife."

She lifted a brow. "In name only, lest ye forget that Gordon blood still ran hot through those veins. My sister and I are bound by blood to my father."

"And so I am reminded..." Ruairi shook his head. Why he thought his wife or her sister would've changed was beyond his comprehension. He wasn't sure what he was thinking at the moment, but he knew he needed to get back to the matter at hand.

There was a heavy moment of silence.

"That's where ye and I differ, Ruairi. I will do anything to benefit my clan, and my father will acquire his men whether ye support him or nae. Ye know 'tis only a matter of time before the king's forces are defeated. Ye need to decide where your loyalties lie and choose a side, the right side."

"Is there naught ye wouldnae do?" he asked with disgust. He didn't expect her to answer.

Cotrìona shrugged. *"Tha mi bòidheach is glic."* *I am beautiful and clever.* She tucked a stray piece of hair behind her ear. "I've learned that most men give me what I want. *Cha bhreug ach sgeul dearbhta e."* *It isn't a lie but a proven fact.*

He spoke through clenched teeth and the words seemed strange on his tongue. *"Tha thu 'nad luid."* *You are a slut.*

She shrugged with indifference. "What ye think of me doesnae matter. Are we through here?"

"Och, lass, we are far from through." He walked

around the desk and sat down on the edge. "When did ye decide to steal my coin?"

"Now donna go and get your kilt all in a twist about it. That only happened fairly recently, after my father paid ye a wee visit. Believe me when I say I tried to stay as far away from here as possible. When Father told me that he asked ye to renew your alliance with him, I knew ye ne'er would. Donna try to deny it, either. I thought the least ye could do was support our cause."

Ruairi silently prayed for patience. "How did ye know about the tunnels?"

"How daft do ye think I am, Ruairi? Anna told me everything. Ye know we were verra close. When ye nay longer shared her bed, she spied on ye several times in the wee hours of the night. She thought mayhap ye sought your pleasures elsewhere, but imagine how pleasantly surprised she was to find your secret hiding place." Cotrìona gave him a look of amusement. "That was verra clever of ye, I must say."

He wasn't sure how much more of this conversation he could take. Between the lack of sleep and Cotrìona's words, his head had started to ache. He rubbed his fingers over the bridge of his nose and sighed. "So ye've been stealing my coin to support your father's machinations. Did I miss anything else?"

"Nay. I donna think so."

He shook his head in awe. "Ye will stay here until your father comes on the morrow."

She nodded her head in agreement. "'Tis fine with me. I wouldnae mind seeing my sister's old chamber again."

"Och, lass, ye will nae be staying in her chamber."

The door opened, and Ravenna stretched her back when the healer came into the room. Her eyes burned dryly from sleeplessness.

"And how is young Torquil doing this morn?"

Ravenna felt as hollow as her voice sounded. "I'm afraid he hasn't moved all night. I've talked to him and held his hand, and frankly, I'm not sure what else to do. Does Laird Sutherland know you're here?"

"Nay, Mistress Denny. I didnae see him when I arrived."

Ravenna stood. "Pray excuse me. I'm sure his father would want to talk with you. I'll go and find him."

"Verra good."

When Ravenna reached the great hall, her stomach promptly rumbled and reminded her that she hadn't broken her fast. No matter, she could attend to those needs later. She saw Fagan and followed him out into the bailey.

"Fagan," she called after him.

He turned and gave her a tired smile. "How's Torquil?"

"The healer is with him now. Have you seen Ruairi?"

"Umm... He has important matters he is attending to."

"All right, but where is he? I'm sure he'd want to speak with the healer." If she didn't know any better, she'd swear Fagan was keeping something from her. The man looked away from her, shifted his weight, and ran his hand through his hair in a nervous gesture, which only further confirmed her belief. "Is he in his study?"

"He's looking over the accounts and said nay one goes in. I'll be sure to tell him for ye." When she turned on her heel, he asked, "Ravenna, ye're nae going to the study, are ye?"

"What is the matter with you?"

"I'll be sure to tell Ruairi. Ye donna want him bringing his wrath down on ye when he said that nay one is to open that door."

She lifted a brow. "Why are you being so…odd?"

"I'm always odd."

She laughed. "Well, you won't hear any argument from me." She paused as he waited for her to respond. "Very well, but I don't know why you're—"

"Odd. I know."

Ravenna walked into the great hall and froze in mid-step. One of Ruairi's guards escorted a woman, holding her roughly by the arm. Her brown hair was pulled back into a tight bun and she wore a black cloak. Her skin was pale and her face was pinched tight. When the woman spotted Fagan, she stopped.

"Fagan, do be a good dog and tell your master to release me."

"Move along," said the guard.

"Who was that?" asked Ravenna, still watching the woman until she was out of sight.

She turned to Fagan and he mumbled under his breath, *"Dùinidh mi mo dhòrn. Is ann a shaoradh dòchainn a thàinig mi staigh."*

"English, Fagan."

"I will close my fist. 'Tis to efface evil speaking that I have come within."

Ravenna shook her head. "I don't understand. You think that woman is evil?"

"I donna think she is evil. I know it to be true."

Sixteen

RUAIRI WAS SURPRISED WHEN HE OPENED THE DOOR TO Torquil's chamber and found only the healer by his son's bed. Perhaps Ravenna had finally gone to the kitchens to have something to eat. He hadn't missed the deep shadows under her eyes and didn't like the fact that her usually lively expression had darkened with weariness.

"Mistress Denny said he hasnae moved, my laird."

Ruairi walked around the bed and placed his hand on Torquil's shoulder, which seemed to make his son's frame that much smaller. When dark thoughts invaded his mind again like a pecking bird that refused to cease, he pulled his arm away.

The healer gave him a compassionate smile. "There is naught else we can do but wait. I know this is one of the hardest things to do, my laird, but we've done everything we can for the lad. The rest is up to him... and God."

"I know. Thank ye for looking in on him."

"There is naught we wouldnae do for Torquil. He's a good laddie and everyone wishes him well."

Ruairi sat down in the chair and didn't respond. He couldn't. He was perfectly aware of how much his clan loved his son.

"Would ye like me to stay with him for a while?"

"Nay, ye can take your leave. I'll call upon ye if… er, when he wakes up."

"Verra well, my laird."

The door closed, and Ruairi balled his hands into fists. He still had a hard time grasping that this was truly happening. How could someone be so full of life and then have it stripped away in one careless moment? He knew he wasn't making any sense. After all, he'd seen men die on the battlefield for less, leaving their wives and bairns behind as a result of only one heated moment. But those men were warriors, placing themselves in harm's way for a purpose. They chose to be there at that moment. Their sacrifices were willingly made to country and clan, but Torquil… There was no reason for this. The boy had not yet lived. He had not yet loved. The thought of possibly having to bury one's child was unthinkable.

Hell.

That was where Ruairi felt like he was trapped. This had to be one of the cruelest tortures for a parent to endure. He was mad with worry. He placed his elbows on his knees and lowered his head into his hands.

"Torquil, I'd verra much like for ye to wake up right now. Please, I beg ye." He knew his words wouldn't miraculously make his son open his eyes, but he lifted his head and looked anyway in the event that God decided to grant him a boon.

With Torquil, Ravenna, Cotrìona, and the Gordon, how much more could one man possibly take?

❧

Little did Fagan know that his unwillingness to shed some light on the arrival of the mysterious captive made Ravenna even more curious. If no one would tell her about the woman in the great hall, she was determined to find out on her own. But not right now. That would have to wait because she wanted to be there for Ruairi when he talked to the healer.

She climbed the steps and walked to Torquil's chamber, deciding to wait for Ruairi there. When she opened the door, Ruairi sat next to the bed alone. That's not what she wanted him to be. The man needed to have someone there for him, whether solely for company or for a shoulder to cry on.

"I was looking for you. The healer was here," said Ravenna as she closed the door.

"I saw her. She already took her leave."

When he gazed at Torquil, she could see Ruairi's eyes were brimming with tears of frustration. "Ruairi…" She walked over and placed her hand on his arm. "Ruairi, please look at me." He turned his head and tired, worn eyes looked up at her. "Please lie down and get some rest. Will you at least lie on the bed with Torquil and try to get some sleep? Lack of sleep is not doing you any good. Come now, Laird Sutherland. Do not make me force you to bed."

"Ye've ne'er had to force me to bed, Ravenna. I assure ye I went verra willingly."

"I didn't mean—"

"I know what ye meant. 'Tis good to laugh. Otherwise, we might weep."

Ravenna guided Ruairi to the bed, and he lay down next to Torquil. She bent and kissed him on the cheek, covering him with a blanket. "Sleep well, my laird."

She closed the door and paused in the hall. There was no way she could've questioned Ruairi about the prisoner. The man had enough troubles. Furthermore, if he'd wanted her to know about the woman who was being held captive, he would've told her. That's why Ravenna decided to find out on her own.

She didn't have any difficulty discovering that the woman was not being held in the dungeon. Praise the saints for small favors. Besides the fact there were no guards, Ravenna had her doubts that Ruairi would've considered placing a woman down there. That meant the woman had to be somewhere in the castle, guarded.

Ravenna made her way to the servant's quarters, and when she walked to the end of the hall, she saw a guard placed in front of the door to her old chamber. The man was big and brawny and looked as though he hadn't budged from that spot since he took up residence there. Knowing the guard would never let her pass, she turned on her heel. She had an idea.

She grabbed a tray in the kitchens and jumped when a kitchen maid walked up behind her.

"Do ye need something, Mistress Denny?"

Ravenna knew she needed to be cautious so as to not make the young girl suspicious. "Ah, yes. Laird Sutherland has not yet eaten today. Do you have some bread and wine? I'd like to take a tray up to him."

"Of course," said the maid, becoming much more agreeable when she thought the food was for Ruairi.

While the girl arranged the tray, Ravenna watched, feeling the same trace of guilt she always felt when she became the English spy. She would love to have a day when she could simply be Lady Ravenna Walsingham, the aging daughter who cared for her sisters and would never wed.

"I can take the tray for ye if ye'd like."

"No, that's quite all right. I can manage."

Ravenna was careful not to be spotted by Fagan. When she reached the door of her old chamber, the guard turned to face her, his hand resting warily on the hilt of his sword. The man made his point, but he apparently didn't realize his actions weren't necessary, since his stance was daunting enough. His massive body almost took up the entire breadth of the door.

"Could you please open the door?" she asked, playing the helpless female. In her experience, men perceived the fairer sex as weak, which she definitely had used to her advantage more than once. If they only knew...

"The laird said nay one goes in or comes out, Mistress Denny."

"And I respect that you are following Laird Sutherland's command so admirably, but did he also tell you the woman was to starve?" When she saw him pause, she quickly added, "I didn't think so. Please have yourself a look." She lifted the tray. "There is only bread and wine."

The guard lifted the bread and split it in two with his hands.

"As I said, it's only bread." Ignoring her words, he lifted the wine and swirled the contents. "Could you please open the door now?"

"I suppose, but be quick about it."

"Now that might be a problem. You see, Laird Sutherland not only asked me to deliver a tray, but I need to assist the woman during her time." When he lifted a brow, she added, "The woman has her monthly courses. She bleeds."

He shook his head and waved her off as Ravenna knew he would. She found that men—even big, brawny ones—did not like to discuss a woman's time. Ever.

Bloody cowards.

"Be off with ye, then." He gestured her in and closed the door behind her.

The woman sat on the edge of the bed. She wore a plain day dress, and strands of chestnut hair escaped from her bun. A few candles were lit and the room was basically as Ravenna had left it.

She placed the tray on the table and smiled. "I brought you something to eat."

"And why would ye do that?"

"I saw you in the great hall." Ravenna walked over and stood by the bed. She looked around the room and then lowered her voice to a conspiratorial whisper. "Why are you here? Do you want me to send for someone?"

The woman's eyes narrowed. "Ye're that English governess that was sent here to educate Sutherland's son. Tell me, how is the lad?"

Ravenna took a deep breath. She could do this.

"He's doing very well. He's a delightful boy, unlike his father."

She laughed as if sincerely amused. "My brother-by-marriage has that effect on most, but ye of all people should know that, Ravenna. Come now. Ye look about as surprised to see me as Ruairi did when he found me in the tunnels. Pray allow me to introduce myself. I am Lady Cotrìona Gordon."

Anna's...sister? Ravenna's eyes widened. "That was you in the woods. You were watching us."

"Aye, ye were verra brave to send Torquil away to fetch Ruairi and then try to catch me on your own. I've ne'er seen the English move with so much spirit," she said dryly. Cotrìona stood and approached the tray. She took a bite of bread and sat down in the chair. "Thank ye for the food."

"But why would you—"

Her eyes narrowed. "My father said there was an English governess sent here for my sister's son. He mentioned ye were quite bonny and I had to see for myself, but frankly, I donna see what he sees. Ye have a lot of questions for being a governess, unless of course ye are more than what ye seem."

"I was sent here to educate the boy, nothing more. I thought you might need my help, but clearly I was wrong." She turned her back on Ruairi's sister-in-law and started to walk toward the door.

"Mmm...I cannae help but notice how concerned ye are for my sister's son, or mayhap 'tis because ye share Ruairi's bed."

Without hesitation, Ravenna laughed and turned to face Cotrìona. "How dare you insult me! I am

English. I do not lie with Scots," she said with disgust. "I watched Laird Sutherland strike down a defenseless man. He has no honor. When I saw you in the great hall, I thought you needed help. Apparently, you can manage on your own."

Cotrìona took a sip of wine. "Ye're either verra daft or verra clever." She hesitated. "I'm nae yet sure which. My father will be here on the morrow, and the last I require is help from the English."

Ravenna shrugged with indifference. "Very well." She reached for the latch on the door.

"Howbeit there is something ye could do for me."

❧

Ruairi didn't sleep very well. How could he? At least he managed to rest for a few hours. He rose from the bed and resumed his place in the chair by Torquil's side. There was a knock on the door and Fagan entered.

"Och, he is the same."

Ruairi shook his head. "I cannae stand to see him like this."

"'Tis difficult, but donna forget the lad is a Sutherland. He'll pull through this." Fagan sat down. "I checked on Angus. John had him walking around for a wee bit. I think he's getting better."

"I'm glad to hear it."

"I know this isnae a good time, but we need to talk. The Gordon will be here on the morrow."

"As will Ian."

"Ruairi, I know ye're distraught over Torquil and ye have a right to be, but—"

"The safety of my clan doesnae stop because of

my son. The moment I lower my guard is the time I should nay longer be laird." Ruairi rubbed his hand over his brow. "The Gordon and his daughters have played me for a fool long enough. They encroached on my lands, killed my cattle, stole my coin, and then expected me to join them.

"The bastard runs a fool's errand with Stewart and the Setons. I have yet to speak to Ian, but I think he'll agree. We will nae fight the English so my father-in-law can gain the favor of Stewart. 'Tisnae my intention to start a war with the Gordon, but I think 'tis now inevitable. *Dhè beanniach dh'an cheum a bheil mi dol." God bless the steps on the path I take.*

"Ye know I stand by whatever decision ye make. And what of Ravenna?"

"She knows the Gordon comes on the morrow, but that is all she will know." He hesitated. "And I have yet to tell her about Cotrìona."

"Well, whatever ye tell her, ye'd best tell her something soon. A word of advice if I may… Ravenna was in the great hall when Cotrìona was being escorted away."

"Damn. What did ye tell her?"

"Naught. I'm nae daft."

There was another knock at the door and one of the kitchen maids cracked it open. "Pardon, my laird. Was the tray that Mistress Denny brought ye enough until 'tis time to sup? I was wondering if ye wanted anything else to eat or drink."

"I didnae receive… How long ago was this?"

"Oh, 'tis been a wee bit over an hour, my laird."

Ruairi looked at Fagan and both of them stood.

Cotrìona gestured for Ravenna to sit. "Can ye find out for me if the wolf still lives?"

"Why would you concern yourself with Angus?" asked Ravenna. She tried to rein in her frustration.

"'Tis only a matter of time before Ruairi discovers I tampered with the animal's food. He and my nephew have favored the beast since it was a pup. If the wolf dies, I donna think my brother-by-marriage will be so forgiving on the morrow."

A soft gasp escaped Ravenna. "Why would you poison Angus?"

"That isnae your concern. Are ye able to find out about the wolf or nae? 'Tis a simple task that I ask of ye."

Ravenna nodded.

"Good. Return later. If Ruairi will nae release me on the morrow when my father arrives, I'll want to see my nephew. I know the lad will be able to persuade Ruairi to release his aunt."

Shock and anger lit up Ravenna's eyes as she stood. One thing was perfectly clear. Cotrìona didn't give a damn about Ruairi or his son. She was completely callous and would do anything for her own gain. And that made her dangerous. Ravenna knew she needed to tread lightly.

"I must go. The guard will soon be suspicious."

"I'm glad I am nae the only one who sees Ruairi's ways."

Ravenna nodded and then opened the door. The huge Highland guard blocked her way and she tapped him on the shoulder. "Pray excuse me."

The man moved to the side and she stepped around him.

"What the hell do ye think ye're doing?"

"Ruairi…"

Seventeen

Ravenna was so angered by Cotrìona's words and demeanor that she didn't bother trying to mask her own guilt about being there. Grabbing Ruairi's arm, Ravenna led him away from the door. She was blinded by rage and hadn't noticed the assessing look on Ruairi's face. She walked with hurried purpose, leading him through the halls to his study. Once the door closed, she leaned against it and sighed.

"I would begin by offering you apologies for taking it upon myself to find out the identity of that woman, but right now, I'm trying desperately to keep myself from throttling her." She paused and searched Ruairi's eyes. "When did you find Cotrìona in the tunnels?"

"She told ye? And how do ye know of the tunnels?"

"That woman had no trouble telling me what she thought about many things." Ravenna's eyes widened and she reached out to touch his arm. "I'm sorry. How is Torquil?"

"He is the same. Fagan is with him now. Please sit." He gestured to a chair and sat down behind his desk. "Why were ye there, Ravenna? Ye had nay right to be."

She flinched at his tone of voice, and when his eyes darkened, she tried to calm the blood that pounded in her ears. "I was with Fagan in the great hall when Cotrìona was being escorted by your guard. I've never seen Fagan act so strangely, and he wouldn't answer any of my questions. I was going to ask you about the woman, but you were with Torquil. I didn't want to—"

"So ye decided to find out on your own?" He bristled. "Fagan didnae answer your questions for a reason. Ye should've thought this through. Ye ne'er should've… Why in the hell would ye enter her chamber? Ye had nay idea who this woman was. What if she had harmed ye?" He let out a deep breath. "Ye placed yourself in a verra dangerous situation. Again. Why am I nae surprised? This seems to be the way of ye."

Ravenna waved him off. "I'm all right." There was a heavy moment of silence and then she added, "You must know that when I found out the woman was your sister-in-law, I told her I was Torquil's governess and led her to believe that I didn't favor you."

He raised his brow. "Why would ye do that? Ne'er mind. I understand why."

"Ruairi, she told me that if you don't release her to her father on the morrow, she'll use Torquil to persuade you to do so. How could a woman use her own nephew that way?" She threw up her hands in the air with renewed disgust.

He smirked. "Aye, well, I am not surprised. She

is her father's daughter. Ne'er forget that, lass." He paused. "But I donna understand something she said to ye. I told her I would release her when her father comes on the morrow. Why would she think that I wouldnae? I sure as hell donna want her under my roof for any longer than is necessary. She would know that."

Ravenna smirked. "Because she wasn't sure you'd release her once you found out."

"Found out what?"

"She poisoned Angus."

☙

Ruairi slammed his fist on the desk and rose to his feet. *"Mo mhallachd ort!" Damn.*

"Why are you sorry? It's not your fault."

He rubbed his hand over his brow. "Ravenna, ye need to learn your Gaelic. That's not what that means. Och, ne'er mind." He rounded the desk and started to pace.

"I don't understand why she'd go to such lengths to poison Angus," said Ravenna with exasperation.

He smirked. "I'll tell ye why. Because Angus stood guard with Fagan. She wanted Angus out of the way so she could carry out her true purpose... to steal my coin."

"Steal your coin? Why would she want to do that? She was taking a big chance by coming here. Why risk being caught?"

"After the Gordon's visit, he told her that he'd asked to renew an alliance with me. Cotrìona claims she only set foot on my lands after her father was here.

She knew I would ne'er join her father and thought
the least I could do was support their cause."

"What cause is that?"

He was so deep in thought that he didn't hear her
question. "Up until now, I didnae realize how verra
cunning my wife was. Anna spied on me in my own
home. That's how she found out where I hid the
Sutherland coin. She told Cotrìona some time before
her passing."

A strange look passed over Ravenna's face. Biting
her lip, she looked away. He could see she was as
unsettled by his words as he was. How could his wife
spy on him under his own roof without his knowl-
edge? He was laird. He should've been aware of that
fact. How could he be expected to take care of his clan
when he didn't know what was occurring under his
own roof? For God's sake, Ravenna must think him a
daft fool for not even knowing his wife had betrayed
him, but he didn't have time to dwell upon that fact
now. There were far more pressing concerns.

"What will you do?"

"I donna know, but I want ye to stay far away from
Cotrìona. Do ye understand me?"

She nodded. "You won't get any argument from
me on that one. And what of Torquil?"

"I should go to him now."

"That's not what I meant."

"I know what ye meant. In truth, I donna know.
His aunt is a venomous woman. She ne'er wanted
anything to do with Torquil when my wife was alive.
That's why I donna like any Gordon near my son. I
donna trust the lot."

Ravenna placed her hand gently on his arm in a comforting gesture.

"The Gordon will be here on the morrow and remove Cotrìona from my sight. My main concern is Torquil. Naught else matters." He realized his words sounded harsh and he brushed his fingers against her cheek. He didn't miss the trace of sadness that washed over her face before she quickly masked it.

"I'm truly glad that I met you, Laird Ruairi Sutherland." And that was all she said.

                    ✷

Clan politics were something Ravenna didn't think she'd ever master. She knew games were played among those at King James's court. This lord or that lord sold secrets to the French, a husband had a mistress, a wife had a lover, but no one she knew had ever stolen coin from their own family for political aspirations. And Cotrìona's actions made Ravenna ponder something further. In fact, one question weighed heavily on her mind.

What did Laird Gordon want Ruairi to do?

The man had asked Ruairi to renew his alliance. Why? She wanted to put all the pieces together, but her head was puzzled by new thoughts. When she opened the door to Torquil's chamber, Fagan met her gaze.

"I'll keep watch now, Fagan."

He rose and approached her. For a moment, he was silent and his expression was troubled. "I know where Ruairi found ye. Ye stay away from Cotrìona for your own safety, lass."

Too tired to argue, Ravenna merely nodded.

The door closed and she resumed her place by Torquil's side. She sighed and brushed the back of her hand across his cheek. "What are we going to do?" She could've sworn the boy's eyelids fluttered in response and she stared at his face, trying not to blink. "Torquil, can you hear me? Can you do that again?"

Ruairi walked through the door, and for a moment, Ravenna thought to tell him what she thought she'd seen. When he sat down beside her and a grave expression crossed his face, she decided against it. The man had been through enough. She didn't want to give him false hope, and she wasn't even certain she had seen anything.

"Will Laird Munro be arriving soon?"

"Aye. I expect him either later this eve or early on the morrow. I imagine he will be quite surprised when he does arrive."

Ravenna wasn't sure if Ruairi's words were regarding Torquil or Cotrìona—undoubtedly both—so she decided to keep quiet.

"I donna want ye anywhere near the great hall or my study when the Gordon arrives. Ye will keep to your chamber or stay with Torquil."

"I understand. Would you like me to get you a tray with something to eat?"

He raised his brow. "Mmm... Is that your way of telling me that ye will again seek out Cotrìona and try to slip through my guard?"

She lowered her voice and shook her head. "No, Ruairi. I—"

"I was only jesting with ye because I certainly hope ye learned your lesson the first time."

"All too well, I'm afraid."

"Have a maid bring something for us both." She stood and he grabbed her hand. "If ye're nae back within the hour, I will come searching for ye." When her eyes widened, he slapped her playfully on the bottom.

She opened the door and turned around. "I'll be back soon."

Now that Ravenna had time to think about her actions, she had to admit that forcing her way into Cotrìona's chamber was not one of her best ideas. Having been placed in these predicaments so many times before, she was usually skilled at thinking of a quick explanation. Yet, Cotrìona had made her lose all sense of reason and she had been unable to give Ruairi a logical excuse for her presence. There was no sense dwelling on that further.

She walked to the kitchens, where the maid placed bread and meats on a tray, as well as a wine flask. Carrying the tray, Ravenna walked into the great hall and froze when a bunch of burly men strode into the room. They wore kilts of red, green, and blue. The same colors as the… God, she couldn't remember. The tartan was either Munro or Gordon. The brawny Highland men all appeared the same to her, the only difference being the colored tartan each of them wore with pride.

She didn't even realize she'd released the breath she held until Laird Munro came into the hall. He spotted her and his eyes twinkled. Placing his hand on the hilt of his sword, he walked toward her.

"Ah, Mistress Denny, isnae it? A pleasure to see ye again."

"And you as well, Laird Munro. I was just taking this tray up to Laird Sutherland."

Laird Munro smirked. "Since when does Ruairi take his meal in his bedchamber?"

"Oh, he's not... I'll let him know you've arrived." She lifted her foot and reached the first step when his voice halted her.

"Now I remember ye."

She heard herself swallow. "Pardon?" she asked in an innocent tone.

"I told Ruairi I ne'er forget a face. I thought ye looked familiar when I saw ye here before. I remember ye now. I saw ye the last time I was at court."

"Oh, I don't think so. Perhaps you are mistaken."

"Nay, I'm sure that was ye. Ye were with Lord Mildmay."

Uncle Walter.

⁓

The door swung open and Ruairi opened his eyes. He hadn't even realized he'd fallen asleep. His back ached between his shoulder blades, the chair an uncomfortable bed partner as of late.

"Ian just arrived," said Fagan. "Ravenna is coming along right behind me with a tray from the kitchens. Ye donna think we need to be concerned about the lass seeking out Cotrìona again, do we?"

"Nay. Ravenna is a wise woman. She doesnae want to bear Cotrìona's presence any more than we do."

Fagan folded his arms over his chest and leaned against the wall as they waited—and waited.

"Will ye stay with Torquil for a moment? I'll see where she is."

Fagan nodded and Ruairi stepped out into the hall. Surely the lass wouldn't go back on her promise. When he reached the landing, he saw Ian speaking in hushed tones with Ravenna below. As Ruairi descended the stairs, he kept in mind that his friend always had a way with the lasses that was difficult to understand, but from the look on Ravenna's face, she was not too happy with Ian at the moment.

Ian cleared his throat. "What is amiss around here? Ye all look as though someone has died. Please tell me luck is on our side and mayhap 'twas the Gordon—although one would think ye'd all be a wee bit more enthusiastic if the bastard met his demise. What the hell is going on?"

Ruairi slapped Ian on the shoulder. "Much has happened since I've seen ye last." Ruairi turned to Ravenna. "Fagan and I must speak with Munro. Could ye please see to Torquil?"

"Of course." She handed Ruairi the tray. "Why don't you take the food for yourself and Laird Munro? I'm sure he must be hungry after the journey." She lowered her voice. "And please make certain you eat as well."

"I will, thank ye. Could ye please send Fagan down to join us?" She nodded and he watched her climb the steps.

Ruairi turned and escorted his friend to the study. When he gestured to a chair and pulled out the ale, Ian smirked.

"Why is it that I always find myself needing a wee drink or two around ye of late?"

"When ye hear what I have to say, ye're going to need several," Ruairi said dryly.

Fagan closed the door and took his seat beside Ian. Ruairi filled their tankards, not even bothering to wipe the fallen drops that had escaped the flask and landed on his desk. He lifted his cup in the air and saluted his closest friends.

"Slàinte mhath." Good health.

"Do dheagh shlàinte," the men replied. *Your good health.*

Ruairi placed his tankard on the desk and fingered the lip. "Torquil isnae well."

Ian's cup froze in midair and he looked at Ruairi over the rim. "What do ye mean?"

"He fell down the steps to the great hall. His head cracked on the stone floor and he isnae yet conscious."

"Och, Ruairi. Will the lad be all right?" With a solemn look on his face, Ian placed his tankard on the desk. "Then take me to him. I must see him, wish him well."

"There is naught ye can do. In truth, there is naught any of us can do until he wakes up. Ravenna, Mistress Denny, stays with him now."

There was a heavy silence.

Ian leaned forward and tapped his hand on the desk. "If there is anything I can do, anything at all, please let me know. Torquil is like my blood. Damn, Ruairi. How do *ye* fare?"

He shrugged. "I've had better days. Although my son's health worries me greatly, there are other matters upon us. The last time we spoke, I know we discussed that ye'd return and we'd tell the Gordon to go to hell together, but some things have changed."

"What do ye mean? What things?" asked Ian warily. When Ruairi took a moment to respond, Ian added, "*Sput a-mach e*, Ruairi." *Spit it out.*

"My beloved wife's sister has been stealing my coin."

Ian's jaw dropped. "Surely ye're jesting."

"I wish I was. I discovered Cotrìona in the tunnels, coin in hand."

Ian slid his cup toward Ruairi. "Fill it up."

Eighteen

RAVENNA STOOD, HER BACK TIGHT WITH STRAIN. SHE shivered with chill and fatigue. It had been an uncomfortable night sitting in the hard chair as she kept vigil over Torquil. She knew she could've rested beside him on the bed, but she wanted to stay awake for Ruairi—who never came. God, she was so tired of sitting, tired of standing and, frankly, tired of waiting. She was by no means a healer, but she was sensible enough to recognize that the longer Torquil remained in this state, the more difficult it had to be for the boy to wake up.

She approached the washbowl with a cloth, then wrung it out and walked over to the bed. When she wiped Torquil's face, a tiny bead of water dropped on his eyelid. She could've sworn he squinted. Pulling back, she watched him, studying every move he did or did not make. To her dismay, he made none. There was a knock on the door and the healer entered, followed by a maid.

"Mistress Denny, Laird Sutherland asked me to bring ye a tray. He said he'll join ye later after his guests depart."

"Has Laird Gordon arrived, then?"

The maid placed the tray on the table and wiped her hands on her apron. "I donna know, Mistress Denny."

"That's all right. Thank you."

The maid left the room and the healer approached the bed. She lifted Torquil's bandages and checked his wound. Now that Ruairi wasn't around, Ravenna couldn't pass up the opportunity to question the woman.

"I didn't want to mention anything to Laird Sutherland in the event I was mistaken, but I think I saw Torquil possibly move on two different occasions. Not much, mind you, but I'm hoping I didn't imagine it."

"'Tis quite possible ye didnae imagine it, but since the lad hasnae opened his eyes, I'd have to say what ye saw might be his muscles twitching a time or two."

Ravenna slapped her hands together and stared at them. She hadn't noticed the strained tone in her voice. "Is there *anything* I can do? Anything at all?" She was so frustrated that she started to pace. "His head stopped bleeding. Ruairi…er, Laird Sutherland and I have checked the bandages, we've bathed his face, held his hand… Praise the saints. There has to be *something*."

"I'm afraid we've done everything we can. The rest is up to him."

"Then think of something else," Ravenna bit out. When she realized her words had come out more harshly than she intended, she added, "Please, perhaps there is some kind of herb treatment that we haven't yet thought of."

The healer smiled at her with compassion. "*Tha mi duilich*, Mistress Denny." *I am sorry*.

Ravenna didn't need to understand the Gaelic words to comprehend their meaning. She merely nodded and resumed her place by Torquil's side. "Thank you for all you have done."

∽

The Gordon and Cotrìona were escorted into Ruairi's solar. Thank God for Fagan and Ian because Ruairi didn't think he could manage this one on his own. He needed his friends close by to make certain he didn't reach over the desk and kill the Gordon and his daughter.

The Gordon shook his head almost regretfully, and a muscle ticked in his jaw. "I didnae know my *daughter* was stealing your coin."

Ruairi smirked. "She's been stealing my coin to support your damn cause."

The Gordon leaned forward, placing his arm on the desk. "Understand this, Sutherland. When ye wed my daughter, ye were supposed to protect her. She was under your roof, your protection, and now she's dead."

"Anna's death was an accident."

"So ye say." The Gordon sounded like he didn't believe Ruairi's words. "Ye know our alliance was important to Anna, and of course Cotrìona was close to her sister. But where Anna failed, Cotrìona yearns to succeed. I donna make excuses for Cotrìona's behavior and I donna agree with the way she went about stealing your coin, but I understand why she did what she did. She is my blood. She knows where her loyalties lie. Nevertheless, I will make certain she gives ye back all the coin she has stolen from ye. I promise ye that." He turned to Cotrìona and gave her a pointed look. "Isnae that right, Daughter?"

Ignoring her father's question, she gazed at Ruairi. "What are ye going to do now? Will ye give my father what he asks of ye or nae?"

"Tha I beag-nàire," spat Ian. *She's got no shame.*

Anna whipped her head around to Ian. *"Trusdar. Dè do ghnothaich!"* *Bastard. Mind your own business!*

Ian stood and his expression was flat, unreadable as stone—at least for the Gordon and Cotrìona. But Ruairi recognized that look. Ian's eyes were filled with dislike.

There was a heavy moment of silence.

"Please donna let my daughter's stupidity interfere with the matter at hand. Patrick Stewart's son, Robert—"

"Illegitimate son," said Ruairi.

"Robert Stewart needs armed men in Orkney. If ye and Munro join us, we will be seven hundred strong," the Gordon said, his voice rising proudly. "First, we will seize the Palace of Birsay, then Kirkwall Castle and St. Magnus Cathedral. We will restore justice in Orkney once and for all. 'Tis verra important that we regain control because we sure as hell donna want King James and his bloody laws coming to the Highlands any more than they already do. By reclaiming Orkney, we take a stand. We send a message to the English that our Scottish blood runs hot and cannae be tamed."

Ruairi's eyes narrowed. "I cannae help but wonder why ye tell us this so freely, Gordon. I donna think

Stewart would take too kindly to ye having told us his stratagem."

"Och, Sutherland, one thing is for certain. Ye and I may have our skirmishes, petty reiving and the like, but we Highlanders are united and stand together for one cause. We both hate those English bastards. And that ye certainly cannae deny."

Ruairi stole a glance at Fagan and Ian. This was their last chance to change their minds. The time was now or never. As he had expected, Ian gave him a subtle nod and Fagan simply smiled.

❦

Torquil moaned and Ravenna flew to her feet.

"Torquil, can you hear me?" When he didn't answer, she said the only thing she knew in Gaelic. *"Ciamar a tha sibh?"* How are you?

"Tha mo cheann goirt." When she didn't answer, he must've realized she didn't understand because he quickly added, "I have headache."

She laughed and rubbed her hand gently over his head. "I'm sure you do. You gave us all a scare. Can you see all right? Can you move?"

He opened his eyes and gave her a wry grin, just like his father, "I see ye." He lifted his hand to his head and groaned. "Where is Da?"

"He's below stairs with… I'm sure he'll be here soon." She walked hastily around the bed and swung open the door. She called for a maid and had the woman seek the healer.

"Shhh…Ravenna, donna scream overmuch, my head. How is Angus?"

She moved and sat down beside the boy on the bed. Seeing the pained expression on Torquil's face, she lowered her voice and spoke in hushed tones. "John has been caring for him in the stables. He's doing much better. I know he misses you, too."

"What happened to him?"

"John thinks it was something he ate, but I assure you, Angus is well. I'm certain you'll be able to see him soon."

"Good. I worried."

"Worried? You, my dear boy, had us all worried about you. You've been out for days."

"Days?"

"Yes, days. We've barely left your side. Your father has been mad with worry. He's going to be so relieved to see you're all right. Does anything hurt besides your head? Can you move your arms and legs?"

"Aye, but I donna want." He raised his hand and held it again to his head. "Every when I move, my head hurts."

"Every *time* you move?"

"Ravenna, nay correct me. Be thankful I nae speak Gaelic to ye. English pains me enough."

She laughed. "Torquil, as long as you're awake, you could speak anything to me."

The healer entered the room and smiled. "'Tis wonderful to see ye awake, laddie."

"Please be silent. If I donna hold my head with hands, it fall from shoulders. It hurts."

"'Tis to be expected. Ye took quite the fall down the stairs. Your head is still healing."

He turned and looked at Ravenna. "I want Da."

Ravenna bent and gave Torquil a gentle kiss on the forehead. "I'm so relieved to see you are well." Her fingers squeezed the tip of his chin. "I'm going to go fetch your father now, but you do what the healer tells you to do."

"Aye."

She made her way through the halls, and even her walk had a sunny cheerfulness. Her heart sang with delight. Torquil was all right. This dreaded nightmare had finally come to an end. Ruairi was more than likely meeting with the Gordon, but she knew Ruairi's son meant more to him than the beastly Cotrìona or her conniving father. Although Ravenna had given a promise not to intervene, she knew Ruairi would want to know Torquil was awake.

Reaching the study door, Ravenna was lifting her hand to knock when she heard raised voices from within.

"I was hoping my daughter's actions didnae weigh against our cause, because we move within a fortnight. I want four hundred of your finest men."

There was a brief silence.

"My father asked ye for men," spat Cotrìona. "At least give him the courtesy of an answer."

"I donna believe ye comprehend how this is going to work, Gordon. Cotrìona will repay all the coin she has stolen from the Sutherland coffers. Ye will repay me and the Munro five cattle *each* for slaughtering our animals on our own lands. Ye will take Cotrìona home with ye, and she will ne'er again set foot on my lands. And most importantly, both of ye are to stay away from Torquil. In turn, ye are free to take your leave and I will nae have my men raise arms against ye."

"Ye cannae be serious. Give my father the men he requires to take back Orkney from the English. Ye owe him that much for my sister's death."

"Silence, Daughter!" the Gordon bellowed.

Ruairi smirked. "That's the wisest thing I've ever heard ye say."

"This is far from over, Sutherland. Who's to say what will come next for ye? Mayhap cattle this day, a bonny governess the next?" He turned to Munro. "The same for ye, except for the bonny governess, of course."

"The time for games has passed. If any of your men set foot on my lands or Munro's, we will hold nay mercy. Blood will be spilled."

Nineteen

Ruairi opened the door to his study and waited for Cotrìona and her father to depart. The sooner he could get the Gordon and his devil daughter out from under his roof, the better. As the men had predicted, the Gordon wasn't surprised by Ruairi's refusal. He had denied his father-in-law's requests so many times that the man should've come to expect it. One thing was evident. The Gordon was thirsty for power—now more than ever. Ruairi would be sure not to take his threats lightly.

The Gordon, Ian, and Fagan walked down the hall. When Cotrìona reached Ruairi at the door, she stopped and stared at him. He wished she would move along. The woman was poison, defecating on everything and everyone around her. She cared for no one but herself and her father. Ruairi stiffened when she reached out and placed her hand on his chest.

"Just answer me one question. How could ye?"

A war of emotions raged within him. He looked down at her hand and swept it away hastily, as if her mere touch carried the plague. "Let me make something perfectly clear to ye, Cotrìona. This has naught to do with ye, even though ye might find that difficult to believe. I think of my son, my clan, their future. I am nae a fool. I will nae raise arms against the English to help the Gordon gain Stewart's favor. The conditions I made to your father left nay room for misunderstanding. Let me be the first to remind ye." His voice hardened. "Ye arenae to set foot on my lands again, and ye and your father are to stay far away from Torquil. Do ye hear me? Do ye understand?"

She shrugged with indifference. "I donna seek to establish any kind of relationship with him. My sister gave ye your heir. Do with him what ye will." She made a dismissive gesture with her hand. "All Anna and I ever sought was for ye to honor my father, and ye've ne'er fulfilled the duty that ye were sworn to do. I only wish my sister could've been here to see this. She could ne'er stand the sight of ye before, but who knows? Mayhap after this she would've thrown ye off the cliff in her stead." She leaned forward and tapped him playfully on the chest. "I wish ye and your son well, Ruairi. I'd also watch your back because ye donna know who will try to stab it."

He glowered at her and turned away. As he listened to Cotrìona's footsteps tread down the hall, he closed his eyes and thumped his head back against the door several times in frustration. His eyes flew open when a hand reached out and touched him.

"Ruairi…" Ravenna's face was pale and pinched.

He stood to his full height. "What is it? What has happened?"

"It's Torquil. Your son is awake."

❦

"Och, Torquil, God has given me the greatest of gifts on this day." A cry of relief broke from Ruairi's lips.

Torquil's eyes widened when his father's body shook. His small hand rubbed Ruairi's back. "Da, please donna cry for me. *Tha mo cheann goirt*, 'tis all." *I have a headache.*

Ruairi chuckled and when he lifted his head, the tears were gone, as if they had been evaporated by a rush of wind. "All ye have is a headache, eh? Howbeit ye worried me greatly." He looked over at Ravenna and held out his hand, gesturing her beside him. "Ravenna hasnae left your side. She talked to ye, held your hand through the night."

"She said the same of ye." Torquil brought his hand to his head and moaned. "It pains me to talk."

"Then be silent. As long as ye're awake, 'tis all that matters."

"I'm hungry. Time to sup?"

Ruairi laughed. "I think my son is getting better."

Ravenna gave Ruairi a smile and then placed her hand on Torquil's shoulder. "I'll get you something to eat. Is there anything else I can do for you?"

"Aye, I'd like Angus."

She nodded. "I'll see what I can do."

Ravenna felt as though her head was going to explode. She was relieved that Torquil was awake and Ruairi's heavy heart was finally lifted, but she was so confused. The bloody Gordon wanted Ruairi and Laird Munro to give him men and arms to use against the English. She knew the Scots hated the English, but she didn't believe for a single minute that Ruairi shared the Gordon's views. At least, she hoped not.

It was nearly time for the midday meal when Ravenna went to the kitchens. While she instructed the maid to deliver the tray to Torquil, a warm voice spoke from behind her.

"They finally took their leave," said Fagan with a heavy sigh.

She turned around and smiled. "I assume Cotrìona returned with her father, then?"

"Praise the saints for small favors. Ian departed as well."

"Did you hear the good news yet?"

He lifted a brow. "I could use some about now," he said dryly.

"Torquil is awake."

His eyes widened. "Truly? Is he all right?"

"He's fine. Do you want to take this tray of food up to him? I promised I would try to fetch Angus from the stables."

Fagan chuckled. "Are ye sure ye donna want to take the tray and I'll fetch Angus?"

"The thought had crossed my mind, but no, you go. Torquil will be glad to see you. Ruairi is there with him now."

He grabbed the tray with a wry grin. "I assume ye will—well, yell or *scream* if ye need anything."

She rolled her eyes and shooed him away. "Off with you."

Ravenna made her way to the stables. She would've given Torquil anything he'd asked of her if only to see him hale. She opened the door, and when the musty smell of hay tickled her nose, she let out a loud sneeze. She turned her head and smiled when the horses stood in a line side by side, heads all staring in her direction. She called for Angus, and when she didn't see or hear anything other than the occasional whinny, she walked out behind the barn. Perhaps she could find John.

She didn't have to look far because he was there shoveling muck out of the stalls. Huge mounds of horse manure were scattered about. She lifted her skirts and walked on the tips of her toes to approach him, mindful to avoid the mess.

"Be careful where ye step, Mistress Denny."

"I can see that." She wrinkled her nose at the foul smell in the air. "I have some good news. Torquil is awake."

John stopped and rested his arm on the top of the shovel. "Now that is verra good news indeed. He is well?"

"He's already asking for food."

John chuckled. "A Sutherland after my own heart. Be sure to wish him my best."

"I will. Have you seen Angus? I promised Torquil I'd bring him up to his chamber." When a wry grin played John's lips and his eyes twinkled with amusement, she asked, "What is it?"

"He's right behind ye, lass."

Ravenna turned around slowly and saw that the wolf's cold eyes were close, too close. "Angus…"

She was attempting to lift her hand when without warning the wolf's massive paws landed on her shoulders, pushing her backward. She landed flat on her arse, as Ruairi would say, and her eyes widened when she realized her landing was a little softer than she'd imagined it would be.

"Och, ye've gone and done it now, Angus. Ye'd better run off before Mistress Denny kills ye. Go on, off with ye!"

Ravenna closed her eyes and bowed her head. She knew her predicament was indeed as bad as it seemed. As a warm, sticky substance oozed between her fingers, she cringed. The wicked wolf of the Highlands had dropped her into a pile of horse manure. She thought she heard a chuckle from behind her, and then John cleared his throat. A hand grabbed under her arm and assisted her to her feet. When John pulled her up, muck was caked on the back of her dress.

"That wolf drives me completely mad," she said through clenched teeth. She flung the manure from her fingertips, only to throw spots of it on her dress again. "Ugh!" She held out her hands, shaking them in frustration. "And to think I tried to nurse that beast back to health."

"Now, lass, Angus didnae toss ye into the heap on purpose."

"*Angus* is going to be the death of me yet." She gave John a steely gaze when he chuckled.

"My apologies, Mistress Denny. 'Tisnae every day I get to see a governess thrown into a pile of horse sh… er, manure."

"I'm glad you find this so amusing," she said dryly.

"Why donna ye go and get yourself cleaned up, and I will take Angus to Torquil for ye."

She nodded. "I think that would be best."

"'Tis about time ye woke up, lad. I was beginning to think ye were going to sleep away your days."

"'Tis good to see ye, Fagan," said Torquil quietly.

He raised a cup to his lips and guzzled down the contents.

"Slow down. Ye need to take it easy," said Ruairi.

Torquil nodded and then took a bite of oatcake. There was a knock on the door, and as soon as it cracked open, Angus pushed his nose through and darted to Torquil's side. Two big paws sprung onto the bed and his son encircled the animal with his arms.

"Angus!"

The wolf placed his head on Torquil's shoulder, almost as if Angus understood how to give the boy a hug. Ruairi's thought was interrupted and he couldn't help but smile when Angus's animal instincts took over. His jaws discreetly turned to the side and he hastily stole the piece of bread on Torquil's tray. Once he'd snatched the food, the wolf tried to move undetected to the corner of the room.

"Da, he ate my bread!"

"Angus is happy to see ye, but he saw the food and couldnae resist."

John cleared his throat. "I'm glad ye're awake, laddie." He gave Ruairi a slight nod. "He looks well."

"He will be."

"I'm glad to hear it. If ye'll excuse me, I must be getting back to my duties, my laird," said John.

"Where is Mistress Denny? I thought she was going to bring Angus herself."

John tried unsuccessfully to mask a smile. His eyes

watered from laughter and he brought up his sleeve to wipe them, turning slightly away from Ruairi. When the man laughed, he looked ten years younger. "Ye see, my laird, Angus leaped on Mistress Denny and pushed her down into a pile of horse manure."

When a couple of Ruairi's men passed in front of Torquil's door carrying a tub, Ruairi stared at John and then turned to Fagan as the men burst out laughing. Fagan threw back his head, slapping his hands on his thighs.

"You couldn't just leave well enough alone, could you?" asked a voice from the hall.

Ravenna stepped into the room and the men gazed at her with wide eyes. When Angus rose and attempted to move toward her, she held up her hand to stay him. "Don't. You. Dare. You wicked, wicked beast. I've had enough of you for one day. Sit down!"

When Angus sat on command, Fagan murmured, "Bloody coward."

Ruairi approached her and studied her dress. "Your dress doesnae look too bad. If John didnae tell us, I would have ne'er even known. I only see a wee bit on the edge of your skirts."

"Ruairi, what is that *smell*?"

Ravenna shot Fagan a murderous glance. "I am in no mood for your games, Fagan. Pray excuse me while I seek my bath."

She spun on her heel, and the entire length of her was caked with muck. Ruairi tried to compose himself, but he couldn't speak for the captain of his guard or his son.

Fagan roared with laughter and Torquil chuckled.

"I hate men," said Ravenna, lifting her head and trying to walk away with some amount of dignity.

֍

Ravenna tilted her head back and covered her face with a warm cloth. She let the soothing water lap against her skin. She'd certainly seen better days. She'd bundled up her skirts in the corner, attempting to mask the foul smell, but the ungodly stench lingered in the air. Her dress was surely ruined, as well as her pride.

"Ye are beautiful, lass."

She jumped and tried to move the cloth over her breasts to hide as much skin as she possibly could.

"There is nay need to hide yourself from me. I've seen ye before."

"That doesn't make any difference, Ruairi. I'm not exactly comfortable having you sit there and watch me take my bath."

He shrugged with indifference. "Ye smell much better."

She balled up the wet cloth and threw it at him. He caught the material with one hand as water dripped onto his tunic. When the beastly man had the nerve to laugh, she wanted nothing more than to wipe that smug expression from his face.

"I'm afraid my dress is ruined."

"I'll have another made for ye," he said quickly.

"That's not what I meant."

"I know what ye meant."

She paid him no heed. "Was everything all right with Laird Gordon?"

Ruairi paused. "Cotrìona has returned under her

father's roof. She will nae come back, and Torquil will nae be told of his aunt's actions. 'Tis better for everyone that way." He tossed her back the cloth and pulled a chair next to the tub. "There is something I'd like to say to ye."

She again placed the cloth over her breasts. "You can't wait until I get out of the tub?"

"Nay. I would rather sit and enjoy the view." He paused with a concentrated look on his face. "I cannae thank ye for all ye've done for Torquil, but I think ye already know that. The time we've shared... together...I will ne'er forget, lass. Ye know that I care for ye. To be honest, I've come to realize that I care for ye quite a lot."

His eyes never left hers.

"Ruairi..."

"Let me finish what I've come to say. I wouldnae feel right if I didnae say this at least once. Stay with me. I donna want ye to leave."

Ravenna was speechless. Perhaps she had taken the meaning of Ruairi's words out of context. She had to be mistaken because he knew she would return to England to her sisters. As he sat and stared at her with an unreadable look on his face, she returned a nervous smile. She felt the tepid water in her bath suddenly turn cold.

"I don't understand." She rose from the tub and he handed her a drying cloth. She wrapped the material around her wet skin and stepped out of the water carefully—but not because she was afraid she would slip or fall.

"What is there to understand? I donna believe 'tis my imagination that ye've grown to care for Torquil."

She nodded.

"And I have enjoyed the time I've spent with ye, and nae just in my bed." He gave her a raking gaze. "Believe it or nae, I've actually come to like having ye around, even if ye are English."

There was something warm and enchanting in his humor, and she appreciated the gentle sparring as much as he did. But certain questions weighed heavily on her mind and she wanted—*needed*—the answers to them.

She turned away from him and donned her chemise. "What about Laird Gordon?" she asked over her shoulder.

"I donna want ye to worried about him. I donna think he will be a problem."

"And how can you be so sure?" When he didn't respond, she pulled her day dress over her head and turned around to face him. "How do you know that he won't be a problem?"

A muscle ticked in his jaw.

"Ruairi…" She reached out and he tensed when she touched his arm. "You asked me to stay, but you don't trust me?"

There was a heavy moment of silence.

"Ravenna, this would be difficult for ye to understand. In truth, I wouldnae even know where to begin. 'Tisnae easy to explain matters of politics to someone who knows naught about them."

She folded her arms over her chest. "Because I'm English or because I'm a woman?"

He shrugged. "Both."

"Then try. Explain to me the politics of the

Highlands." She sat down and patted her hand on the bed. "Come and sit beside me. Start with Laird Gordon. What did he do?"

Ruairi rubbed his hand over his brow and sat next to her. For a moment, she didn't think he was going to say anything because he just looked down at the floor. Finally, he cleared his throat and spoke solemnly. "I told ye that when I wed Anna, she and her father wanted me to join their cause. What I didnae tell ye was that even back then, she wanted me to give her father men and arms to stand against the English."

Ravenna masked her expression. "Please go on."

"Life in the Highlands is so damn hard. Between the harsh winters and trying to keep my clan protected, sheltered, and fed, the last the Sutherlands needed—*I* needed—was a war with the English."

A slight smile of uncertainty played at the corner of his lips, and she nodded for him to continue.

"The king thinks the Highland lairds are naught but a bunch of barbarians. In a way, I can see why King James thinks the way he does. What he doesnae understand is that by forcing Highlanders to speak only the king's tongue, he is making us give up our heritage." Ruairi shrugged. "I donna know. Mayhap the king does realize this and that was his intention all along. Nevertheless, his laws are ridiculous—sending Torquil to the Lowlands to learn the English language. God's teeth! The lad's nae even English. He's a Scot."

He threw up his hands with disgust. "And let's nae forget about the king forcing the Highland lairds to appear in Edinburgh every year just because he commands it so." Ruairi smirked, his eyes narrowed, and his expression clouded with anger. "Attempt to leash a wild dog and ye're going to get bitten."

Ravenna raised a brow and Ruairi shook his head as if he realized he'd wandered far from the path of the conversation.

"As I said, I refused the Gordon's request to raise arms against the English, and the man's resented me for it ever since."

"I understand that much, but you said you didn't think Laird Gordon would be a problem. I can't see how he won't be now," she said dryly. When he hesitated, Ravenna added, "You've shared this much with me."

"'Tisnae that. I just have a feeling ye're nae going to like what I have to say."

"Ruairi, you're one of the kindest men I know. I assure you that I won't think poorly of you. How could I?" When she realized the words she had spoken were how she truly felt in her heart, she quickly lowered her gaze.

"The Gordon attempts to raise arms against the Crown in Orkney. He thinks that by seizing the Palace of Birsay, then Kirkwall Castle and St. Magnus Cathedral, he will restore justice to Orkney once and for all."

"But surely he doesn't have enough men."

"He has the help of the Seton clan, and he has asked Munro and me to join forces with Stewart's men."

"Stewart?"

"Aye, Robert Stewart."

The Earl of Orkney's son.

Ravenna spoke hesitantly. "Mmm...I imagine

Cotrìona and her father are rather unhappy that you and Laird Munro won't be aiding them. What will you do if Laird Gordon reciprocates the gesture and not in kind?"

"Kill him."

❧

When Ravenna's jaw dropped, Ruairi knew she didn't understand. There was no way an English lass— let alone a woman—would be able to fathom what he and Ian intended to do if another one of the bastards set foot on their lands. Freskin de Moravia had cleared the Norse from Scotland in his time, and Ruairi would follow in his ancestor's footsteps. Whether that meant protecting his clan from the invading English or the neighboring clans, Ruairi was determined to rid his lands of any vermin that encroached on them. The unwelcome tension stretched even tighter between him and Ravenna, and he hesitated in the silence that engulfed them.

"The less ye know the better, and this doesnae involve ye." She was about to speak, but he reached out and placed her hands in his, rubbing the tops of her fingers with his thumb. "I didnae come here to talk about the Gordon. I want to talk about us. I asked ye to stay with me."

There was a heavy moment of silence and he took a deep breath.

"I ask ye to stay with me because I love ye, Ravenna Denny."

She stiffened as though he had struck her. "Ruairi, I wish everything was different. I really do, but we can't refuse to acknowledge the fact that you have an entire clan to protect and I still have a family, my sisters, who need me."

"I've thought of that. Ye can bring yer sisters here."

She laughed. "You have no idea what you're saying, my laird. You wouldn't know what to do with Grace, let alone Kat and Elizabeth."

"We'll figure that out, as long as we're together. 'Tis all that matters."

She smiled at him and two deep lines of worry appeared between her eyes. "I'm sorry, Ruairi, but I simply cannot."

He studied her thoughtfully for a moment. "Answer me this... Do ye love me? I will have the truth."

She briefly closed her eyes. "It's not that simple."

"'Tis a simple response, lass. Aye or nay."

Her voice softened and sounded almost regretful. "My answer doesn't matter because there is nothing we can do. I must return to England and you have many responsibilities here."

"If ye love me, we will find a way for ye to stay."

"And would ye give up your clan and come to England to be with me?"

He snapped his mouth shut, stunned by her question. He'd never thought of it that way. "'Tisnae the same and ye know it."

❧

Ravenna's heart pounded. She stood up, surprised and now more uncertain than ever. Ruairi said he loved her—well, not exactly *her*. Ravenna Denny, not Lady Ravenna Walsingham. When she heard his words, she felt a tremendous amount of guilt for deceiving him. She didn't deserve a man like Laird Ruairi Sutherland, and she wasn't ready to have this conversation because deep down, she knew she loved him, too.

The admission came from a place beyond logic and reason. She shook her head as she realized her vow not to become involved with him had been shattered some time ago. For God's sake, she was a spy, and he didn't even know her true name. She had to stop this now before any further damage was done. She didn't want to hurt him, but she couldn't give him any false hope of something that could never be.

She sat back down on the bed and faced him. "Torquil means a lot to me and so do you. I care for you both *very* much." Ravenna forced herself to look him in the eye and not falter. She could do this. She had to, for both their sakes. "But I do not love you. I'm sorry that's not the answer you wanted to hear." For a moment, he looked surprised, and then he quickly turned away from her. His wounded expression felt like a dagger straight through her heart.

"Can ye at least stay another fortnight? I donna want to leave Torquil unattended, especially since his head—"

Ravenna loved the boy. How could she refuse such a request? "Of course."

Ruairi stood and walked to the door. He reached for the latch and hesitated. With his back to her, he spoke in a solemn voice. "I'll be with Torquil."

There was an uncomfortable silence.

"I want ye to know that nay woman has ever held my heart like ye do. Ye brought light into my life and my son's." He lowered his head and his voice. "I'd give ye the moon and the stars. I'd give ye anything ye'd ask of me. It doesnae matter that ye donna feel the same for me because ye'll always be in my heart. *Tha gaol agam ort*, Ravenna." *I love you.*

He opened the door, and when it closed, Ravenna burst into tears.

Twenty

FAGAN AND HIS MEN RODE OUT TO THE BORDER.
Ruairi had given them strict orders not to lower the
guard until he felt confident things with the Gordon
had settled down, not that they ever would. They
couldn't afford to be careless, and he knew it was
only a matter of time before the Gordon brought
his wrath down on the Sutherlands. Even though a
fortnight had passed since Ruairi and Ian denied the
bastard, they still needed to be cautious. And Fagan
didn't have to remind Ruairi or Ian about that devil
Cotrìona. Who knew what tangled web she might
yet weave?

Since everything was silent at the border, Fagan
turned his mount for home. He had almost reached
the castle when an approaching carriage caught his
attention. The wheels stopped on the path and the
driver hastily stepped down. Fagan thought he recognized the carriage, and for a moment he hesitated. A
woman walked with hurried purpose around the man
and made her way up the path toward the castle. The
driver ran after her and grabbed her arm. She shook

him off, and they became involved in a heated argument in the middle of the road.

Fagan rode up and dismounted. The woman didn't even notice that he and two of his men were there. He recognized the driver as the man who'd first brought Ravenna.

"What are ye doing here?" asked Fagan.

The woman spun around to face him. Her dress was the color of the sky, accented with a gold ribbon and a low neckline that only heightened the milky color of her neck. A belt around her waist defined its smallness, and her enchanting young body and wholesome good looks made him smile. Her oval face was daintily pointed, and the wind gently ruffled her brownish-gold hair. She was beautiful…and then she spoke.

"Whatever do you mean?" she asked in a haughty English tone, lifting her chin. When the driver tried to speak, the woman simply talked over him. "I am here to see Lady Walsingham."

Fagan lifted a brow. "Who?"

"Do not be coy with me, sir. I've come the whole way from Edinburgh."

He shook his head. "What are ye blabbering about?"

"What?" The woman wrinkled her nose and turned to the driver. "Perhaps this man does not understand my words because I can barely understand his." She took a step forward and looked him in the eye. "La-dy Wal-sing-ham…"

Fagan's eyes narrowed. "I heard ye the first time. Listen to me, *bhana-phrionnsa*," he said with a heavy dose of sarcasm. *Princess*. "Ye have wandered verra far from home. I suggest ye turn around and be on your way because I donna know who 'tis ye seek."

"Pardon?"

He rubbed his hand over his brow. "Give me strength." He spoke slowly, patiently. "There is nay Lady Walsingham here."

The woman closed the gap between them and pointed her finger at his chest. He thought he heard one of his men chuckle behind him. "Now you listen to me. I've just made a very long journey to see my sister, and I'm not leaving until I do." She lowered her voice. "She may be with child."

"I can assure ye there isnae anyone here named Lady Walsingham, let alone one who is with child," he said with exasperation.

She tipped her head back to look up at him and placed her hands on her hips. "I demand to speak with Laird Sutherland, and I'm not leaving here until I do." Every curve of her body quivered with defiance.

"Ye're out of luck, lass, because he is rather indisposed at the moment." Fagan regarded the woman with subtle amusement, which infuriated her even more. That's when he decided to do the only thing that came to mind.

He winked at her.

Her body stiffened. "How dare you! I am a *lady*, and you are most definitely not a gentleman."

"Aye, well, I ne'er claimed to be." He shrugged with indifference. "I suppose there is nay changing me now. Besides, ye're a verra long way from England. We do things differently in the Highlands." He gave her a roguish grin. *"Fàilte gu Alba."*

"Pardon?"

"Welcome to Scotland, lass."

"My lady," said the driver in a nervous tone. "Perhaps it is best if we take our leave and return at anoth—"

"Absolutely not, George," she scoffed. "I'm not leaving until I see Ravenna. I know she's here. Where else could she be?"

"Ravenna?" asked Fagan.

The woman looked at him as if he'd lost his mind. "Yes, my sister." She turned away without waiting for a reply.

"And tell me, this Lady…Walsingham is Lady *Ravenna* Walsingham?"

She looked back at him, a shadow of annoyance crossing her face. "Yes. For heaven's sake, what is the matter with you?" Clearly dismissing him, she turned back to the driver. "Do all Highland men act this oddly?"

The woman's answer hammered away at Fagan, his mind refusing to comprehend the significance of her words. His thoughts darted vaguely around until he realized exactly what he had to do. "Aye, I know where your sister is." He gestured her toward the castle. "Come, follow me and I'll take ye to her."

The lass hesitated and her face clouded with uneasiness. "Why didn't you tell me you knew who she was when I asked you to begin with?"

"Because we hadnae been properly introduced." He gave her a slight bow. "I am Fagan Murray, captain of Laird Sutherland's guard. Let me take ye to your sister, Lady Walsingham."

"Very well. George, the walk is not far. Gather the carriage and I'll meet you in the bailey."

The driver looked pale and uncertain. His face was closed as if he guarded a secret, a secret that would shortly be unveiled.

Fagan returned to the bailey with the lass and driver in tow. He led them into the great hall and gestured the woman forward. "Why donna ye have something to eat and drink while ye wait?"

"That would be delightful. I am a bit parched."

He had a maid bring some food and drink. He was determined not to leave this woman's side. Ruairi had enough troubles. Fagan would be sure to keep his friend at bay until he knew what was afoot. Moreover, he needed to see Lady Ravenna Walsingham's eyes when she saw her sister and realized she had some serious explaining to do.

While the uninvited company sat in the great hall, Fagan listened to the woman's endless prattle. Although she spoke in a low tone, he could still hear every word. Meanwhile, the driver hadn't uttered a single peep. Who knew? Perhaps he was unable to get in a word or two.

"The castle is beautiful. Don't you think so, George? I'm not surprised my *sister* has been away for so long if she's been living like this. Our small manor house doesn't even begin to compare. Why do you think the tapestries have nothing but swords, shields, and scenes of war, and what is that imbedded into the mantel over there? It looks like a giant cat sitting upright. I despise cats as much as Ravenna despises dogs."

When there was a moment of blessed silence, Fagan said a silent prayer that the rant was over. Of course he spoke too soon.

"The Highland men and women certainly dress differently than we do, even when we're out in the country. Why do you think the Scottish men wear those ridiculous skirts, George?"

Enough was enough. Fagan approached the table and gave her a roguish grin. "'Tisnae a skirt, lass. If I wore something under it, then it would be called a skirt."

As if on cue, the woman's face deepened to crimson and Ravenna walked into the great hall and stopped dead in her tracks.

Her sister cleared her throat. "Hello, Ravenna."

"Oh, bloody hell."

The driver finally found his voice. "My apologies, Lady Walsingham."

Ravenna paled, and Fagan permitted himself a withering stare.

❦

"What are you doing here?" asked Ravenna as she approached the table. "Has something happened? Elizabeth and Kat?"

Grace studied her from head to toe. "You're not with child."

Ravenna found herself clenching her teeth. "I told you before and you did not listen. Are Elizabeth and Kat all right? What are you doing here?" she repeated in a tone that demanded an answer.

"Hello to you too, Sister." When Ravenna's eyes narrowed, Grace waved her off. "Yes, yes, Elizabeth and Kat are fine. You were supposed to meet me in Edinburgh, remember?"

A hand came down firmly on Ravenna's shoulder. For a moment, she was afraid to look. She knew who that grip belonged to. What could she possibly say to the man now? She soon realized it didn't matter because he spoke before she had the chance.

"Lady Walsingham, would ye like to speak to your sister first or to me?" asked Fagan.

Ravenna flinched at the tone of his voice. When she turned to look at him, the first thing she noticed was that his eyes had darkened like a summer storm. If she'd suddenly been struck by a bolt of lightning, she wouldn't have been surprised. A warning voice whispered in her head, and she knew that she needed to handle the situation delicately.

"Fagan, would you mind if I spoke to Grace alone?" She didn't bother to give him a smile because he just might decide to run her through with his steely gaze. "Please, I promise then I will explain everything. You have my word."

He stood there, tall and most definitely angry. "Use Ruairi's study because after ye're done with your sister, we will most definitely have words."

She nodded. "Follow me, Grace."

For once in Grace's life, her mouth was shut as Ravenna led her sister through the hall to Ruairi's study. Too bad the damage was already done. As soon as the door closed, Grace whirled around, her eyes ablaze.

"Where the hell have you been? I've been worried sick. We received your letter that you'd meet me in Edinburgh and then not a single word from you."

"The laird's son had an accident. You shouldn't have come."

Grace walked casually around the study. "The girls are staying with Uncle Walter. I told George I was coming here with or without him. He made a wise choice by bringing me to you." Awkwardly, she cleared her throat. "If you are not with child, then I can only presume Uncle Walter has spent the last of our coin. What I cannot understand is why you would travel here to the Highlands, of all places, to work."

"Uncle Walter has not spent our coin. We have more than enough. Why can't you ever listen to me?" she asked in exasperation.

"Because nothing that comes from your mouth is ever the truth. How many times have you disappeared until the early hours of the morn and offered me a lame excuse as to where you have been? I even caught you, Ravenna, dressed as some kind of harlot. For God's sake, have you no respect for yourself?"

Praying for patience, Ravenna shook her head. "Grace…"

"I really grow tired of you playing the martyr all the time." Grace sat down in a chair and fingered her skirts in a nervous gesture. "I received a marriage proposal from Lord Casterbrook. Uncle Walter refuses to give his answer until he speaks with you. You don't have to do this anymore. Come home. I will marry Lord Casterbrook and he will provide for us. I will make it so. When will you see that I'm no longer a child? You don't need to coddle me like you're my mother. Let me help you and our sisters. You don't have to carry the burden alone. We are family."

Ravenna sat down in the chair beside Grace and sighed. "You don't need to remind me of how old you are," she said in a solemn tone. "You're right. You are practically a grown woman. It's time I treated you as one. Please understand that every choice I made, I made for our family so we could stay together. Our mother and father were taken from us far too soon, and yes, it's now time that you know the truth."

Grace's expression was bleak. "What are you talking about? You're speaking in riddles."

Faltering in the silence that engulfed them, Ravenna felt sourness in the pit of her stomach. She wasn't ready to do this. She had never wanted her sister involved. The less Grace knew, the better for everyone. But now Ravenna had no choice in the matter and that irked her.

She settled back, disappointed she was about to have this particular conversation. Added to her disappointment was a feeling of guilt for having deceived her sister, her family, her own blood. "I wish I could protect and shield you from what I'm about to say, because once you know, there is no turning back time. My words will be difficult for you to understand, but please hear me out."

"All right, but you're behaving as though you've robbed someone," said Grace with concern. "Whatever this is about, I'm ready to hear the truth. I've been ready. I believe it's long past due."

"I'm a spy for the Crown."

Grace's jaw dropped. "I can see it in your eyes. You're not jesting."

"No."

There was a heavy moment of silence, and Ravenna knew her sister was torn by conflicting emotions. Welcoming the confusion her confession had caused,

Ravenna took a moment to gather her thoughts. She couldn't imagine what her sister must be feeling. A wave of apprehension swept through Ravenna and gnawed at her confidence, especially when she noticed the troubled look on Grace's face. Her sister was always quick to speak her mind, and Ravenna couldn't help but notice that her sister had yet to speak a single word. When Grace finally spoke again, her tone was far from pleasant.

"We're family. How could you not tell me? How could you keep this secret from us?" She crossed her arms and pointedly looked away. When Ravenna didn't answer, Grace's voice became quiet and held an undertone of cold contempt. "All this time…What do you think Father and Mother would say? What about Uncle Walter? He is supposed to be our protector." Grace turned as Ravenna lifted her brow and gave her sister a knowing look. "Dear God, they know."

Ravenna nodded. "Father was a spy for Queen Elizabeth, and Uncle Walter has always worked for the Crown."

"And you never thought this was important enough to mention before?"

"The less you knew— anyone knew—the better for everyone involved."

Grace stood and a suggestion of annoyance hovered in her eyes. Her accusing gaze was riveted on Ravenna. She thought Grace might have even snarled at her. "This whole time I've been concerned about you, thinking you're selling yourself, and it turns out you're a bloody spy." Grace frowned.

"You're doing goodness knows what, making our

world a better place, while all I've been worried about is having the perfect gown and looking my best to find a husband. I've spent weeks asking myself: What if no one offers for my hand? What if I grow old and become a spinster like Ravenna? Now I find myself willing to give about anything just to be you. I can't imagine the political intrigue, the excitement and adventures you must have."

The conversation had taken such a dramatic turn that an alarm sounded in Ravenna's mind. She held up her hand to stay her sister's wild misconceptions before the situation was even further out of control. "Wait a moment. You need to understand that what I do is very dangerous and is not to be taken lightly. This is no life for anyone. There are many sacrifices that I've made and still continue to make, all for the sake of Crown and country."

Grace knelt before Ravenna and took her hand. "You must teach me. You must talk to whomever you need to talk to. I want to do this. I want to serve His Majesty. Give me a purpose. Please."

Ravenna shook her head, shocked. "You have no idea what you're asking. My answer is no. Father wanted nothing but the best for us. He wanted you and the girls to have an ordinary life. I will not allow you to throw yours away. If you want to wed Lord Casterbrook, marry him and start a family of your own. Working for the Crown is a lonely, solitary life. No matter what, you always end up hurting good people that you had never meant to hurt."

"My life is not for you to decide. You are not my mother or father."

Ravenna stood. "No, I'm not. Nevertheless, I am the only one who knows what's best for you, Grace. Perhaps you've forgotten, but your little trip to the Highlands has placed me in a very dangerous situation. The clan knows me as Mistress Denny, governess to Laird Sutherland's son. I am no English lady, especially not Lady Ravenna Walsingham."

"Oh, my God. What have I done? What are we going to do? Why were you sent here to be a governess? Are you spying on that laird?"

"Ruairi is a good and honorable man."

Her sister's eyes widened and she stood. "Ruairi? You call the laird by his Christian name? His captain is right. They certainly do things differently in the Highlands. God help us, Ravenna. That Murray man heard George and me call you Lady Ravenna Walsingham. I'm so sorry. What are we going to do?"

"*You* aren't going to do anything. I don't want you involved in this. Do you hear me?"

"I understand, but you're going to have to tell him something he'd truly believe since you certainly can't say, 'Although I was sent here by His Majesty to be a governess to Laird Sutherland's son, Mistress Denny is not my name. My true name is actually Lady Ravenna Walsingham and I'm a spy for the Crown.' What do you think he'd accept as true?"

The door swung open and Fagan stood there perfectly still. He looked as though he could've killed them both. "Donna worry upon it because I will only accept the truth, and I just heard it."

Seeing that Fagan's face was contorted with shock and anger, Grace moved without hesitation, placing herself between him and Ravenna. Grace lifted her fingers to his chest, and her hand looked small against his massive frame. "I don't know what you're thinking, but you stay away from my sister."

His eyes never left Ravenna's. "And which sister would that be? Mistress Denny or Lady Walsingham?"

"Grace, leave him be."

Ignoring Ravenna, Grace stood her ground and refused to budge. "You know very well they are one and the same." She nodded her head toward Ravenna. "Gather your things and we will leave." When Fagan took a step forward, Grace renewed her hand on his chest. "You'll have to get past first," she warned.

A muscle ticked in his jaw. "That will nae be a problem." He grabbed Grace by her arms, lifted her from her feet, and moved her to the side.

"Unhand me at once, you big brute!" When he released her, she kicked him in the shin with her boot. The man didn't even flinch.

"Grace, enough!"

When Fagan moved farther into the study, Grace hastily pulled on his arm. "I'm warning you, Highlander, take a step closer to my sister and it will be your last," she said firmly.

Fagan paused and looked down at Grace's restraining grip. "And if ye know what's good for ye, ye'd remove your hand from my arm." His angry gaze swung over her, and she swallowed hard, lifted her chin, and boldly met his eyes.

"Grace, please stop this."

"I'm not afraid of you," spat Grace. "I don't care

if you're the bloody laird himself. You're not getting any closer to my sister or touching a single hair on her head. Do you hear me?"

Fagan shook off Grace's arm and advanced another step. That's when Ravenna should've known her sister would do something stupid. Grace moved between them and hastily reached down, pulling her dagger from under her skirts.

"I warned you, Highlander."

Ravenna grabbed Grace's arm. "Put down your blade. He will not harm me."

"Ye should listen to your sister before I reach out and strangle ye with my bare hands," Fagan growled through clenched teeth.

To Ravenna's dismay, her sister only renewed the grip on the dagger. "Now there you go again making threats, Mister Murray. How can I ever trust your word?"

Fagan's eyes darkened.

"Grace, this is not a game. You are only making matters worse. Listen to me. Put down the dagger!"

Fagan struck Grace's arm and the blade dropped to the floor. Without warning, Grace pulled back her arm and rammed her fisted hand into his face.

They all froze in stunned silence.

If Fagan's looks could kill, her sister would already be dead. A soft gasp escaped Grace, and Ravenna took a quick breath in utter astonishment. At first, she was too startled by her sister's actions to offer any words. When she was finally able to find her voice and lift her fallen jaw, she mumbled hastily, "Grace, give us a few moments alone, and if I were you, I'd move fast."

Grace bristled. "I'm not leaving you alone with him. He was ready to kill you only a moment ago."

Fagan's breathing was labored, and he raised his hand to touch his eye. "Lass, if I wanted to kill either of ye, ye'd already be dead. At this moment, I think *ye* have more to worry about than your sister. I'd heed your sister's advice before 'tis too late."

Grace placed her hand to her throat. "Don't be cross with me. You're the one who refused to listen."

"Grace! Get out!" Ravenna gestured toward the door.

"All right, all right, but I'm not leaving you alone with him. I'll be standing outside the door."

Ravenna shook her head, and Fagan's eyes narrowed. "What should I call ye? Mistress Denny or Lady Walsingham?"

"Why don't we start by you calling me Ravenna."

Twenty-one

GRACE HAD INSISTED THEY TAKE THEIR LEAVE, BUT Ravenna was no coward. She refused to take the easy way out. She owed Ruairi the truth and didn't want him to hear it from the captain of his guard. She could at least give him that much. Fagan had placed Grace in Ravenna's chamber so that her sister could pack Ravenna's trunk. She also thought Fagan's actions were to keep from him throttling Grace, something Ravenna had no trouble understanding.

Ravenna opened the door to Torquil's chamber. The boy slept, and Ruairi looked up from the chair. "May I speak with you a moment?" When he hesitated, Fagan stepped around her and walked into the room.

"I'll stay with him."

"What happened to your eye?"

Fagan shrugged, and Ravenna didn't miss the look he shot her before he quickly turned back to Ruairi. She was surprised the man didn't run her through where she stood.

As Ravenna led Ruairi to his study, she gazed at his

face slowly, feature by feature. She wanted to remember him like he was now, at this very moment, before he despised her. When she saw the heart-rending tenderness of his gaze, an inner torment began to gnaw at her and a suffocating feeling tightened her throat.

When the door closed, the pit of her stomach churned. Her voice broke miserably. "I know you're weary."

"Is everything all right? What is amiss?"

She was filled with a sense of foreboding, but she knew this needed to be done. She straightened her spine and gestured him to a chair.

"Lass, the last thing I want to do is sit right now."

"My apologies, I wasn't thinking."

"Why donna ye tell me what this is about?"

Ravenna wished the man would've sat or at least put his rump on the edge of the desk. When he stood, he was so tall and overpowering. She took a deep breath and forced herself to look him in the eye.

"Ruairi, there's something I need to tell you, but first, I have to say something more than likely I shouldn't." He was about to speak, but she held up her hand to stay him. "Please, you must let me finish or I won't have the courage."

"I will admit ye have my curiosity."

"I know I do not give you any reason to believe me or my words, but before I say what I must, you will have the truth."

He placed his hands on her shoulders in a possessive gesture, and she wished he wouldn't hold her so close. "Ravenna, ye know ye can tell me anything. What troubles ye?"

"I never wanted to come here. Like everyone else

in England, I've heard tales of the wild Highland lairds. I knew you did things differently here, but you, my laird, were definitely not what I'd expected to encounter. I've been in this position many times before, and I've never allowed myself to get too close to those I've been sent to...er, assist. Torquil is such a delightful young man and it was never my intention to hurt him."

He lifted a brow. "I'm nae sure what ye're trying to say."

She briefly turned away from him to gather her thoughts. She continued to speak in a solemn tone. "I know it's not possible for us to be together, but you must believe me. I love you, Ruairi. I'm not exactly sure how and when it happened, but I love you with all my heart. The last thing I ever wanted to do wa—"

He spun her around and pressed her open lips to his. Ravenna's thoughts spun, her emotions whirled and plunged, as blood pounded in her brain, leaped from her heart, and made her knees tremble. It was divine ecstasy when he kissed her. She reached up to feel the muscles of his chest beneath her fingertips. When something clicked in her mind, she pulled back, lowering her head to his chest.

Ruairi held her.

"Ye have just made me the happiest man in the world, lass."

She lifted her head and gazed at him with despair. The pain in her heart had become a sick and fiery gnawing. She couldn't do this any longer. Tears blinded her eyes and choked her voice. "I'm a spy for the Crown."

For a moment, he merely stood there and looked at her. When she heard his quick intake of breath, she actually trembled. To her surprise, he showed no other reaction, and then there was a slight hesitation in his hawk-like eyes. A war of emotions raged through her and she could see the torment that raged within him, too. The news of her blunt confession was met with an expression of incredulity. Ruairi turned and stepped away from her.

She reached out to touch him and then decided against it. "Please say something."

When he finally faced her, he was not the same man she had known. She felt an acute sense of loss, and her throat ached with defeat. His expression was grim as he watched her. She did not miss his flare of temper and sudden curses, and then he shook her into gasping silence.

"Why? Why in the hell would ye do this to me and to Torquil? All because I didnae pay homage to my liege at the English court?" His voice was heavy with sarcasm. "Ye came into my home, lectured my son…shared my bed. Everything ye've done and said is a lie."

"It's not all a lie," she said with a hint of desperation. "Please understand. I have to do what I'm told. I don't have a choice. I didn't even know you." She paused. "I didn't… I *won't* tell the king anything as I'd promised."

He smirked. "I know naught about lasses, but there is one thing of which I am certain. Ye are made from the same cloth as my wife and her sister."

Ravenna's sense of loss was beyond tears. "I cannot apologize for who I am. I meant my words, although I can see there is no use repeating them. My family was all that ever mattered to me, and whether you believe me or not, that was true until I met you and yours."

"Why do ye tell me this now?"

She looked him in the eye. "I was so worried about Torquil that I forgot to send another letter home and did not meet my sister in Edinburgh as we'd planned. My sister traveled here because she was concerned about me. Fagan found out, and I insisted on being the one to tell you."

"How verra convenient and kind of ye, Mistress Denny. Is that even your name?"

She bit her lip. "My name is Ravenna."

He shook his head in disgust. "I assume ye know how to find your way back to England."

She closed the distance between them. When she lifted her hand to his cheek, he did not move. "There will not be a day that goes by that I don't think of you. I wished, prayed, that things could end differently between us. I will always remember our time together, and you and Torquil will always hold a special place in my heart. I give you no reason to believe me, but I speak the truth. I do love you, Laird Ruairi Sutherland."

"*Leig cead dhìot, a ghràidh,*" he spat. *Enough of you, my love.*

Ravenna was about to ask him the meaning of his words, but then she lowered her hand, deciding against it. By the tone of his voice, she knew the answer would not be a pleasant one. "I think it best if I take my leave now. May I say a proper farewell to Torquil?"

"Only for the sake of my son. Nae for ye. Do ye understand? *Nae* for ye."

Ravenna nodded and closed the door, leaving behind the only man she'd ever truly loved.

∽

Ruairi escaped to the parapet. He needed air because he found that he couldn't be within arm's reach of that English spy any longer. He'd had more than enough. He was furious. He felt murderous, and if he was being truthful with himself, he was heartbroken.

Although the woman was nothing but a conniving English wench sent to spy on him in his home, he'd openly expressed his love for her. He smirked at the thought. Love was an emotion that meant nothing to her. The way he felt at the moment, she might as well have ripped his beating heart from his chest and fed it to Angus on a platter.

Ravenna, if that was even her real name, had played him for a fool. Who was he kidding? He was a fool, and that's what disturbed him the most. He could now admit that he knew absolutely nothing about women, for they were as merciless as any army he'd ever faced on the battlefield, even worse because they left no prisoners in their wake.

Ruairi leaned back against the cool stone wall. Anna, Cotrìona, and Ravenna—how he wished he'd never known of their existence. Three women in his life with whom he'd felt the bitter sting of betrayal. At least the first two were Scots, but the last woman was Ruairi's own mistake, an Englishwoman.

He'd let the enemy get too close.

When he heard a loud commotion in the bailey, he looked over the wall. Ravenna's trunk was secured and he saw a flash of a skirt climb into the carriage. Let them leave and report back to the king how uncivilized he was. He didn't see any of the Highland lairds sending their women to spy on the English—although perhaps they should. And the English had the audacity to say Highlanders were barbarians!

Ruairi watched the carriage as it traveled through the gates, taking with it another woman who had trampled his heart.

❧

Ruairi hadn't slept at all. His last memory of Ravenna was from two days earlier, when she had walked out of his study, rode through the gates, and left his life without as much as a backward glance. Praise the saints for small favors. By now, she was traveling back to her beloved country, proud that she had played him for a fool. He rose from bed and hastily dressed, knowing that he needed to occupy his thoughts with something other than the woman who had betrayed him. He opened the door to Torquil's chamber as his son rolled over on the bed.

"Da, ye leave?"

"Aye. The healer will be coming shortly. I take my leave to make rounds with Fagan. Go back to sleep."

Ruairi quietly closed the door behind him. He walked out into the bailey and the sun had already started to rise. The crisp morning air was just what he needed. A few men readied the horses, and Fagan shook his head when he spotted Ruairi.

"Ye're riding along again, my laird? I assure ye the men know what to do."

"Good. Then they will nae mind if I come. I want to see the look on the Gordon's face when he decides to raise arms against us, only to find our men ready and waiting. He thinks he's clever, but he isnae. It has taken some time to learn, but I know how the arse thinks."

For a moment, Ruairi was silent.

"Ye look troubled. Is something else on your mind?" asked Fagan.

"I've been remiss not to mention… Ye should know something I didnae tell ye before. I made a grave error in judgment. Ravenna knew of the Gordon's plans on Orkney."

Fagan shifted from foot to foot. "Damn, Ruairi."

"Aye."

"Do ye think she'll send word to the Crown?"

"It doesnae matter. My bollocks are nay longer my own. The lass knew I purposefully disobeyed an order from the king, and she knows perfectly well how I feel about the bastard."

Once again, Fagan held an inscrutable expression on his face. "Mmm…be that as it may, I saw the way Ravenna looked at ye. I would be surprised if the lass said as much to the king. She's a smart woman. She'd know her words would seal your fate."

Ruairi gave Fagan a subtle warning glance.

"Och, Ruairi. If it makes ye feel any better, ye can tell me all ye want that her English blood doesnae fire yours. But I saw the way ye looked at her as well. Ye ne'er looked at your wife that way, even when ye were wed and she was alive." His friend shook his head as if he'd realized what he'd said.

"Mount up and cease your tongue."

"Why? Because I speak the truth?"

Ruairi paid no heed to Fagan and his prodding as they rode in glorious silence. Until of course Fagan found it necessary to broach the subject again. "I must know… What do you think of her? I will have the truth."

"Donna be daft. Ye know what I think of her. 'Tis why she took her leave." Ruairi wasn't about to point out that he'd been deceived again by yet another woman. He'd never hear the end of it.

"Ye must admit, ye donna make the best decisions when it comes to the lasses, Ruairi."

"Thalla gu taigh na galla." Go to hell. "Hand me a drink and shut your mouth."

As Ruairi stood at the border with a handful of his men, the sound of leaves rustled in the wind. His land was beautiful with its lush foliage, rock cliffs, and mossy green grass. For a brief moment, he thought about never being able to share this view again with Ravenna, and then he turned and looked at Fagan for a much-needed distraction.

"Ye're supposed to be a strong warrior. I cannae believe ye were bested by a lass, an English lass nonetheless." Ruairi shook his head in disgust. "The captain of my own guard. I must say that your eye is verra colorful and quite becoming on ye."

Fagan's eyes narrowed. "Just because ye're angry at Ravenna doesnae give ye leave to jest at my expense." He paused. "I told ye before. Ravenna's sister caught me unaware."

"I should say."

"Àrdanach, aineolach, mòr-bhriathrach, beag-chiallach,

gann-rianach…" Arrogant, ignorant, big of speech, small of sense, scant of reason.

Ruairi lifted a brow. "Are ye through?"

Fagan looked up at the sky and let out a heavy sigh. "I suppose, but I donna want to hear another damn word about the color of my eye or how I was bested by a lass. How long do ye think the Gordon will wait until—"

His captain didn't need to finish his words because the sound of thundering hoofbeats came over the mountain pass as riders charged toward them at break-neck speed. Swords were drawn at the ready, while battle cries were carried by the wind. Ruairi spotted a flag with a lone stag head and knew the moment was upon them. The forthcoming battle was long past due.

There would be no more mercy. The time had come to stand and fight. Ruairi loved his country and would do anything to keep tyranny out, even if that meant cleaning up Scotland from within its own ranks. He shouted orders at one of his men to summon the waiting guard, and the man whipped his mount around and rode like the hounds of hell nipped at his heels. From the looks of things, there were at least a hundred Gordon men.

After a brief moment, eighty of Ruairi's finest men emerged on horseback from the forest behind him, ready for their laird's command. Ruairi and Fagan unsheathed their swords, their mounts prancing beneath them. Fagan lifted his blade to his forehead and gave Ruairi a mock salute.

"Always by your side, my laird. 'Tis my great pleasure to send Gordon men to their maker. The helmet of health about your head. The corslet of the covenant about your shoulders. The breastplate of the priest about your breast to protect ye in battle and the combat with your enemies."

"Neart teine dhut. Gliocas fithich dhut." The might of fire to you. Wisdom of raven be yours.

As a sea of men flowed toward them, Ruairi and Fagan held back their mounts. Ruairi would give the command when he was ready. He wasn't about to rush into battle foolishly, especially with the Gordon. The man had no honor and could not be trusted. Ruairi wouldn't put it past the bastard to do something completely shifty and deceitful.

When the Gordon's men were within range, Ruairi waved his archers forward and they showered the heads of his enemy with arrows. A few Gordons fell from their mounts and others continued to ride with arrows lodged in their bodies. The Gordon's army was then greeted by a wall of well-armed Sutherland men who were able to barricade the border. No man who wished to live would ever make it to the castle alive. Ruairi's instincts were usually right, and he was glad he had trusted them this time. He had kept his men on alert, only waiting for the time when their enemy would arrive.

The sound of metal against metal rang through the air. Men fell and blood was drawn, cries of death and despair spreading in the wind. Ruairi and Fagan dismounted and stood shoulder to shoulder with their men in battle, quickly removing a few choice Gordon men from the battlefield. Two men charged Ruairi, and Fagan brought one to his knees with a slice to the gut. Ruairi deflected a blow and, with a twist of his wrist, disarmed the man. Within seconds, the man was no longer of this world.

Only a few moments passed, and if Ruairi hadn't seen it with his own eyes, he would never have believed it. The Gordon stood to the side, watching. When Sutherland men hastily sent his guards to meet their maker faster than the Gordon would've liked, the man mounted his horse. How appropriate that the bastard would try to save his own arse and leave his men behind. When he spotted Ruairi, the Gordon's eyes narrowed and he gave him a mock salute. He turned his mount away from the battle and Ruairi called after him.

"Chan eil ach dearg amadan!" You're a bloody fool!

The Gordon looked over his shoulder as Ruairi leaped on his mount. Ruairi hefted his weapon in the air and thundered after his father-in-law as the man's eyes widened and he paled.

A horse moved in front of Ruairi's path.

"Cotrìona!" shouted the Gordon.

"What the hell do ye think ye're doing?" she asked Ruairi. Her eyes conveyed the fury within her as she held her mount firmly in place.

Ruairi dismounted and approached her with long, purposeful strides. He reached out, firmly grabbed her arm, and pulled her from her mount. "Return home at once! This is nay place for a woman." His steely tone gave her no room for debate.

She shook off his arm. "How dare ye try and kill my father!" Her expression was thunderous.

"Ye've nay reason to fear." Ruairi pointed to the

Gordon. "He runs like a bloody coward with my guard fast on his heels."

Before he knew what she was about, Cotrìona leaped on her mount and gave chase to the Sutherland guard. Ruairi grabbed the mane of his horse and swung his leg up over his mount. As he charged after her, he heard Fagan calling him from a distance.

"Cotrìona! Cotrìona, stop!" As if Ruairi's words fell on deaf ears, she continued to urge her mount faster to come to her father's aid.

"Father!"

Two of Ruairi's guards were able to cut off the retreating Gordon and two of his men. While Ruairi's guard currently occupied those men in battle, the Gordon dismounted and tried to inch away from all the thrusts and parries.

Cotrìona still proceeded hard and fast. Ruairi needed to reach her, stop her. No matter what his feelings were toward her, he would never place a lass in harm's way—ever. Even if his sister-in-law was spawned from the devil, she was still his wife's sister.

She reached the men before Ruairi and jumped from her mount with purpose. One of the Sutherland guards shifted his stance and managed to slice the Gordon's arm with the blade. In an effort to shield her father, Cotrìona threw herself against the front of Ruairi's man. At the same time, Ruairi hefted his broadsword to ward off a forceful blow, but the guard quickly fell to the ground when Ruairi sliced his neck.

The Sutherland guard shoved Cotrìona away from him. As if everything moved in slow motion, she fell into her father and gasped suddenly. She looked down, and her eyes widened.

She was impaled on her sire's sword.

Without words, the Gordon pulled out his blade and Cotrìona slid to the ground. Ruairi fell to his knees beside her and rolled her over into his arms. Cotrìona watched as her father backed away slowly, retreating.

"My apologies, Daughter, but ye fell into my blade. I told ye before. I donna need ye to save me. I am a Gordon."

"Mo mhallachd ort," said Ruairi through clenched teeth. *My curse on you.*

"Father..." She reached out her arms but the Gordon turned his back on her, sheathing his sword. Tears welled in her eyes and slowly found their way down her cheeks. She loved her father with a wide open heart, and when she realized her sire had taken his leave, Ruairi almost took pity upon her. The bastard had abandoned his daughter to die in the arms of his enemy.

Ruairi placed his hand over his sister-in-law's wound, and his fingers pooled with her lifeblood. She gasped for air, her breathing shallow. "'Tis all right, Cotrìona. I'm here with ye."

"Why?" she asked in a hushed tone.

"Because ye're Torquil's aunt."

She lifted her hand to his cheek. Her eyes closed and Ruairi heard her take her last breath. He gently lowered Cotrìona to the ground and stood. Only a few Gordon men were left standing, and they were quickly bested by Ruairi's men. His land looked like a river of blood. It was a far cry from the mossy green grass and fresh air he had reveled in only a short time ago. Now there was nothing but the stench of death.

He turned to one of his men. "Please see to Lady Gordon. We will take her back with us."

"Aye, my laird."

Fagan studied his sword as he turned it from side to side. "What say ye? Should we have a wee bit of sport with your father-by-marriage, then?"

Ruairi's eyes darkened. "He was ne'er my father."

When Ruairi had watched the Gordon take his leave from his dying daughter, his temper had became almost uncontrollable. He was so furious he could've struck down the man where he stood. But deep within his soul, he knew he could never let his sister-in-law die alone.

Shaking his head when the obvious was confirmed, Ruairi smirked. The Gordon was a daft fool. His heedless actions had set the Sutherland clan on a mission, given them a single purpose, and they would not stop until they caught the bastard.

Ruairi, Fagan, and a few of his men rode hard after the Gordon. When Ruairi spotted the man fleeing for his life in the field below, he pushed his mount faster and thundered after his enemy. At least the Gordon didn't get very far. That revelation came as no surprise since he was undoubtedly trying to crawl back under the rock from which he'd come. The man had the audacity to abandon his men and his dying daughter. The force of Ruairi's anger was so strong that only one thought came to mind.

The Gordon would die. He would accept nothing less. Ruairi charged across the open field, and when he was finally able to rein in his mount next to his enemy, blood pounded in his ears. His breathing was labored and his nostrils flared with fury.

"Gordon!"

The man glowered at him, and then he tried to turn his mount away from Ruairi in a cowardly gesture. Ruairi was tired of games. He was more than ready to bring this to an end, something he should have done a long time ago. He released the reins and leaped from his horse, tackling the Gordon to the ground with a heavy thump.

The Gordon stood and fumbled for his sword.

Ruairi held up his hand and stopped his men. Turning to Fagan, he snarled. "Leave the man to me."

Fagan shrugged with indifference. "Aye, well, let me know if ye want me to have a go at him."

The men watched as Ruairi faced the Gordon in a field of heather. A field of thistle would've been a more suitable place for the bastard to meet his demise, but who was Ruairi to choose? Consumed with hatred, Ruairi was about to strike down his enemy once and for all. When the Gordon waved his sword in front of him, Ruairi turned and looked over his shoulder, knowing Fagan would never let Sutherland men interfere.

"My daughter's death was an accident. I would ne'er have caused her harm."

"So was Anna's." Ruairi pulled the sword from his scabbard, and his wrist curved around with blade in hand. "Yet ye left Cotrìona to die and ran like a bloody coward."

The Gordon's expression darkened and his eyes

narrowed. "What do ye care? Ye ne'er cared for Cotrìona, and ye didnae love Anna."

"But I stayed with Cotrìona in her final moments and offered her comfort, while ye abandoned your daughter, your blood, who died by your own hand!"

The Gordon's voice was cold and lashing. "Nay. She died by yours, Sutherland. I should've known ye would ne'er aid me with Stewart. Ye always were a pain in my arse."

"I am nae foolish enough to send my men to be slaughtered. Ye used both your daughters because that suited your purposes. Cotrìona died for *your* cause, a cause that was only to gain Stewart's favor. For God's sake, she was your daughter."

"Aye, and Cotrìona was your sister-by-marriage. Anna was also the mother of your child, my *ogha*." *Grandchild.* "What's your point? I grow tired of your endless words."

Ruairi's eyes blazed with fire. "Nae to worry because I am done talking."

❧

Torquil ran into the great hall like a whirlwind. Ruairi had lost track of how many times he'd told his son to stop and take it slow. He supposed the lad was relieved to escape the confines of his chamber, but his son needed to take it easy. It had only been a fortnight since the healer said Torquil could leave his bed, and he certainly hadn't wasted any time in complying with that command. If only he listened to his father with that much enthusiasm.

A chuckle greeted Ruairi as well as a pat on the

back. Fagan pulled out a chair and sat down beside him. "A lad after my own heart. Naught can keep a Sutherland man down, eh?"

"'Tis good to see Torquil and Angus up and about."

"I have to ask something of ye. Now that your son is well and the Gordon is dead, *dè nì thu?*" *What will you do?*

Ruairi knew perfectly well what his friend meant because everything out of the man's mouth lately was regarding a certain subject that he didn't want to discuss. He didn't appreciate being tortured by Fagan's words.

Ruairi shrugged with indifference. "I donna know. Mayhap ride out to see the Munro."

"Ye know damn well what I mean, Ruairi. What about Ravenna? I know she's been in your thoughts more often than ye care to admit, and ye're perfectly aware how much your son misses her. Nae a day goes by that he doesnae say as much. I know ye love her, and I believe the words she said to ye to be true. She wouldnae tell the king. Remember, *tha am pòsadh coltach ris an t-seillean, tha mil ann 's tha gath ann.*" *Marriage is like a bee—there's honey in it and a sting too.*

"Says the man who has ne'er been wed. I've had far more sting than honey with the lasses, I assure ye."

"Aye, but mayhap 'tis because ye've ne'er found the right woman. Did ye ever think 'tis finally time for ye and Torquil to have kin again? And that particular lass, although she was English, was verra fond of ye. I am sure of it."

Ruairi held up his hands. "I donna want to talk about Ravenna."

God knew he didn't want to talk about the lass

because he couldn't stop thinking about her. When she left, he'd felt an extraordinary void. Once the anger finally subsided and he was able to clear the cobwebs, he was able to recognize an emptiness within him that he couldn't quite explain.

The feeling made no sense.

Ravenna was an English spy. He knew that, but a little voice inside his head kept reminding him that the lass had been sent to his home to betray him before she'd ever met him. The more Ruairi thought about it, the more the idea drove him mad.

He didn't think he had imagined Ravenna's happiness with him, but the admission was dredged from a place beyond logic and reason. Although she'd managed to place a dagger through his heart, he wanted to believe with every fiber of his being that their time together had meant something. He'd lost count of the number of times he'd pondered Ravenna's words, remembering the way she'd said them, the way she looked, the way her eyes met his. She'd said she loved him. Was that true? He wasn't sure what to believe.

There was a heavy silence.

"I want everything back the way it was, except for the Gordon and Cotrìona's machinations. The harsh weather will soon be upon us. At least there will be nay more slaughtering of our animals and our people will be fed. I can now sleep at night knowing my coin isnae being stolen under my own roof. Our clan and the Munro's are both safe for now. But I donna like the way the English keep coming farther and farther into the Highlands. 'Tis inevitable that they will continue to take what isnae theirs, but until then, I want to keep the peace for as long as possible. Mayhap I should attend court and take Torquil to the Lowlands next year. 'Tis my hope that if King James notices our attendance, mayhap he'll leave us the hell alone."

Fagan's eyes grew openly amused. "Or mayhap if ye donna attend court or send Torquil to the Lowlands, the king might send a certain bonny governess to your door again."

"Sometimes I donna like ye."

"And sometimes I'm the only one who knows what's best for ye."

Twenty-two

UNCLE WALTER SAT IN THE CHAIR IN HER FATHER'S study and tapped his finger on the top of the desk. He leaned forward, studying Ravenna intently. He showed no signs of relenting anytime soon. She knew he waited for her response, but truth be told, his incessant prodding was grating on her nerves.

"I'm not ready."

"So you've said for the past six months. I think I have a fairly good idea what happened in Scotland. Grace is really concerned about you, as am I. She said you've been sleeping with that…er, blanket every night. I told you not to get involved. You knew better than that, and yet you continue to pine for that…*Highlander.*"

"I wish you wouldn't say it like that. The man has a name," she said in a chiding tone. "And that blanket is called a plaid."

"Be that as it may, you've been through this many times before. I don't understand what made this man so different."

"Because he *was* different." There was a softness in her voice as she remembered every detail of Ruairi's face. "He was…*is* nothing like we thought him to be. He's a proud and honorable man, even more so than some of the English lords we know."

Uncle Walter sighed. "So what Grace tells me is true, then. You love him."

She detected a hint of censure in his tone, and her annoyance increased when she found that her hands were shaking. "What exactly do you want to hear, Uncle Walter? That I was a fool? It doesn't matter what I feel or don't feel. The assignment is over, done. There's nothing else to discuss."

"Ravenna…" His tone held warmth and concern. "You know your father and I were good friends before he fell in love with your mother, my dear sister. The life you choose to lead is a solitary one, but your father never thought he'd wed, either. When he met your mother, the rest was history. You don't choose who to love, my dear niece. Love finds you and, yes, sometimes even in the oddest of places like the Scottish Highlands."

She propped her elbow on the desk and leaned her forehead in the palm of her hand. "You didn't see the way he looked at me. I'll never forget the expression on his face. He looked at me the same way he looked at his sister-in-law, and believe me, that was far from pleasant."

He chuckled. "I remember the look on my sister's face when she found out that not only did your father work for the Crown but her own brother did, as well."

"This is an entirely different matter, and you can't compare the two. You and my father did many things for the Crown, working on the same side. I was under Ruairi's roof as the enemy. He felt betrayed."

"You need to come to court. King James is very pleased with your efforts, and I'm proud of you. It's not every day that the king boasts to me that my niece was solely responsible for stopping an uprising on Orkney. Setons were captured and Stewart was imprisoned, all thanks to you. I'm sure it will only be a matter of time before Laird Gordon is brought to justice as well."

When Ravenna didn't respond, he added, "Word has spread of Lord Casterbrook and Grace's betrothal." He stood. "You know how much Grace wants to attend court. She should go. Elizabeth and Katherine will stay with us, and I'll send a carriage for you on the morrow." He walked around the desk and placed his hand on her shoulder. "You need to leave the manor house on occasion. This will be good for both you and Grace."

She reluctantly nodded.

❧

He hated the London court almost as much as he hated the Gordon. There were so many warm bodies in the same space that Ruairi pulled at his restricting doublet, trying to get a fresh breath of air. The women wore fanciful gowns and the English men looked much the same—well, that wasn't entirely true. The men wore breeches, and he shifted his bollocks underneath his kilt just thinking about it. He knew their proper English clothing was as restricting as their openly haughty attitude toward the Scots.

"I see the look on your face, and donna whine to me. Remember ye're the one who insisted we come to court," said Fagan.

Ruairi smirked. "Only because ye wouldnae leave me the hell alone. Ye're like an incessant female. And aye, I wanted to come, but I donna have to like it."

"Do ye think Ian will be able to find him? 'Tis been three days already, and he's had nay luck."

"'Tis my hope that he finds him verra quickly because I donna know how much longer I will be able to survive this."

A hand slid up Ruairi's arm and he turned. "Would you like some company this eve?" The woman's low-cut bodice left little to the imagination, and her wild blond locks were tossed carelessly around her shoulders. She pressed her breasts into his chest and looked as though she'd been bedded many times before. Her breath reeked of ale and something else he couldn't quite discern.

"Nay." He gently pushed her away.

The woman didn't even have enough wit to be offended before she immediately set her sights on another target. "And what about you, handsome?"

Fagan shook his head and wrinkled his nose. "I donna speak English."

She tapped her finger on his chest. "Now that's just too bad, but we really don't need to speak at all."

Fagan waved her off and shivered from head to toe as the woman slithered away. "Perhaps she left to crawl back under the rock from which she came. I have a sudden urge to bathe."

"Ruairi, *thig an seo*." *Come here.*

He looked over his shoulder to see Ian gesturing them over.

"It wasnae as simple as I thought it would be, but I finally found him. *Tha e leis-fhèin*." *He was alone.*

For a moment, Ruairi hesitated, wanting to make certain he knew exactly what he wanted to do. When he paused a little too long for Fagan, his friend didn't hesitate to give his opinion.

"Why are ye still standing here? Please make haste. *Tha mi ag iarraigh dol dhachaigh*." *I want to go home.*

"Where is he?"

Ian pointed at the dark-haired man who stood by the open door to the garden. At least Ruairi wasn't the only one who was miserable in this heat. Now was the perfect opportunity to speak with the man. If he didn't do it now, he wasn't sure when he'd get another chance. He wasn't exactly thrilled to get involved with the English, especially since he'd spent his life trying to avoid them, but he knew Fagan and Ian would remain close at hand if he needed them.

Ruairi approached the man, meeting his gaze. "Pardon me, but are ye Lord Mildmay?"

"Yes," the man answered hesitantly.

"I've come a verra long way to find ye."

"Me? Whatever for?" The man looked around and shifted his weight as he leaned against the door.

"Ye used to have a governess in your service, Mist—"

"I'm sorry, but I believe you're mistaken, my good man. You see, I've never had a governess and all my children are grown."

Ruairi was momentarily speechless. Ian had sworn he'd seen Ravenna at court with Lord Mildmay, and when his friend had confronted her in the great hall, she'd claimed to be this man's governess. A cynical inner voice cut through Ruairi's thoughts.

What if she was his lover?

Ruairi needed to think fast. He didn't want to say Ravenna's name for fear he'd place her in harm's way and because he wasn't sure of the extent of her involvement with this man. He certainly didn't want to compromise anything she'd already done. Furthermore, the last thing he wanted was to become an enemy of the Crown because he'd opened his mouth and said something stupid. Ruairi's uncertainty seemed to amuse the English lord, but at the same time a warning voice whispered in Ruairi's head that he should not question the Englishman further.

"My apologies for wasting your time." Ruairi turned and cursed under his breath. How could he have thought that finding Lady Ravenna Walsingham would be easy? Nothing in his life ever was. He should've known the English wouldn't give any information freely, especially to a Scot. Since no one would tell him where he could find Ravenna, this English bastard was Ruairi's last hope. And he failed again. He was starting to walk away when the man spoke.

"Do you love her, Laird Sutherland?"

Ruairi froze.

He turned and walked back with long, purposeful strides. "What did ye say?"

"You heard me. I asked if you love her."

"*Who*? And how do ye know who I am?"

"You were very careful not to mention her name

so I assume the answer to my question is yes." When Ruairi stiffened, Lord Mildmay added, "The woman is not my lover. She is my niece."

"How did ye know what I—"

"This is your only chance. You will not have another. I ask you again, Laird Sutherland, do you love her?"

Ruairi did not hesitate. "Aye, with all my heart. 'Tis why I am here. Please tell me where I can find her."

A devilish look came into the lord's eyes, and he patted Ruairi on the shoulder with a friendly gesture. "Let's take a walk in the garden, shall we? We need to have a chat." He turned and spoke over his shoulder. "And please, leave your men here. If I wanted to kill you, you'd already be dead."

Ruairi liked this man already.

❧

Ravenna watched her sister look around the crowded hall and smile. Grace was still quite taken with court, even though Ravenna knew it would only be a matter of time before the enchantment wore off and Grace recognized this place for what it truly was— nothing but a home for political games and stifling heat. The public clamoring was enough to drive anyone mad.

"You look beautiful, Grace."

Her sister smiled, but it did not quite reach her eyes. "Please," she said, exasperated.

Ravenna waved her off. She didn't realize her foul mood was ruining her sister's moment. Grace had become very skilled at reading her feelings as of late.

"I told you I'm all right. Quit your worrying. Now who's being the mother?"

"One of us has to be," said Grace under her breath. "How long are you going to be like this? The man didn't even try to stop you when you took your leave. The only one who followed you was that black wolf, and even he turned around after a while. Quit pining after someone you will never have. Uncle Walter is right. The sooner you take another assignment, the better. And don't forget that I still want to help you with your next orders. I think I should start with something small. What do you think?"

Ravenna forced a smile. "Where is your betrothed?"

"I'm not sure. Why don't we go and find him?"

They walked through the sea of people, and Grace looked as though she was a small child on market day. Her head whipped from side to side, not wanting to miss anything of importance. She smiled in greeting to everyone she passed and she was happy. Ravenna remembered that spark of excitement, what it was like to live fully in the moment. She was lost in her own reveries when Grace reached out and grabbed her arm. At least her sister had sense enough to lower her voice.

"When you're searching for someone, how far back do you remain? I'm sure you wouldn't want to get too close for fear of discovery."

Ravenna knew her sister meant well, but Grace's relentless questions were becoming—well, relentless. Perhaps if she answered one of Grace's more innocent inquiries, her response would satisfy her sister's craving for learning how to master spy craft. Ravenna stopped and leaned her back against the wall.

"Listen to me very closely. If you're following someone, a public place often provides the perfect cover. For instance, if you're at the market, at—"

"Court."

Ravenna smiled. "Yes, at court. Anywhere there is a crowd. You want to make certain you're dressed appropriately to mix in with those around you. You don't want to stand out. That is one way to lessen your chances of discovery."

Grace's eyes widened. "That's why you were dressed as a harlot that night."

"Yes, that's why I was dressed as a harlot."

Her sister's smile broadened in approval. "Ravenna, that is so exciting! You must simply tell me how you do it."

"Look over there. Do you see your betrothed?"

Grace turned and nodded. "Yes, I see him."

"Why don't you try to follow him and see how long it takes for him to notice you? I'll be watching from over there."

Joy bubbled in her sister's laugh and shone in her eyes. "What a brilliant idea! I'll be a spy for the Crown before you know it."

Ravenna's brief amusement swiftly died. "Great, that's exactly what I wanted to hear."

Grace didn't hear her sister's words because she was off before Ravenna had even finished them. Ravenna walked along the edge of the crowd as she had done so many times before. She found an unoccupied wall and quickly claimed it as her own. She laughed aloud when she spotted Grace, who tried not to be readily conspicuous behind a stone pillar.

"I'm so glad you decided to come with her. You look beautiful."

Ravenna didn't even bother to turn. "Thank you, Uncle Walter."

He stood beside her and leaned against the wall. When he noticed Grace peek her head around the corner, he sighed. "I'm afraid to ask."

"I wouldn't if I were you. I really don't want to encourage her. Perhaps Lord Casterbrook will deter her wild ways."

"Do you honestly believe that?"

Ravenna shrugged. "We could always pray for a miracle."

"Will you follow me for a moment? There's someone I'd like you to meet."

She lifted a brow. "Is that truly the best you can do? I told you I'm not ready."

"Since when do you pass up an easy assignment? This will only take a moment of your time." He waited for her response, and she knew he would never leave her be until she agreed. "Ravenna…"

"Oh, very well."

She took her uncle's arm and walked with him out into the garden. The cool spring breeze felt wonderful against her hot skin. Perhaps a brief respite would do her some good. The firelight from the torches illuminated the gravel path, which crunched beneath her feet. When Uncle Walter stopped, she looked around.

"Are we meeting someone?"

When he didn't respond, she heard a noise behind her and a dark figure stepped from the shadows.

Instinctively, she stepped back and lowered her hand to reach for her dagger, and then her jaw dropped.

"Laird Ruairi Sutherland, pray allow me to introduce you to my niece, Lady Ravenna Walsingham."

Ruairi gave her a low bow. "'Tis a pleasure to make your acquaintance, my lady." He brought her fingers to his lips and brushed a brief kiss on her knuckles.

Ravenna stammered with confusion.

"I see I've rendered her speechless," said Ruairi. "They say there is a first time for everything."

Uncle Walter placed his hand at her back. If he hadn't, she undoubtedly would have fallen to her knees. She suddenly found that her legs were shaking and could barely support her.

"I'll leave you two to talk."

She didn't even notice that Uncle Walter had taken his leave.

Her hands trembled, her body quaked, and she floundered before the man she loved. She felt his hand brush the hair away from her neck. She gulped hard, hot tears falling down her cheeks. He wiped them away with his thumb and gave her a tender smile. His arms encircled her, and she buried her face against the corded muscles of his chest. She'd missed his spicy scent, his touch, his companionship, his love. He filled the void that she didn't even know she had. He made her whole. He completed her. He made her realize what life was all about.

"I take it ye're pleased to see me then," he said in that lovely Scottish accent she had grown to adore.

She sniffled. "Yes, very much. I don't want to let go. I'm so afraid that if I open my eyes I'll wake up from this dream. I'd die now if only to be held in your embrace one last time."

He rubbed his hand gently over her back and kissed her on the top of the head. "Och, Ravenna, I have missed ye so. 'Tisnae a dream, lass. I am here, *a ghràidh*." *My love*.

Pulling back, she wiped her eyes. "I am so sorry, Ruairi. Not a day goes by that I don't regret causing you pain. I never meant to—"

He placed his finger to her lips. "Shhh… There is nay sense in talking about the past. 'Tis done. I'm here at this moment to talk about our future."

"What do you mean?"

"After I stayed the desire to kill ye," he said dryly, "I knew I meant what I said before. Whether ye are Mistress Denny or Lady Walsingham, I love *ye*. I know the lass beneath the surface well enough to recognize that the woman is one and the same. I want to be with ye. I cannae imagine my life without ye in it. Torquil and, aye, even Angus miss ye greatly. Come home, Ravenna. Come with me."

She lifted her hand to his cheek. "Ruairi, there is nothing I want more, but you know I can't. I have my sisters here in England. They depend on me, and you have your clan."

He took a deep breath. "There is something I need to tell ye. Cotrìona is dead, by her father's hand, nay less. And there is naught to fear from the Gordon. Nay one will ever find him, but 'tis best if ye donna ask me how I know that. I came here to find ye with the help of Ian. I spoke to your uncle and I have his blessing. Your kin is my kin, what's mine is yours. As long as we're together, naught else matters. We'll figure all that out later, together. If ye will have me, ye'd make me the happiest man alive."

Ravenna was so caught up in the moment that she didn't quite know what to say. It was hard to remain coherent when he stood so close. He lowered himself on bended knee before her and held her trembling hands.

"Ravenna, *am pòs thu mi? Tha gràdh agam ort.*"

She shook his arm and thought she may have even squealed in delight. "English, Ruairi, English!"

He laughed. "Ravenna, will ye marry me? I love ye."

"Oh, yes, Ruairi! Yes!"

She pulled him to his feet and kissed him with reckless abandon. The man was right. As long as they were together, nothing else mattered. Whether England or Scotland, London or the Highlands, love had finally found her and Ravenna had no intention of ever letting him go.

Read on for an excerpt of Victoria Roberts's

X Marks the Scot

Winner, *RT* Reviewers' Choice Award,
Best Medieval Historical Romance

Royal Court, England, 1604

"GET UP, YE WHORESON."

Praying he was still in an ale-induced state and only dreaming, Declan MacGregor of Glenorchy slowly opened his eyes as he felt the prick of cold steel against his throat. A man with graying hair at his temples stood a hairsbreadth away from the bed, dagger in hand.

A muscle ticked in the man's jaw. "Get up," he said through clenched teeth.

The blonde in the bed next to Declan—what was her name?—gasped and tugged up the blanket to cover her exposed breasts. Her eyes widened in fear.

"Ye defiled my daughter," the stranger growled.

Declan raised his hands in mock surrender. "I assure ye that I didnae." He stole a sideways glance at the woman and silently pleaded for his latest conquest to come to his aid.

"Papa?" The fair-skinned beauty sat up. "What are ye doing here?"

Glancing at his daughter, the man spoke in clipped tones. "This whoreson had ye and will wed ye."

"Now just a bloody minute. I..."

The enraged father glared at him, repositioning the dagger—much *lower*. Feeling the contact of the blade, Declan took a sharp intake of breath while the woman sprang from the bed as though it was afire. Hastily, she started to don her attire.

He silently chuckled, realizing the irony of the moment. What would Ciaran think? Declan had chosen to remain at court in order to escape his older brother's scrutiny, now only to be thrown deeper into hot water. In fact, it was scalding.

The lass rolled her eyes at her father. "Really, Papa, ye must cease your attempts at matchmaking. I donna wish to wed him."

She pulled on her father's hand, thankfully removing the blade from the most favorite part of Declan's anatomy. He breathed a sigh of relief when he reached down and felt his most prized possession was still intact.

What the hell had he gotten himself into? The gods knew he had needs, but if he wasn't more selective of the women he bedded, the fairer sex would surely be the death of him.

He needed to escape.

Declan threw back the blankets. While father and daughter were huddled in deep conversation, he donned his trews, pulled on his tunic, grabbed his boots, and simply walked out—unnoticed and unscathed.

When would he learn that ale always led him into trouble? Perhaps there was some truth to his brother's ramblings on how he was destroying his life. Not wanting to contemplate that revelation, Declan proceeded out the door.

"MacGregor!" Sir Robert Catesby called, waving him over.

In the fortnight Declan had attended court, he had met Sir Robert Catesby and Thomas Percy several times. Upon his approach, both Englishmen smiled in greeting.

Declan nodded. "Catesby. Percy."

"We head to shoot targets," said Catesby, holding up his bow. "Would you like to join us?"

The corner of Declan's lips lifted into a teasing smile. "The first time I bested ye wasnae enough?"

Catesby slapped him on the shoulder. "Perhaps it was purely luck the first time around, eh?"

"Come with us. I challenge you to a match, and we'll see if you can equal my skill with a bow," said Percy with a sly grin.

Declan refrained from commenting that Percy barely had any skill with a bow.

A bit of sport was exactly what he needed after this morning's spectacle. Engaging in some healthy competition might cleanse his spirit, so to speak.

He nodded. "If ye are up for the challenge, it would be my pleasure to have ye *attempt* to best me again."

The men made their way to the targets. The sun was shining and the winds were relatively calm, a great day for shooting. When they arrived at the area, a handful of men were gathered and the boards were already in place. When Declan turned, it felt like he had been punched in the gut.

Lady Liadain Campbell stood in the distance and brushed an errant curl away from her face. Her hair was the black of a starless night and hung down her back. Her high, exotic cheekbones displayed both delicacy and strength. Her lips were full and rounded over even teeth. The flush on her pale cheeks was like sunset on snow. She looked ethereal in the sunlight. Enchanting—well, that's what he had thought the first time he held his dagger to her throat.

Percy cleared his throat. "What say you, MacGregor? Let's have some practice shots before we compete."

Declan laughed, reaching for the bow that Percy held. "'Tis fine with me, Percy. Ye need all the practice ye can get." Declan adjusted the arrow and took aim. He focused on the board and shot, the arrow flying out of his fingers. His eyes never left the mark.

Dead center.

"Well done, MacGregor! Come now, Percy. Do not let me down, young chap," said Catesby, handing Percy his bow.

Percy adjusted the arrow. He raised the bow and took aim. At the last moment, his elbow moved and he shot far to the left.

Catesby shook his head. "Clearly not your best shot, man."

Declan gave Percy a knowing look. "Do ye still wish to challenge me?"

"I never back down from a challenge." Something unspoken clearly passed between Percy and Catesby before they masked their expressions.

Catesby reached out to hand Declan the arrows when Declan spotted the swish of a skirt out of the corner of his eye.

The daft woman leisurely walked along the edge

of the forest. He stifled a sigh, trying not to let his displeasure show. Quickly making his apologies to Catesby and Percy, Declan followed the lass with purposeful strides. Where did she think she was going without an escort? He had lost count of how many times he'd lectured her about that.

Lady Liadain Campbell—healer, half sister to the late Archibald Campbell, seventh Earl of Argyll— was a thistle in his arse. He strived to be patient with her—after all, Ciaran had recently slayed her brother, the bloody Campbell, the right-hand of the king.

When the Campbell had disobeyed King James's orders and abducted members of the MacGregor family, Ciaran had been left with no alternative. Declan supported his brother completely in that regard. His nephew's screams of terror still plagued his thoughts. Since Ciaran still nursed a shoulder injury, he'd ordered Declan to attend court on his behalf to explain the circumstances. To Declan's relief, Liadain Campbell had not only affirmed her brother's treachery, but the king exonerated Ciaran.

She was a ward of the court, which meant there was no suitable male presence to watch over her. And with a clan debt to be paid, he could not abandon her to all the courtly vultures. He at least owed her that much. Although he had no problem watching over her from a distance, a very far distance, times like these that drove him mad.

Someone had to keep a watchful eye on the wily minx.

Declan thundered after her, his temper barely

controlled. "What the hell do ye think ye are doing?" he bellowed. "Didnae I tell ye nae to—"

The obstinate woman lifted her chin, meeting his icy gaze straight on. "*Ye* arenae my husband, MacGregor. Ye have nay right to tell me what I can or cannae do!" She tossed her hair across her shoulders in a gesture of defiance.

He reached out to clutch her arm.

She held something close to her chest and tugged away from him. "Careful, ye fool. I donna want them broken."

"What is that? Sticks?" Puzzled, he pointed to her bundle.

The lass responded sharply, "They arenae just any sticks, ye daft man. This is willow bark for healing."

Declan smirked. "Willow bark? And they donna have enough for ye at court?"

She brushed past him and increased her gait. "I donna expect ye to understand."

He grudgingly trailed behind her. "I donna *want* to understand. Ye need to cease wandering off by yourself. Do ye hear me?" He quickened his pace to catch up with her.

"Of course I can hear ye. Ye are bellowing at me," she called over her shoulder.

He grabbed her shoulders and spun her around. His eyes narrowed and he studied her. Was she completely daft? Did she have no idea of the dangers that could befall a woman without an escort? He remembered a time not long ago when he sprang out from under the brush and startled her. He could have killed her. Did she not learn a lesson?

Apparently not.

She stiffened at his silent challenge and her emerald eyes were sharp and assessing.

Declan chuckled. "Tell me, *healer*. What if a man found ye out here alone?" He gave her body a raking gaze. "What would ye do since ye have nay escort?"

Every generous curve of her body bespoke defiance. "I came this far without your assistance and I donna need it now." Turning on her heel, she started walking back without him—again.

Who was he to argue with a stubborn Campbell? She could bloody well walk back on her own.

Still, his conscience hammered away at him. "Wait, healer." His voice softened. He ran up beside her and extended his arms. "Here. I will carry it for ye and promise to be careful."

Damned twigs.

Reluctantly, she released the bark into his care and they continued to walk silently. Declan was grateful for the quiet because if he heard her sharp tongue again, he might just take her back into the trees and show her what could befall a woman who was caught out here alone.

Acknowledgments

A very special "thank you" goes out to the following people:

To my agent, Jill Marsal, for keeping me afloat in the murky waters.

To my editor, Cat Clyne, for supporting my dreams.

To the unsung heroes at Sourcebooks, it truly takes a village.

To Ravenna Ours Redman, for the use of her beautiful name. I recognize a strong heroine when I meet one.

To my family, for their patience and understanding of all things kilted.

To Sharron Gunn, my resident Gaelic expert, *mòran taing!*

To Mary Grace, for her brutal honesty, constant praise, and endless encouragement. To the woman who never blinks an eye when asked to read the same chapter five times, and to the lass who always appreciates a good kilt when she sees one. It is kind of fun to do the impossible, and because of you, this endeavor is possible.

To my readers, for your posts, emails, and pictures, and for being so incredibly supportive. Thank you for helping me bring my love of Scotland to life.

About the Author

Award-winning author Victoria Roberts writes Scottish historical romances about kilted heroes and warriors from the past. She was named by *RT Book Reviews* as "one of the most promising debut authors across the genres" and was also a 2013 *RT* Reviewers' Choice award winner for *X Marks the Scot*. Victoria is a member of Romance Writers of America and several local chapters, as well as a contributing author to the online magazine *Celtic Guide*. When she's not plotting her next Scottish adventure, she's dragging her clan to every Scottish festival under the sun. Visit Victoria at www.VictoriaRobertsAuthor.com.

Stay tuned for the next book in award-winning
author Victoria Roberts's Highland Spies series…

Kilts and Daggers

Highland Spies
by Victoria Roberts

❦

When Fagan Murray is charged with escorting Lady Grace
Walsingham back to her home in England, he expected tension
with the headstrong lass. But he didn't expect to be waylaid by
Highland rebels. Fagan soon realizes he'll do anything to protect
Grace, even if he has to protect her from himself.

Lady Grace Walsingham hated the Scottish Highlands—
well, one Highlander in particular. Ever since she discovered
her sister was a spy for the Crown, Grace has yearned for
adventure. But the last thing she wanted was to encounter
danger in the Highland wilderness, needing the one man she
despises to protect her.

❦

Praise for *My Highland Spy*:

"An exciting Highland tale of intrigue, betrayal,
and love." —Hannah Howell, *New York Times*
bestselling author of *Highland Master*

For more Victoria Roberts, visit:

www.sourcebooks.com

Temptation in a Kilt
by Victoria Roberts

She's on her way to safety

It's a sign of Lady Rosalia Armstrong's desperation that she's seeking refuge in a place as rugged and challenging as the Scottish Highlands. She doesn't care about hardship and discomfort, if only she can become master of her own life. Laird Ciaran MacGregor, however, is completely beyond her control...

He redefines dangerous...

Ciaran MacGregor knows it's perilous to get embroiled with a fiery Lowland lass, especially one as headstrong as Rosalia. Having made a rash promise to escort her all the way to Glengarry, now he's stuck with her, even though she challenges his legendary prowess at every opportunity. When temptation reaches its peak, he'll be ready to show her who he really is... on and off the battlefield.

"Wonderful adventure with sensual and compelling romance." —Amanda Forester, acclaimed author of *True Highland Spirit*

For more Victoria Roberts, visit:

www.sourcebooks.com

X Marks the Scot
by Victoria Roberts

❧

**He's fierce, he's proud, he's everything
she was warned against.**

Declan MacGregor hadn't a care in the world beyond finding
a soft bed and willing woman…until he had to escort Lady
Liadain Campbell to the English court. The woman needles
him at every turn, but he can't just abandon her to that
vipers' nest without protection.

Liadain wasn't thrilled to be left in the care of her clan's
archrival. It was as if the man never had a lady tell him no
before! And yet as whispers of treason swirl through the
court and the threat of danger grows ever sharper, her bitter
enemy soon becomes the only one she can trust…

❧

Praise for *Temptation in a Kilt*:

"Well written, full of intrigue, and a sensual,
believable romance, this book captivates the
reader immediately." —*RT Book Reviews*

"Filled with everything I love most about
Highland romance…" —Melissa Mayhue, award-
winning author of *Warrior's Redemption*

For more Victoria Roberts, visit:

www.sourcebooks.com